STEALING ANNABELLE

BELLES AND ROGUES
BOOK ONE

STACIA KAYWOOD

Dad and Mom, there are days when I am astounded that I ended up here. I never imagined I could have written one book, let alone two. But without a doubt, this was only possible because of your unwavering love and belief in me.

To my children E and L, never forget that dreams are yours to bring into reality, and that I am here to slay the dragons that block your path.

CHAPTER ONE
ANNABELLE

April 1822

I t was a truth universally acknowledged that an impoverished debutante must be plagued with a meddlesome aunt. Annabelle Greene cursed her misfortune of being born without a fortune after suffering through yet another *ton* event wearing slippers that pinched while her aunt dragged her through London on a fruitless quest to snag the slipperiest prize of the season–the unattached aristocrat. She threw herself onto the bed and screamed into a pile of dusty rose pillows.

Winston was not impressed. The orange tabby froze midlick with its hind leg pointed into the air. Its notched ear twisted once, before it resumed its nightly bath.

"You realize that if I am not wed by season's end, I must return to Hampshire. Do you know what that means?" The bath continued as the cat gnawed at a tuft of fur. "You will be kicked outside to live in the gutter. No more pillows for sleeping and plates of fish," she said. A fat tear splashed upon the silk bolster pillow. She chided herself for crying, where had it ever gotten her before?

The frustration of an unsuccessful start to her only season wore on her tattered nerves. The stakes were too high. The consequences should she remain unmatched were too dire to contemplate, but continuing the rigmarole required of a debutante was exhausting.

Winston stretched, then bumped its head against Annabelle's nose. She buried her frustration in its soft coat until its purrs worked their feline magic, calming the urge to shout down the roof. The cat collapsed next to her, pawing at the loose fringe of her cotton nightrail.

She straightened the tangle of bedding and reclined against the smooth oak headboard. The bed curtains remained open, allowing the final remnants of the fire in the hearth opposite her to cast the room in a golden glow. Unfortunately, the sputtering flames did not provide enough light for reading, leaving her with only thoughts and no other distraction save for the cup of chocolate cooling on the bedside table.

Residing with Aunt Silvia did come with advantages. Cups of chocolate being the primary. Silvia's generosity funded the cost of the season, there was no complaint there. It was simply that what constituted a suitable match did not align.

Annabelle desired an amiable husband, who made her feel both wanted and appreciated. Aunt Silvia was interested in income, breeding, and desperation—not exactly the virtuous qualities to tout in an ideal spouse. It might also explain her aunt's penchant for her own short-lived marriages, all four of them.

The husband hunt would be expedited if Annabelle had a dowry attached to her name or if she were a remarkable beauty like her mother. However, no dowry and being a touch too plump and too short with topaz-colored eyes instead of blue meant she was anything but de rigueur. At least her bloodline was solid, being the granddaughter of a well-respected viscount. Whether it was enough bait to lure a man into a matrimonial trap, remained to be seen.

Annabelle felt like anyone but herself when she was paraded through the *ton* like a broodmare at a Tattershall auction. She was surprised she did not have to flash her teeth for inspection before being asked to dance. No one seemed to desire her. Except for... oh, she must not fantasize about roguish viscounts with terrible reputations and delectable lips. Oh heavens. Fortunately, no one knew about *the kiss*. Not even her closest friends.

She giggled. Winston meowed and stalked over to her elbow. Well, maybe her cat knew a little.

Her aching feet forced her back to reality. She rubbed them together, hoping to ease the persistent throb while sipping at her cup. Winston took displeasure in her movement, knocking into her elbow and upsetting the cup of chocolate. Splat! A trail of brown liquid snaked across the front. For a moment she contemplated changing, instead she used a handkerchief to dab up the access. Then she yanked the heavy chintz bed curtains closed, dousing her bed in darkness. Sleep would be a blessed reprieve after tonight.

Silvia's desperation had increased tenfold as the season moved into full swing. Annabelle knew it would be her only. How many times had her aunt reminded her of that fact? If she had a shilling for every mention of her unfortunate circumstances, she would not be in such unfortunate circumstances.

Choice was no longer an option. She stifled a sob, choking it back. Scolding her display of self-pity. It did not mean her future husband would be terrible. If she fully weighed her options, she might find one pleasant enough. Though tonight's available suitors did not embody any of the qualities she desired. Dancing with bachelors so far in their dotage that she had to lead them through the steps, certainly fueled her trepidation.

"Drat," she said. Winston yawned and stretched, digging his claws into the pile of blankets before turning twice to collapse onto the coverlet. "If I am not successful, you will have to return to hunting for your nightly meal."

Winston blinked his remaining eye as if to say, *I am not concerned.* Arrogant feline. It would worm itself into another house, while Annabelle would be homeless. Or living again with her father. Marriage or servitude to a neglectful father? Neither sounded particularly appealing.

Thump! A heavy object slammed against the outside of the townhouse. It was not windy. There were no trees to scrape against the outside–unlike her house in Hampshire–where branches scratched and clawed at windows giving rise to the fears of little children that witches lurked in the darkness.

Annabelle waited. Hearing nothing for long moments. She debated peeking through the bed curtains, but in truth, the thought of a nefarious someone lurking beyond the fabric was too terrifying to chance. So, she drew up the covers and began reciting her nightly prayers.

It was silent. Even the fire stopped popping and crackling. Her prayers were complete, so she held her breath. Waiting. Willing whatever might be outside her window to simply go away. A bang followed by the groan of the sash lifting stole the last bit of breath in her lungs. She heard a person tumble to the floor. A great crash followed by a vulgar exclamation with a voice she did not recognize.

She struggled to find the ability to scream. To say more than a whispered, "Wh-wh-who is th-there?"

No answer. Nothing but the creak of floorboards and heavy footfalls. She yanked the blankets over her head, clutching the material in her tightened fists. A muffled chorus of "go aways" stuttered from her mouth.

The steps ventured closer. Winston did not stir, a heavy weight resting on her ankle, the only warmth she felt as fear cooled her body and goose pimples erupted over her skin. Closer and closer.

Schlink! The bed curtains slid apart, revealing a face more shadow than defined. Winston, disturbed from its rest, launched with paws extended. Cat and intruder knocked into a table, upsetting the candle and dousing the flame. It extinguished the light, except for a few glowing embers in the far hearth.

Lying in bed was not Annabelle's idea of being a free-thinking woman. No! Action demanded that she throw off the covers, but her feet snagged in the bedsheets. She tumbled to the ground. However, Winston kept the trespasser distracted.

Weapon. She needed a weapon to bash his head. Finishing school did not prepare her for such violence, but she had read enough. Knew the weaknesses of a man. So, she picked up a book. It was heavy, but more was necessary to inflict damage. She tossed it to the side, choosing a hideous porcelain piece of bric-a-brac.

Just before she brought it down on the man's head, he managed to dislodge the harassed feline by flinging it away from him, losing his balance in the process. He smashed against a chair. The wooden piece was no match for his momentum, shattering beneath him.

"Ouch," he hissed, shaking off what had to be a ferocious sting. He looked up and smiled. Twin dimples creased his face. "Funny meeting like this. Me down here. You up there," he said, far too happy for an average housebreaker. Far too confident for a man seconds away from having his head caved in by a Dresden shepherdess. "Come give me a kiss hello, Annabelle."

"Lord Linscott." The statue clattered to the floor, rolling away to hit against the heels of his boots. "I believe I instructed you to call me Miss Greene."

He smirked and repeated her name with the proper address.

"Do you mind explaining why you are in my room, dressed all in black with a length of rope coiled around your hands?"

"Certainly," he replied, unwinding the rope, "we are going on a little adventure."

CHAPTER TWO

JACK

March 1822

J ack Davenport woke to sandpaper scratching over his eyelids. He wondered where in the hell he was until the patterned navy and cream curtains came into focus. Home it was. Good thing he was not in the streets asleep on a pile of leaves with a dead rat for company. An unfortunate incident during his eighteenth year had demonstrated the necessity for proper companionship whilst imbibing in intoxicating substances. However, he might need a reminder given his current state of overindulgence.

Perhaps a bottle of port followed by two bottles of claret exceeded his tolerance. The layer of cotton lining his mouth was an ill omen for any future plans. If fortune smiled upon him, a half-empty bottle was near, as this morning's remedy called for the hair of the dog.

Relief was on the bedside table if he could only shift through the tangle of silk sheets and pillows. He tossed them aside and uncovered a shapely calf, then a bare hip. Blurrily, he sorted through the bedding to reveal a blonde head. The rest of her was as voluptuous as the leg pressed against his side. Ah, it was a good night.

Back to his quest. On the table, he discovered a silk stocking. A pair of ribboned garters. A half-smoked cheroot stubbed out in a hunk of crusty bread. Victory at last, a glass! Instead of liquor, he tasted water laced with laudanum his thoughtful valet had left behind. Thomas truly was a godsend.

In greedy gulps, Jack drank, grateful to quench his thirst. Hopefully, the throb pulsing in his skill might abate. Why did he feel it in his teeth?

Silky hair brushed against his arm. It was not the blonde who stirred, rather the dark tresses belonged to another. Yes, it had been a good night indeed.

A servant scratched at the door. The blonde threw a pillow over her head and the brunette grumbled, "Go away."

"Come in!" Jack laughed at the brunette's pinched scowl. A grumpy bit of goods.

Thomas braved the den of iniquity, breezing through the doorway. He rolled his eyes, the single acknowledgment of the blatant display of carnality. A sight he was entirely too familiar with after serving as Jack's batman during the war and now as his valet.

Jack felt not an ounce of remorse. The hefty salary he paid Thomas abated any potential guilt that might creep in due to his unrepentant lifestyle.

"My lord, Mr. Parker is downstairs. He appears a bit out of sorts." Thomas drew open the curtains.

The flash of daylight forced Jack to retreat under the coverlet, but not before he yanked it free from the blonde. She hissed a protest he ignored.

"Out of sorts" was typical for Parker, but Thomas fetching Jack before noon spelled trouble.

While he shaded his face from the vicious sunlight, he managed to extract himself from the bed, swatting both women on their derrieres as he rose. "Apologies, my lovelies, but business before pleasure."

The brunette pouted. The blanket slipped from her shoulder and revealed her creamy breast.

"Come back to bed, Lord Linscott," she purred.

At least she remembered his title, clever vixen. "I will. If you can recall the color of my eyes." He lifted his hand to cover them lest she decided to cheat.

She chewed her lip and nudged her blonde friend for help.

The blonde shrugged.

"Brown, my lord," the brunette hazarded.

"Ah, a fair guess, but wrong." He dumped their clothing on the bed and ignored Thomas, who held a dressing gown open for him. Retreating to the adjoining bathing room, he washed quickly.

As he toweled off, he heard the bedroom door slam shut. Cleansed from the night of excess, he felt moderately restored even without a good soak. Enough to pull on a pair of trousers and return to his bedroom, where he waited patiently for Thomas to shave him.

"Really, Linscott." In private, Jack permitted a more casual form of address. After all, they owed each other their lives. "Perhaps you should consider your father's demands to wed. I grow tired of cleaning up after whores and overindulgence."

"They were not whores."

Thomas slammed a bowl of heated water on the dressing desk and motioned impatiently to the chair so that he could shave off the night beard that shadowed Jack's jaw. "Whatever name you want to call them. They pocketed half the silver before emptying the cellarette. Cook refused to make your breakfast after she noticed her favorite platter had gone missing."

Now, that was the final straw. No cinnamon scones? How was a man supposed to recover without his favorite morning-after breakfast? "No meal to break my fast?"

"She made you kippers."

Jack's stomach protested the thought.

"She threatened haggis for supper."

"That Scottish witch! She has gone too far. Fire her." When he hired the woman, she swore she would never make that awful dish. Now she was threatening it as punishment for light-fingered courtesans. The nerve.

"You do it. I am afraid of her knife skills."

Jack glared into the mirror.

Thomas was unfazed.

"What a loyal staff I've amassed."

"You need a wife. Cook's talents are unappreciated working for a bachelor. And the housekeeper is down two more house-maids. They quit when they saw the state of your parlor."

"What happened in the parlor?" Jack asked.

Thomas wrinkled his nose. "We threw out the Persian rug. There was no saving it."

Jack's temples pulsated with every irritating syllable. He opted for silence over more irritation. A wife? He no more needed a wife than the bayonet scar puckering the skin of his shoulder.

Dressed and refreshed by a pot of strong coffee, Jack made his way to his study to speak with his frantic secretary.

Mr. Herbert Parker had worn a path across the burgundy carpet with his chronic pacing. The man wiped his florid face with his wrinkled handkerchief. He stopped in his tracks when he noticed Jack enter the room, switching to pepper his speech with his usual litany of my lords.

"Get on with it, man!" Jack's patience had ended the minute he woke up. He snatched a glass and decanter then poured himself a more bracing fortification. Light-headed from the night before and with no scones to sop up the liquid that gurgled in his stomach, he all but collapsed into the leather chair behind his desk. It was a sturdy and practical piece of furniture with an expansive top and nearly empty drawers.

Jack propped his feet on the blotter and braced his free hand against his temple, so the room no longer tilted to the side. He needed to practice some sort of temperance. Cut back at the least.

Parker's stuttered explanation grated on Jack's frayed nerves. "My...my lord. It is...it is your fa-ther. He b-bid me to tell you—"

"For God's sake! Drink this!" he shouted before he shoved the glass toward the man.

Parker approached the desk, accepted the drink, and downed it greedily. His ability to consume the entire whisky without pause surprised even Jack. "Better, thank you, my lord." Parker set the glass down and gulped air before he spit out the reason for his early visit. "You are overdrawn."

"What?" The chair clattered to the floor as Jack staggered to his feet, grateful the desk remained steady as the abrupt movement nearly sent him toppling end over end.

"When I attempted to withdraw funds to pay your tailor and the wine merchant, I was informed your account was overdrawn."

Impossible, he easily had ten thousand in reserve. "Did you speak with my father's steward?"

Parker swallowed deeply, then nodded. "Yes, there are no more funds."

"No funds?" Jack asked, his tone caused Parker to flinch.

"That is what the steward said."

"What of my investments? The rents from the Sussex estate?"

"There is nothing, my lord," he whined. "What do I say to your wine merchant?"

"Tell him to speak with my father."

Parker patted his dewy forehead. "What are you going to do? If you do not have the funds to pay—"

Jack cut him off. "Do not worry. I will find the means to pay your salary."

Parker sighed in relief. "And your tailor?"

Jack drummed his fingers across the desk's mahogany finish. "Baron Crayfield will know a way out of this mess. I promised him I would attend the Boucher affair tonight. If all else fails, I will appeal to my father. By tomorrow, this will all be resolved."

Parker worried the brim of his hat until the material warped under his hand. The man had far too many doubts about the success of Jack's schemes. It probably explained why the secretary's head refused to grow any more hair. "Your father bought you a commission and sent you off to war after you last faced money trouble."

Curse Parker's infernal memory.

"No doubts or second guesses," Jack said.

He wanted to discuss investment properties he might sell at a profit to keep him solvent until he discovered the leak in his finances. He should have plenty of funds at his disposal. He was no spendthrift. Something rotten was afoot.

A distressed Parker was utterly useless. When the man finally complained of a megrim, Jack sent him home. Besides, if he needed to play the part of a bore at a London affair, he had a ball to prepare for. A fact that delighted his housekeeper and cook. Better to keep the women in his life happy, but not overly so. He still drew the line at leg shackling himself to a wife.

CHAPTER THREE

THE BALL

reathe. Open your mouth. Inhale. Breathe. It was the fifth time in as many nights that Annabelle rode in a coach through Mayfair on the way to yet another *ton* event. Aunt Silvia droned on about the available bachelors expected to make their appearance, while Annabelle wanted to sink into the velvet upholstery and disappear. *Ten more minutes.*

Lord and Lady Boucher's home could not be much farther away. She counted the passing beats of her heart. Trying to calm her racing thoughts. The carriage was steady. There was not a cloud in the sky. Safe. Especially if she scooted a bit further to the middle of the bench. Away from the windows. *Breathe.* She wanted to scream. To cry. To break into hysterics.

Silvia's pinched scowl did ground Annabelle a bit into reality. Her aunt fished through her reticule and withdrew the dreaded *List*. It would not be a society function if *The List* did not make an appearance detailing with exactitude every available bachelor from the ages of eighteen to six-and-eighty. Incomes. Properties. Eye-color. Sporting preferences. It read like a who's who of London society. For a desperate debutante, it served as a handbook to navigate the season. Ideally, the information would help procure the perfect match or rather a match.

Too bad she did not agree with her aunt on what constituted an ideal husband. Fat, ancient, and flatulent were the common attributes of Silvia's top choices. Granted Annabelle's might be a tad unrealistic. Did attractive men under the age of thirty with bright smiles, who were kind to animals, and compassionate to a woman with a fear of carriages exist? She had yet to meet one. Those topping her aunt's list predominated the market.

"I have it on good authority that Lord Welsham is in attendance tonight." Silvia chirped, smoothing out the billowing layers of her plum satin gown. Her dark brown hair was piled on her head in a cascade of sausage curls with three raven-black feathers waving in the air. "His son is not expected to survive through summer." Silvia lifted her brow, whispering "Consumption" as if the word itself might be catching. She pressed her hands together for a tiny prayer before finishing her thought. "He is looking to produce a second heir, but with his fortune, there is not a necessity for a bride with a large dowry."

"Which makes him suitable. What a coup," Annabelle said as her head fell back against the plush velvet cushion. The lord was short, wide, ancient, and reeked of pomade. There had to be another.

"No, a coup would be the Duke of Sambridge. He too will be in attendance. Do you remember him? You spilled cake down his front at Baroness Landry's picnic." Silvia's finger traced over the paper, tapping against particular names.

"It was a dog that upset a tray. Not I." The duke was attractive with peridot-green eyes, but he seldom smiled. Fastidious in dress, slightly older than thirty, those were not strikes against him. However, calling the dog an ill-bred, flea-ridden cur was. "I believe he should be crossed off of the list. A man with his connections and wealth would not be interested in me." *Unless he is ninety-five and desiring a companion to rub his bunions.*

"Do not start." Her aunt was in high dudgeon tonight. She waved her index finger and issued her commands. "You will dance with no less than five eligible bachelors. You are not to spend the night chatting with your friends or hiding behind pillars."

Annabelle should be more gracious. It was entirely due to her aunt's generosity that she was in London instead of rotting away in Hampshire along with her father and his pile of books. Then there were her friends, all of them former students of Mrs. Maxwell's School for the Education and Deportment of Fine Ladies. There she met Cecilia Hammond, Isabel Howard, Vivian Stratham, and Francine MacKinnon. They made the season bearable.

The carriage rolled to a halt behind a line winding around the driveway as lords and ladies of the *ton* exited in all their finery.

Annabelle plucked the periwinkle sarsenet fabric, wondering if she would fit in. Her gown was lovely. Ivory satin scallops lined the hem, and a gauzy scarf was tied around the high waist. Capped sleeves and long ivory gloves completed the ensemble. Her modiste was a true talent with a needle and thread.

Her aunt exited the carriage in a waterfall of plum silk. She waited with a half-smile curving her lips and her fan waving away the stagnant air. It might be March, but it was unseasonably warm.

Annabelle took a footman's man, but her slipper caught on the step. She toppled forward, falling against the outstretched arms of Lady Boucher's liveried servant. The man was far more graceful than she. He maintained his footing and eased her down to the ground.

"Thank–"

"You do not address servants. Come, Annabelle." Her aunt bobbed along with the crush towards the entrance.

"–You," Annabelle finished, shrugging an apology to the footman, whose lips curled in a private smile.

"My pleasure, Miss. Glad to be of service." He turned to address the coachman.

An extraordinarily tall man exited the next vehicle, settling his black silk top hat on his head. Exquisitely dressed, he blended in except for the humor evident in his gaze. Not bearing the typical bored visage of the average aristocrat. He was intriguing. He quirked his brow, the single sign that he saw her. Annabelle's head dove into a pool and swam off without her.

Nudging Silvia, she tried to gain her attention. Perhaps an introduction could follow once inside, but the singular focus of the woman made it impossible to alter the course. She made a beeline for the front entrance. For now Annabelle chose to admire the home.

It was grand, blazing with candles shining from all the windows. Torches lined the drive, creating a sunny glow in the fading twilight. The home oozed opulence from every corner, obvious that no expense was spared. The walk through the entry was even more impressive with statuaries that rivaled Elgin Marbles.

Lord and Lady Boucher greeted Aunt Silvia and Annabelle with an enthused welcome. The ladies chatted, while Lord Boucher acknowledged the tall stranger, who had been following close behind. Eavesdropping was forbidden, but who would notice with such a crowd. Annabelle leaned ever so slightly, hearing only the quiet drone of male voices. Drat.

The butler announced them, receiving very little notice from the gathered crowd. She hesitated, waiting for the name of the tall man, but Silvia pulled her along, whispering furiously about properties. All she caught was the title of Viscount. The good that did her. There were hundreds of viscountcies in the whole of England.

Moving past the entry, aunt and niece stepped down into the grand ballroom. Spectacular. The Viscountess Boucher had decorated her ballroom with swags of bunting in nearly every shade of pink. It hung from the marbled pillars and draped over windows. Six heavy crystal chandeliers flooded the room with candlelight. Couples twirled while a quartet played *Invitation to a Dance* rescored for strings.

Silvia looped her finger through Annabelle's sash, gently pulling her to the side of the room closest to the doors. "Stay here. I know your friends are gathered in the corner, but I demand your company. If you dance with five suitable bachelors, you may flit about and gossip. For now, focus on having your card filled with names."

Annabelle fiddled with the string securing the dance card to her wrist. Five bachelors. The previous ball she attended included a singular dance for her, offered by Baron Crayfield in sympathy of sorts. He was the elder brother of her dearest friend, Cecilia Hammond. Amiable and kind, he was not on the top of either Annabelle's or Silvia's list of potential husbands for it was well known he was on the hunt for an heiress.

"There is Lord Welsham." Her aunt pointed across the room. The plump earl bowed, escorting the towering Francine MacKinnon to the floor for a country dance. "He will work his way over to us shortly. Now, what about Lord Stratham?"

"He is my friend's father, and he has an heir."

"Yes, yes. But he is unwed." Silvia tapped her fan against her open palm.

"And not looking."

"Captain Hunter is here." Her aunt lifted her nose toward the front entrance as a discrete indication of who walked in the room.

Handsome, young, and head over heels for Cissy. "When he asks, I will accept." That was two potential partners. Three more and she could find a brief reprieve for the night.

They lapsed into silence and watched the spectacle of pastel-clad debutantes with lords in superfine dress coats flutter past.

A prickle crept along Annabelle's nape, an awareness that a person was looking at her. There he was. The stranger from the drive, lifting his glass in salute across the crowded room. She felt her skin burning, flushing under his regard. To acknowledge her presence with no formal introduction? It was the very definition of a rogue. This was not the type of man she should even entertain, yet—how could she explain it? He churned feelings she did not know could exist. Lud, she was interested.

He had curling brown hair, broad shoulders, and a trim waist. His features were a series of harsh lines, angled sharply with high cheekbones and a thick brow. But it was those eyes. Bright, humor-laced eyes she could feel across an entire ballroom.

He waved while Annabelle quickly averted her gaze lest someone witness the impertinence.

"Aunt Silvia?" Annabelle leaned in closer, pulling her away from a conversation with a group of matrons. "Do you know the gentleman conversing with Baron Crayfield? The one wearing a black stock instead of a cravat?"

Silvia craned her neck, standing on her tiptoes. "Where is he?"

"Near the twin pillars, directly across from us."

"Oh." She looked at Annabelle, then again to the stranger. Her eyes were two round saucers as she shook her head. "That is Viscount Linscott. Stay away, he is the worst sort of rake. Detestable reputation."

"Is he unattached?"

Silvia looked at Annabelle like she had sprouted a second set of eyes. "Yes. But reputations are reputations. While his father is regarded well, displaying both fairness and affability, his son..." Pulling her niece in closer, she lowered her voice. "Favors courtesans and liquor. He is the type that will leave his future wife miserable and alone."

The warning should be enough to scare Annabelle away, yet her body lit with tingles and shivers she had felt only once before. And that was at a concert hearing an orchestra fill a theater with exquisite music. A man had never evoked such pleasures.

"If he is single," she began.

"My first husband was a similar type. While I would not refuse his pursuit simply because I want to see you wed, I also want my niece to find happiness. Something I have searched for through four marriages. Learn from me, my sweet niece. Trust that your old aunt has a lesson or two still to teach." She squeezed Annabelle's hand.

A shadow drifted into view followed by the clearing of a masculine throat, the sound richly vibrant.

"Miss Greene." A man bowed, brushing a set of firm lips across the knuckles of her glove. "Perhaps you remember me. I am the Duke of Sambridge. Your cousin Marcus introduced us when you visited him last summer."

"Yes, I almost did not recognize you without a coating of purple icing."

His chiseled face broke into a wide smile that softened his

features as the candlelight reflected in his eyes. "My valet never could remove it from my waistcoat. He has forbidden me from any more fetes the baroness hosts."

"What a terrible shame. I recall a delightful afternoon, falling trays excluded." His geniality eased her worries, but better to be on guard. Lest she inadvertently say the wrong thing.

Aunt Silvia brushed against her elbow to curtsey before him. "Your Grace." She whispered to Annabelle to stand up straighter from behind her fan. "How charming it is to see you again."

"Countess Brighton, the pleasure is purely mine. I wanted to inquire if Miss Greene might do me the honor and agree to a dance."

Before Annabelle could reply, Aunt Silvia nudged her forward. "Of course, Your Grace. She would be delighted to accept. How kind of you to ask."

He offered his arm. What would it be like to say no? But who was Annabelle fooling? No one said no to a duke.

Sambridge chatted about the bland and uninteresting. Weather. Refreshments. Decor. The topics were safe but provided little insight into the man now holding her in an almost familiar embrace. It had to be a waltz. Not a quadrille or country dance.

On a turn, she spotted Lord Linscott dancing with a nameless debutante. The two spun around the room as if the waltz was played solely for them. He winked at Annabelle and wicked dimples creased his handsome face.

Oh, but how he could dance! With graceful, sinuous steps, his partner was barely able to match the intricacies of his footwork as he glided across the floor.

Annabelle realized the duke addressed her and dragged her attention back to him.

"Miss Greene, I had no idea you were such a capable dancer. I thought you were opposed to the activity, since you often sit with the matrons. I dare say, you are rather accomplished."

His tone was off-putting. Arrogant and typical for such rank. Yet, he softened his words with a gentle smile. A crease formed around his mouth. He had a pleasant face. However, a duke needed a more socially acceptable potential bride. The granddaughter of a viscount was not a suitable enough bloodline.

"I do enjoy dancing. Music. Sculpture. Though, to see a theater production would be a dream come true. To immerse myself into the spectacle of actors and words melding in harmonious entertainment," she said.

"You venerate the arts with such heartfelt devotion that your enthusiasm is infectious. I hope one day you will do me the honor and help me complete my erudition, as it is sorely lacking in this area."

The music ended with his request. Annabelle pressed a gloved hand against her belly in the hopes that the odd flutter that took root with his words stilled. He accompanied her to where her aunt stood watch. A gleam in the woman's eye did not go unnoticed.

"I cannot teach you how to enjoy art, Your Grace. It comes from within, not from books or lectures."

His fingers brushed a stray tendril from her cheek. They lingered for a moment against her heated flesh. "Then perhaps my only salvation will be to have you by my side. Goodnight, Miss Greene." He allowed no time for Annabelle to return a farewell. Abruptly, he turned on his heel.

Her head spun. A dance with His Grace. A flirtation with a scandalous stranger. Her aunt was so satisfied with her dance partner, she joined Lord Stalworth for a quadrille. Would wonders ever cease?

A shimmer drew her curiosity upward. She spied a lone spider dangling on a web. Contented to watch, Annabelle studied the weaver as it laced its intricate design through the burning candles of a chandelier until it switched directions. She gasped. The spider slid down its gossamer thread closer and closer to the floor below, floating perilously above certain demise.

She reached out to snatch the tiny creature between her gloved hands. Dodging around the crush, she raced outside. On the terrace, she searched for a haven, all thoughts of dances and men forgotten.

CHAPTER FOUR
ON A TERRACE

Twenty minutes passed since Jack arrived at Lord and Lady Boucher's affair, and he had spent nineteen minutes formulating a plan for a hasty exit. The horde of mothers with their marriage-hungry daughters were indignant, irked by his presence. Especially since he had the audacity to accompany the charismatic but destitute Baron Crayfield.

Why these women feared their progenies' reputations, Jack never understood. He made his one inalterable rule clear to everyone—never dally with an innocent. No, he spent his wanton nights between the thighs of experienced women. Where he should be right now if he still had the funds, instead he sweltered in this oven cleverly disguised as a ballroom.

Entertainment took a new form today. While he was not interested in bedding the creature, he was utterly intrigued and befuddled by the woman in pale blue with ribbons wound through her hair. She was the opposite of every woman he knew. She was plump when she should be svelte. Timid, when she should be brazened.

Her height reached mid-chest; so small he would have to bow to kiss her. Though she did possess a perfect kissable bow-shaped mouth with pouty berry-stained lips. Wide and sensual.

A flock of pastel-colored debs approached, encircling Jack and Baron Crayfield like a pack of savage dogs. He chuckled over the comparison. Crayfield eyed him like he had taken leave of his senses. Perhaps he did. The baron entertained the mass that twittered rapaciously, while Jack continued his survey of the room.

His plump vixen chatted with an older matron. A Lady Brighton if memory served. Hmm. Perhaps an introduction might satisfy his curiosity about the blue-bedecked sprite.

Jack never danced in public, a personal rule of self-preservation, but for her, he would spin circles across the floor. Dancing came as naturally as fornication. The two activities were synonymous, the direction of the bodies the only difference. Well, not always.

Twice he chuckled aloud. The punch must be spiked, though the taste merely hinted of spirits. Not intoxicating, not by any stretch of his imagination.

The Duke of Sambridge approached the debutante. He blocked Jack's view and stoked his ire. How dare Sambridge address the only woman out of hundreds that was the tiniest bit interesting and then have the temerity to escort her to the floor.

Jack's hand flexed with the memory of his latest spar at Gentleman Jacksons when he managed to knock the duke down in five rounds. If only the *ton* made such bouts the headlining event instead of frivolous dances and bland repasts. Or a duel. Now *that* would be entertainment.

"Linscott." Nigel's voice broke through a vivid daydream in which Jack skewered Sambridge with a well-timed riposte.

"Perhaps you might be inclined to dance with Miss Pettigrew. You remember Clive Pettigrew from Oxford. This is his younger sister."

A mask of utter indifference fell across Jack's face. He executed a polite bow to the brunette in cream. Banal was perhaps the best description he could apply to the deb. Time for pleasantries, before he resumed his hunt for a tastier morsel. "Your brother is a champion horseman. How is he?"

"Very well, my lord. He is currently at his country estate with his wife and six children." She cooed with delight.

Jack's stomach dropped. A brood of six clinging to his tail-coat, it was too terrifying to contemplate. Give him six French frogs to take out with his fists. Now that had appeal. He cleared his throat with a long whistle. "Six nieces and nephews, what a terrific blessing."

Her skirts swished as she swayed. "I love being an aunt."

Ah, yes, she probably expects me to opine about the joys of family or some such utter rot. Best to squash that hope. "Would you care to dance, Miss Pettigrew?"

She chirped a yes, which caused her head to bob like a bird.

"Excellent." Without further fanfare, Jack spun the young miss onto the floor. Her grip tightened on his arm as she fought to stay upright while he waltzed them around. They quickly gained on the mysterious young woman with Sambridge.

In contrast to Miss Pettigrew, who struggled with the relatively basic steps, the fairy floated along with the music. The duke, Jack noted with barely veiled glee, remained stiff and maladroit.

"My lord." Miss Pettigrew's voice wavered as they neared the end of the song. "Perhaps you would be so kind as to return me to my mother."

With a graceful turn, he maneuvered them off the dance

floor. Jack handed the winded young lady over to her mother with a kind word that lacked any actual amiability or promise to continue the acquaintance, much to the relief of both parties.

Baron Crayfield still danced with yet another pastel-clad creature, working his way through his personal list of women who required a title and no fortune. Jack returned to his previous post. There his scowl deterred any further distractions from his admiration of the blue confection across the room.

A smoky voice purred in his ear, the sound magnifying his current state of annoyance. Valentina, the infamous Countess of Anworth, his current mistress. He eyed a ruby and diamond bracelet that encircled her wrist, the reminder of his expensive tastes and their exorbitant price grated on his final nerve.

"Jack, why do you brood so? Perhaps the next dance would soothe your ill humor." Valentina's gloved hand rested with stark familiarity on his forearm.

With a roll of his wrist, he broke her hold. "My dear Countess. There are rules to be followed and rules to be broken. To dance in public with you is one I will not negotiate."

For the past month, ever since the mourning period for her husband officially ended, she dropped hint after hint about the direction of their affair. However, venomous creatures were only good for a tumble, never as a wife.

Valentina's fingers dug through the superfine wool of his coat. "You will find, my lord, I am a rule breaker. It is necessary for a woman with any hope for a financially beneficial future to forge a unique path, regardless of the people who might stand in her way. Men do not say *no* to the Countess of Anworth."

"Threats do not become you, my dear."

"Who said I made a threat?" Her deceptive innocence sparked a challenge.

"The Duke of Sambridge finished his dance." He redirected her attention to a far more available and unscrupulous opponent. "Rumor has it, he desires a wife and paramour. Perhaps you might fill the latter as our little arrangement needs to end."

"I hate you," she hissed.

"The sentiment is mutual."

Sambridge had circled the room and now stood before them. "Linscott." His tone dripped with ducal condescension. "Introduce me."

Jack obliged the abrupt command without comment. "My lady, may I introduce to you the biggest horse's ass to graduate from Oxford, Christian Archer, the Duke of Sambridge." The anger bristled within his most fearsome adversary–his nemesis since Eton. "Your Grace, this is Valentina, the Countess of Anworth. A veritable succubus and confirmed Queen of the Damned. Be on guard of both your purse and cock. She has use for both. Neither will be full again after she finishes."

Though Jack had just insulted a duke, most often an unforgivable offense, it was merely their normal exchange. Besides, Sambridge was a horse's ass and Jack fully admitted that he might be worse.

With her gasp of indignation and Sambridge's assurances to defend her honor in the pugilism ring tomorrow, Jack fled the overly crowded room. A quiet terrace offered solitude on a rare night with a sky glittered with stars.

After a night full of unwanted encounters, it should not have surprised him that Fate had other plans, enough to give him pause and contemplate the alteration of his route of retreat when he spotted *her*. *She* fought a losing battle with her glove.

One glance back through the open doorway, he met

Valentina's icy glare, thus confirming his need for a fortuitous exit and an unlikely introduction.

The petite debutante from across the room pleaded in a voice so sweet he tasted it on his tongue. She waved her white-gloved hand erratically above a planter.

"Oh, please, little spider. Do not crawl up my sleeve. This bush right here is the perfect home for you. I should be so lucky to be able to find relief from the suffocation of a ballroom. Out here promises freedom like I will never know."

Jack identified with her plaintive lament. Perhaps she could grant him a similar escape from societal entrapments.

The arachnid refused to obey her piteous pleas, instead, it chose to skitter across her kid glove in the opposite direction. She twisted her forearm before she rolled the hem of her glove to trap it.

"Epp! No, no, no."

Without a word, Jack approached from behind. He enfolded the woman with his body and reached down to remove the makeshift prison with its inhabitant. Gingerly, he peeled the material free from her fingers to shake it out onto the bush. For a frustrating moment, the spider refused to emerge, before it sailed on a silk thread, landing on a leaf. A tiny ballerina pirouetting across a glossy green stage.

With the rescue complete, Jack did not remove his arms. Instead, he took liberties he knew he should not. Liberties his principles cried out for him to forgo, but she lured him like forbidden ambrosia.

He used the light from the full moon to illuminate her innocent face. His fingers skated across her parted lips, tender and moist against his touch. Crave, need, and desire were not large enough words to encompass the urge demanding immediate satisfaction. He was helpless to resist. Entranced by a fairy on a terrace garden. A protector of the innocent.

His lips brushed against hers. She responded not with a slap, which he deserved. Instead, her head reeled back the tiniest distance before she returned with equal vigor. Her hand tentatively held the sleeves of his coat while their lips mingled in quiet exploration.

Not even his first kiss at the age of fourteen had caused his heart to accelerate the way this one did. At once lightheaded and giddy like a virgin, it filled him with a longing he did not know his body possessed. Possession was a word. Who possessed whom, was the question.

When her tongue tentatively brushed against the tip of his own, he broke away. He knew if the kiss continued for a moment longer, all principles would be lost next to a bush on a darkened terrace with a woman whose name he did not know.

"Alas, my rescuer of the unlovable, please forgive my impertinence."

She did not speak, much to his chagrin, as he desperately wanted to hear the melodic notes of her voice. To hold it as a memory, to cherish it during his remaining years as an unabashed rake.

She merely nodded. Her grip gave way as her arms wrapped around her middle, holding herself together.

"Until we meet again." With one hand on the railing, he leapt to the ground. Jack gazed up the half-story to where she stood. It reminded him of Romeo and Juliette in a scene much like this. "*Parting is such sweet sorrow.*"

On the breeze, her words carried across the lawn to complete the line. "*That I shall say goodbye until it be morrow.*"

CHAPTER FIVE
A SUMMONS

The door hinges creaked when Thomas entered. "Sorry about that. I will ask a maid to oil them later."

Jack rubbed his whiskered cheeks before he waved away the intrusion. "What time is it?"

"Half past nine."

Jack grumbled. He knew there was a reason for his valet to wake him so early for the second day in a row, but his mind was preoccupied with visions of tightly coiled twists of honey and eyes the color of a topaz ring he once admired in a Belgium jeweler's case. The taste of an innocent's lips, like a sip of fine French brandy, lingered and fueled his curiosity. How would she taste in other places? As scrumptious or more heady and robust?

"My lord." Thomas handed over a message with a distinct scarlet seal.

Before he broke the wax, Jack knew with certainty that the letter contained a summons. So did Thomas, who readied the shaving implements and ordered a bath.

Jack unfolded the note. The sharp slashes of his father's

handwriting filled two lines on the page. No flowery language, no inquiries about his only son's health. Short, simple, and directly to the point. *Come to Maitland House at quarter past eleven.*

So much for erotic daydreams. Jack flung off the bedclothes and stomped to the bathing room to the waiting hip bath for a quick wash. Answering the earl's summons required expeditious actions.

With the help of the ever-efficient Thomas, Jack dressed in a respectable amount of time. His temperamental cook made a tasty plate of sliced meats, cheese, and cinnamon scones. Hmm, she must have forgiven him for the stolen platter.

In the carriage, Jack mused over the deb in the garden. He had indulged in the kiss as a mere whim, entranced by such an innocent in a sea rife with unscrupulous people. Perhaps egged on by Countess Anworth, he felt dissatisfaction with his current state of affairs.

The carriage rolled to a halt in the exclusive Mayfair neighborhood. A recently built property from the past decade, Maitland House became the Earl's primary London residence, while the older home in Marylebone now belonged to Jack. An ideal location for a bachelor of leisure, out of the purview of a meddling father.

Graves, his father's obsequious butler, showed him to the study.

A fire blazed in the hearth with two ball-and-club-footed chairs situated to face the intricate mantelpiece and the Rembrandt that hung above. Jack occupied the chair nearest to the door.

He poured a full glass of Scottish whisky, then snipped off the end of a cigar. The illegality of the drink did little to deter either man, as both preferred the amber liquor's soothing warmth to fruity fortified wines. He drew the cigar under his nose and inhaled the rich aroma before he used a spill to light it. Puffing on the fine tobacco, a heavy smoke cloud filled the room, one to which his father would vehemently object.

The door opened for his imperious father. Nearly his twin in appearance, save for the silver threaded through his temples.

"Linscott, a pleasure." Though the tone of his father's voice implied the opposite.

"Maitland."

The earl sat in the second chair and glared pointedly at the smoke that circled Jack's head while he poured a drink.

"Rather early in the day to imbibe," Jack noted.

"When in your presence, I feel the extra fortification is a requirement." He raised the glass. "To your mother."

A ritual Jack did not mind, whenever together the earl honored his only wife with a salute. A sign his father actually possessed a heart.

"Do you know why I asked you to Maitland House?" the earl asked as he set his empty glass on the table between them.

"I am sure I could surmise the reason—a cataloging of my failures as your sole heir. A decree to alter my current behavior or risk a number of unpleasant deaths. Perhaps you decided to buy an officer's commission once again, then ship me off to India. Malaria might put an end to my indolent lifestyle. Take your pick, I am through caring."

"Your flippant tone does not amuse me." His father sat rigidly and drummed fingers along the chair's armrest.

Jack slouched against the tufted leather back. "Absolutely it does. I am charming, ask anyone."

"Most of the *ton* find you an unrepentant rake."

This particular arrow hit its mark with a resounding thwack. For once he wished for a milder reputation, though he knew the truth, he was much, much worse than anyone imagined.

"Touché."

From beneath the decanter, his father withdrew a sheet of paper with a list of finely scratched names. "Your birthday is fast approaching."

As if he needed a reminder of the weighty hands that ticked away the remaining years. He neared the dark side of his thirties and was perhaps a bit long in the tooth to continue on his current path of overindulgence.

"Yes." Jack drew out the word as a suspicious feeling stirred low in his gut. Birthdays ending in multiples of five inspired his father's creativity to new levels of devious motivations to toe the line as the only suitable heir to the Maitland earldom. Jack approached thirty.

"My final hope died when I bought your commission. You came back from Waterloo the same unrepentant rake with your ideals firmly entrenched. You are, as always, intractable." The earl flicked the list with his fingers. "I am afraid my earlier entreaties have fallen on deaf ears. You've left me with no choice—marry before you are thirty, or I will cut off every shilling of your allowance."

Whisky spewed from Jack's mouth; he choked on the words as they sunk in. The promised threats that tumbled from his father's thin lips. Blow followed by perfectly timed blow. A twenty-minute bout in the ring with Sambridge's bare knuckles would feel like butterfly kisses after his father systematically destroyed his indolent existence.

"You will receive nothing. Your townhouse in Marylebone will be rented out. I will sell your Arabian because he will no longer have a place in my stables. The salaries of your cook, valet, and secretary will no longer come out of my accounts. It is your decision, naturally, but your income exists solely on my generosity."

"It was you, was it not? The reason I have no more funds at my disposal."

His father did not even bother to feign astonishment at his son's accusation. He picked at the cuticle of his thumb while Jack railed about the injustices served upon him.

"A month! How am I to find a suitable bride in the time it takes to acquire a license to marry?" Jack was partially out of his chair, ready to flee. He gripped his hair in his fists, half-willing to yank on the strands, but knew he would end up bald with the ferocity of his anger.

The earl attempted to hide his smirk, but his lips twitched. "Surely you have encountered a few viable candidates. What of Miss Mattingly? Her father has given her a substantial dowry."

Jack blanched. "Only to compensate for her lack of appeal. The woman has a goiter the size of a crabapple!"

The earl pointed to the paper in his hand. "Miss Sheffield, then."

"She is taking orders. She is almost a nun."

"No, not her. The other Miss Sheffield, Lilly."

Jack raked his hands through his hair, the strands fell in disarray. "Lilly Sheffield is eighteen. The age difference is intolerable."

"My steward and I created a list to help. There are three-and-forty names. At least one should appeal. Choose a ring from the countess's jewels and propose. It is that simple."

"What father will allow his daughter to wed a man with no engagement or proper courtship?" He currently had not a farthing to his name, only an overdrawn bank account. He had already sold a case of brandy to his favorite gaming hell to pay bills and stay out of Fleet. Now he had to marry or remain impoverished?

"Those barriers exist because of your antics and lack of discretion. Any proper young woman with the tiniest drop of blue blood or one from a respectable family will do. Son…"

Jack flinched at the uncharacteristic acknowledgment of their relationship. When did his glass become empty? Jack picked up the decanter and splashed liquid inside before he swallowed it all.

"Find an attractive woman, hie her off to Scotland, and be done with it. Begetting an heir is delightful entertainment. Marriage will make you a contented man. You will no longer have this inexplicable need to live a life of indulgence and indolence."

He blanched at his father's description of sexual congress. "You could have remarried, produced more suitable heirs than me. Do not forget there is Cousin Gregory. Why push marriage now?"

Maitland grimaced at the mention of Jack's buffoon of a cousin. "I constantly try to forget Gregory. No, never a woman for me other than your angel of a mother. Marriage is my only hope of saving you. If I could find you a good woman to care for I would, but we both know you would reject the poor creature simply to spite me. Read the list. I await the opportunity to greet my future daughter-in-law."

With the painfully thorough document in hand, Jack swallowed his protest. Call his father's bluff or agree to a life trapped in a marriage to a woman he did not love? He knew his father did not jest or make empty threats. Signing Jack's life away as a major had taught him that. No more putting off the inevitable. Preferably a non-repulsive sort. Surely his father required grandchildren in the future. He would not put it past the man to threaten to cut him off again if his wife did not bear him a child within a year.

"How exactly do you propose I start?"

His father won; he always won. He managed to defeat Jack at every turn. Wiley bastard.

"Well, I would start with the Nottington Ball tonight, then make sure to attend all events for the foreseeable future." The earl stood to indicate their meeting was now concluded.

As Jack walked through the door with his head lowered in defeat, his father called out one last request.

"John?"

He turned around, surprised to hear the use of his birth name.

"I will be expecting a grandson by this time next year."

The butler closed the door on the earl's hearty whoops.

Maitland addressed Graves, "We have got him hooked. We only have to crank the reel to bring him to shore."

"Yes, my lord. Clever indeed." Graves handed the earl his freshly ironed newspaper and watched his master jump and click his heels, all but dancing to his study. Graves pitied Lord Jack for once, not envious of him being forced to find a bride in a month's time. It took Graves six-and-twenty years before he found his love, but even then, they never married. They remained instead the butler and the housekeeper for the Earl of Maitland. No, he felt no envy today and he whispered as much to Mrs. Putnam when he stole a kiss in the dining room not a minute later.

CHAPTER SIX
THE MORNING AFTER

Annabelle paced the length of the rose drawing room, brushing her fingers over tingling lips. The encounter on the terrace remained fresh in her mind, most likely because of her obsessive replaying of every subtle nuance surrounding *the kiss*. The giddy excitement. Kissed by a mysterious stranger. And it happened to the mousey debutante from Hampshire!

Annabelle could barely believe she allowed a stranger to touch her so intimately. What would it be like to kiss for longer? To feel the bare skin of hands holding hers… a bubble of laughter erupted before she silenced it with a cough. Truly, there was no reason to hide her joy, unless porcelain figurines could reveal secrets. For a fleeting moment, she was alone. Well, except for Winston. But he did not count.

Did all kisses feel the same?

A kiss from a rake. Nothing more, nothing less. Best to be forgotten, or at least remembered only in private. *Rakes mean ruin*, better to remember her aunt's mantra. One of many, but probably the most useful.

She sighed, then picked up her one-eyed cat to rub its notched ear with the tips of her fingers. It melted against her chest, purring.

Winston was the man of her life. Loyal only to its rescuer.

"I once reckoned you were all I needed, my furry knight, but perhaps I was wrong." Winston leapt from her arms, its crooked tail twitching back and forth as it stalked to the basket near the hearth.

Aunt Silvia entered the room. The housekeeper trailed behind scratching furiously on a sheet of paper.

"Annabelle! Have we had any callers?" Silvia turned on her heel to dismiss Mrs. Carter with a wave of her jewel-laden hand.

A maid snuck in with a tea tray.

"Not yet." Annabelle slumped onto a rose-colored settee.

Her aunt lifted her hand with a tut-tut to remind her niece of the proper way to sit.

While Silvia sipped a cup of tea, the lady subjected Annabelle to another of her lengthy tirades about how to land the perfect husband. Long ago she declared herself the expert in matrimonial matches, after she managed to be married and widowed four times. Each marriage brought more wealth, but no children. Now Silvia entered her twilight years to prowl once again with husband number five firmly in her sights.

Annabelle eyed the shortbread longingly while Silvia snatched *The List*. She tapped the tip of her lorgnette as she contemplated the names. With her aunt distracted, Annabelle reached for a biscuit and munched surreptitiously on the end.

"Now, Annabelle." The high-pitched voice pierced the quiet of the room. "It does you no good to act like a wallflower or else men will discount you."

"Yes, Aunt Silvia," Annabelle said firmly as she bit into another piece of shortbread. *The Husband Hunt*, her aunt's favorite topic for discussion. If only they could talk about anything else. The theater perhaps. Or a novel. She just finished a delightful piece from a Miss Austen titled *Emma*.

"Are you even listening to me? What have I said about eating too many sweets? A man prefers a slender frame. Sweets are treats we do not eat." Her aunt ran her pudgy hands over her body as if to emphasize its slenderness. Nothing about Silvia suggested slimness or restraint.

"Yes, Aunt Silvia," Annabelle sighed as she put down the remains of her biscuit to sip her tea.

"You are not getting any younger, as you are already one-and-twenty," Silvia tsked her niece. "Remember your father swore this would be the only season. I know I promised that you would not have to return to such a dreadful place as your father's cottage in Hampshire, but there is little I can do if you remain so opposed to my council. Your cousin is not here to help us. Without the guidance of a younger gentleman, I am afraid we need to consider other possibilities."

Annabelle did not like the sound of this new direction in *The Husband Hunt*. Where was Marcus? Her cousin last wrote from Italy that he was once again extending his Grand Tour. He should be here in London. He promised.

"Perhaps if we send another request to Cousin Marcus, he might delay his plans to visit Greece and help me navigate this season."

"By the time he receives a letter and books passage home, it will be over." Her aunt set down her tea cup. "I saw you did not dance with Lord Welsham as I requested."

"He favored Francine MacKinnon. Then Miss Fitzherbert," Annabelle said.

Her aunt shivered at the mention of the sour-dispositioned debutante. "If he prefers the Fitzherberts, then so be it. Let the man suffer." Silvia pursued *The List* once more. "We should consider more mature gentlemen. Lord Stalworth comes to mind."

Lord Stalworth was at the upper end of sixty, a man old enough to be her grandfather. *Blech.* "His pursuit is singularly focused on you, dear Aunt."

Silvia giggled like a young debutante. "Oh, Annabelle, you do like to flatter an old woman." She waved a fan in front of her powdered face. "Then perhaps Colonel Burton. Though he is an odious man, he is flushed with funds."

Annabelle blanched. "Is there no other? I danced with the Duke of Sambridge. He is quite attractive." Not as handsome as strange men who caught naive debutantes alone on terraces, but Annabelle was not about to give voice to such a thought.

Silvia's head perked up. She tapped her lip with her finger before she shook her head as if she were in a conversation with herself. "Sambridge? As much as we might want a connection with a man of such rank and privilege, it is better to consider other more available candidates."

Her aunt never opted for restraint when unfiltered truth would do. The unwanted shortbread taunted Annabelle with its sugary goodness.

Silvia sighed heavily and consulted her list of eligible bachelors. "This list grows shorter by the minute. What about Baron Crayfield? You are close with his sister Cecilia, are you not?"

"I admit he is rather comely, but he desires, um," Annabelle paused. Discussions about money were crass, but she knew Baron Crayfield, or Nigel as he allowed only Annabelle to call him, would never be interested in her because of the lack of wealth. "...a more financially beneficial union."

Silvia arched her gray eyebrows in disapproval. "Perhaps. And yet, perhaps we need to invite Miss Cecilia to tea. Find out from the sister what her brother requires."

Any argument was a practice in futility, Annabelle reluctantly nodded. She enjoyed Cissy's company immensely, but Nigel's consideration of Annabelle was firmly planted at zero.

Winston jumped onto her lap purring.

"Gah! Why must you insist on such a hideous beast for a pet?" Silvia recoiled and threw her hands up in the air in frustration.

Lovingly, Annabelle scratched its ears, while it butted its head against her palm. "Winston was half-starved when I found him. Just because he is a little rough around the edges, does not mean he should not be loved."

"Rough around the edges?" Silvia scoffed. "That cat has the temperament of the devil. He looks like he got tangled with a threshing machine! If you can love such a ragtag furball like Winston, I have no idea why you object to so many of my suggestions for future husbands."

Annabelle shrugged. Perhaps her aunt had a point, but a temperamental pet and husband were not on par, were they? "You cannot compare this lovely cat to an old goat like Lord Stalworth?"

"But Baron Crayfield?"

Annabelle shrank in defeat. "Fine, invite Cissy to tea. But I will warn you aunt; it is pointless."

Silvia clapped in delight and scribbled an invitation for the next day. Annabelle rested her head against the back of the settee and stroked a contented Winston. If she had to consider anyone to marry, it would be the mysterious Viscount Linscott with his wicked dimples.

CHAPTER SEVEN

THE OBSIDIAN CLUB

One month. Those two words tumbled around Jack's brain while the hired hackney charged through London to St. James Street. Fleeing to the continent was on the forefront of practical ideas. While finding a bride whose family would willingly offer her in marriage in exchange for the security of his income was the least practical. Impossible. Improbable. Intolerable.

His father's list was thorough if not impressive. Jack had no idea so many debs were out this season. Then again, when was the last time he paid attention to the marriage mart? Not even when he returned home a decorated soldier did he bother with the twittering masses.

Escape was a young man's dream. Foolish, too. Frankly, he enjoyed his comfortable home. He stayed abreast of political situations. Studied improved agricultural practices for the tenants on the Maitland estate. He was far more interested in a rising bottom line than sinking into indolence and waste. If only his father would bother to see that. But the earl was single-minded and punishing his only son was his favorite pastime.

Instead of fleeing to France, he chose his gentleman's club. The one he invested in with his former sergeant and well-known bruiser–Arthur Fox.

The Obsidian Club. A modern building nestled among the masculine havens of Boodle's and White's, this was Jack's second home.

The majordomo clapped his meaty fist around Jack's shoulder and gave it a squeeze. "Word moves fast through this town. We have been expecting you." He pointed to the betting book propped on a lectern near the front door.

Fast was an understatement. More like a spy in Maitland's home. Had espionage worked this quickly during the Napoleonic Wars, they would have defeated the emperor during the Third Coalition. From the time Jack left his father's home, confided with his secretary, and arrived at his club—entries for and against his procurement of a bride filled an entire page. The staggering amounts blew his mind, so he tossed in a hundred quid against himself. Sure bets and all.

What he needed was commiseration. He found the perfect partner sitting in the lounge. His closest friend–Baron Crayfield.

Nigel had his head buried in a newspaper, puffing on a cheroot.

Jack slouched in the chair across from his friend, nudging him with the toe of his boot. "I need a wife." The greeting had its desired effect.

The baron lowered his newspaper, while his eyebrows shot past his hairline. "Pardon?"

Jack ordered a bottle of whisky and two glasses. "You know the earl has been threatening me for years."

"How is this threat different from the last?" Nigel folded

the paper and set it aside. "Did he buy you a commission as a naval officer? When do you leave for India?"

Jack chuckled. The waiter returned, pouring two fingers each and leaving the bottle behind. They were going to need it.

They toasted each other's health. Nigel let the glass sit on his bottom lip, savoring the flavor.

Jack drained the contents in one swallow and poured a second. "My father changed the trust. If I am not married in one month, I lose everything."

Nigel choked and cursed. "A month? Your father has gone balmy."

Jack shrugged and removed the list from his pocket to wave it in Nigel's direction.

Tempted by the contents, Nigel snatched it from Jack's fingers.

"My father and his meddlesome steward made a list of three-and-forty different available debutantes!"

"Impressive." Nigel perused the list, shaking and nodding along while he read. "So, one month to wade through this list and marry? The demand is ludicrous."

"I have no choice."

"Then we decide right now who you want to pursue." He sounded certain. Perhaps Jack's luck was changing since he had an expert bride hunter to aid him. "Tell me about your ideal match."

With an irritated grunt, Jack listed the qualities he sought. "Attractive, but not overly so. No one vain and concerned with appearance."

"Then explain your latest paramour." Nigel crossed his legs, looking entirely too comfortable for this discussion.

"Entertainment." It was the only reason Jack allowed himself to be involved with any woman.

"So, it was not Cupid's arrow?"

"With Valentina? You and I both know that while she kept my toes warm, she had her eyes trained on the next target."

Nigel tilted his head and nodded. "I saw her leave with Sambridge. Guess your arrangement is already over."

Jack shrugged. One less hassle to undertake. Then he ticked off more qualities on his fingers. "Desires a title, but not a fortune. She must be malleable. Quiet. Well-read. Able to carry on a conversation. God help me, but I need a mouse."

"Not exactly the fine qualities you expect a husband to want in his future bride. I mean, you will have to bed this woman."

Jack shrugged. "I do not care about an heir. A manageable wife, who stays out of my way is my preference."

Nigel steepled his fingers together, resting them beneath his chin. He sat in pensive silence, while Jack ruminated over a third glass. Whisky had a way of clearing the mind or dulling the pain.

"I have a few ideas. Gladys Fitzherbert. This is her fourth season."

"Four years and no engagement. Something must be wrong with her."

Nigel shrugged. "Perhaps a bit more opinionated than you prefer."

Jack tried to gauge Nigel's expression. "How opinionated?"

"Eh." Nigel tilted his hand back and forth. "More than is de rigueur, but less than Cissy." Nigel referred to his sister, who had no qualms expressing exactly what was on her mind.

"Who's next?" Jack snatched the list from Nigel.

"Vivian Stratham. She has held a tendre for me, but perhaps you might secure her affection."

Jack's eyebrows clashed together. "The curvy blonde? Last ball she attended, she shoved me out of the way to corner you. I nearly landed in the punch bowl."

"I remember." Nigel winced. "It might not be well done of me, but perhaps I can foist her attention onto you. We would both benefit."

"Pass."

"No." Nigel waved excitedly. "It is a perfect idea. It will solve both our problems. She is from a respectable family with vast connections to wealthy enterprises and is a, er, a nice person." The way his lip twitched after he completed the statement only fueled Jack's doubts to the contrary.

"Next suggestion."

"But..."

Nigel protested, but Jack refused to relent. He only had a month to find and wed a woman. Rescuing friends from overly eager debutantes was not in the cards.

"Fine, some friend you are," Nigel said without any actual heart behind the complaint. "What about Isabel Howard? She is more your speed. Beautiful black hair, a little more exotic than ordinary."

"Howard?" A recent scandal involving the name niggled the recesses of his mind. "Sounds familiar. Remind me."

Nigel groaned. "I hoped you would not remember. Another idea is..."

"Wait, tell me more. I am intrigued. I always enjoy the transgressions of others."

"Your father does not."

"If it means I am married, he will look the other way." The woman appealed more and more. Exotic and perhaps a bit outrageous.

"Her father killed the future Marquess of Dannonbury."

Jack lost his grip on his glass. Liquid splashed his trousers. "That Howard? Pass!"

"Thought you might feel that way. Francine MacKinnon."

"Is she related to Leith MacKinnon?" Jack shuddered. He

remembered Leith from Oxford. A bear of a man with a temper to match.

"His sister, but she is far less temperamental. The solitary family resemblance is their unusual height. She has said two words all season."

"That is more like it. I am rather fond of tall women. You wrench your neck less."

Nigel grinned. "Precisely! She will be perfect for you, trust me. No scores of other men to vie for her attention. I forgot to mention the best part, Leith is currently in Scotland. He is rebuilding an estate he inherited. My friend, I could not pick a better victim, er, future spouse for you."

"Any other names stick out?" Reluctant to, as the saying went, put all his eggs in one basket, Jack wished for a few more potential candidates.

"There is Miss Mattingly."

Jack winced. "My God, man! The goiter."

Nigel shrugged. "Annabelle Greene. She is a bit animal mad and quiet. Cissy likes her well enough and is the only one of my sister's friends I find tolerable."

So, this is what has become of him? The once unflappable major now resorted to picking out his future wife like she was a filly displayed at Tattershall. "When is the next *ton* event? My father suggested the Nottington Ball. I need to strategize if I am going to be successful."

"For this situation, I believe intimate functions will better serve your pursuit. Check your stack of invitations, but I am sure there is one for Lady Sinclair's affair on Wednesday. I will not be there as I need to escort Cissy to Almack's, but the lesser-sought-after debutantes without vouchers tend to be invited as they are not otherwise occupied."

"I recall Parker mentioned such an invitation. A dinner if

memory serves. At least I will not have to dance. There should be plenty of good wine. But the conversation..." Jack made a disgusted face.

Nigel laughed in commiseration. "It is all part of the battle, my friend."

"Yes, but unlike you, I have been through real battles. They are far less frightening than marriage-hungry mothers with the parson's noose swinging in their grips." Jack squeezed the bridge of his nose between his thumb and index finger, while he mentally counted the reasons he had to persevere. Why, in the end, he was better off with his purse intact. "Any other suggestions?"

"Gunters."

Jack groaned at the mention of the popular haunt of the fashionable elite. "Not ices."

"On Tuesdays, I escort Cissy when she calls on her friends." Nigel yawned and scratched at the layers of whiskers covering his cheeks.

"If I must. Any other brilliant ideas?" Jack felt his cravat cinch tighter on his throat.

"Walks in the park."

"What am I? A woman who goes out for a daily constitutional?" Jack yanked at the fabric but did not find relief.

"No, a man hoping to meet a woman out for a stroll. You wanted my help, this is part of the hunt. I can throw women at your feet, but short of trussing one up and delivering her to the chapel, you are the one who has to do all the dirty work."

"I would rather be shot at by a squad of French frogs." Jack stuffed the list into his pocket.

Artie Fox entered the room and leaned against the chair Jack occupied. "Heard some interesting rumors all with your name attached."

Jack rolled his eyes. "I thought you had more important things to do, like running your club?"

"Rumors lead to profit." He wore a garish silk waistcoat stitched with outlines of men and women engaged in sexual acrobatics. Offering a cheroot from a silver case tucked into his breast pocket, he motioned to Jack. "There is one we should discuss in my office if Baron Crayfield can spare you?"

Nigel picked up the newspaper and resumed his earlier position. "Please take him. He is in a foul mood and spoiling my good humor."

Artie's laugh echoed in the quiet room. "When is he not?"

Nigel answered with a smirk.

Some friends he had amassed.

Jack followed Artie through a hidden doorway in the paper-covered walls, then up a wooden staircase to the first floor. Another door opened into a lavishly decorated hallway with lush carpeting featuring the same ornate oriental pattern as the paper-covered walls. Artie pushed against a seam along the wall where a door opened into a vast flat.

The décor deviated from overly sensual abundance to a more austere masculine simplicity with heavy oak furniture and few ornaments, save for the regimental sword displayed proudly behind his desk.

"That is a hell of a polish you gave the saber. Practically blinded me." Jack removed a stack of newspapers from a seat in front of the desk before he sat with his legs crossed at the ankles.

Artie groaned, stiffly unfolding his body into his chair. He rubbed his knee before the tightness around his mouth eased. "It was a bitch smoothing out the chip from when I gutted the French lieutenant, but it shined up nicely." They rarely spoke of the war, merely passing references that contained a hundred unspoken thoughts. "I feel compelled to warn you but not where others might overhear."

"I am not concerned about the newest threats from my father. I always land on my feet like a cat tossed out a window."

His friend's scared face broke into a crooked smile before he waved his hands in dismissal. "You do, but that is not what has me worried. The Countess of Anworth is sniffing around my majordomo, trying to bribe him for information about a few of our patrons." He tapped his cheroot against an ashtray, leaned far back in his chair, and assessed Jack. "I smell something foul."

"Probably your boots."

"More likely your cologne. In all earnestness, something's amiss with your light o' love."

"I would not worry. We have severed our relationship. Last night, she left the Boucher affair in the arms of Sambridge." Good riddance too, he had been hunting for a way to end their arrangement for months. Let the duke have her, he could afford her extravagant tastes.

"Perhaps, she is moving up in the world. One would never know her father was a nitwit baron who was duped by a scheming prostitute with a pretty face and brains to match." Artie twisted one of the diamond rings on his massive finger.

"Like mother, like daughter."

"She is not done with you. Not by a long shot."

Jack shook his head in denial. "Be that as it may, she will not have anything to do with me now since I am a pauper. Money is the only language she understands."

Artie smoothed over his unfashionable beard. "You are wrong about one thing. It is not money she craves, but power. Sambridge is no fool either, mark my words. Guard yourself."

Jack doubted Valentina's desire to hold onto a viscount without income. Sambridge was the mark. A true coup for the prostitute's daughter-turned-countess. No, Jack had no concerns, not about Valentina. Though he did wish he could pawn the ruby bracelet he had given her, the funds from it alone might keep him solvent for a year. Then again, what was a year when faced with a lifetime of poverty? Looks like he had a dinner to prepare for.

CHAPTER EIGHT
A VISITOR

Aunt Silvia burst through the parlor doors, frightening Annabelle and chasing Winston under the floral settee. "Why are you not wearing the peach-sprigged muslin? The Duke of Sambridge is walking up our front stoop as we speak, and you are wearing a dress fit for the country."

Annabelle dropped the book she was reading onto the low table in front of her. Tea with Cissy had been a blessed reprieve, but it was short-lived when a missive from the duke arrived, stating his intention to visit tomorrow. Ever since Aunt Silvia had been barking orders to anything that sat still for longer than five minutes.

"We decided on this gown," Annabelle said, holding up the delicately embroidered sleeve. It was a lovely robin's egg blue walking gown with off-centered enclosures and ruffled seams. "You said it accentuated my complexion, while the peach was too soft."

"I have changed my mind."

"We cannot choose a different gown." Annabelle's point was emphasized by the front knocker resounding loudly through the hallway.

Silvia huffed her displeasure, caught between a fruitless argument and the need to impress the biggest catch of the season. Pride always won out.

Coleman entered the room with a visitor trailing close behind. The butler's transformation from drunkard to skillful servant was truly remarkable, thanks in part to the drills Silvia insisted upon. They had paid off with his flawless execution of duties. No one would know of the man's colorful past unless they managed to look a bit too closely at his cravat and spy the tattoo on his neck.

Coleman announced the visitor, ending with a regal bow. "My lady and Miss Greene, His Grace, the Duke of Sambridge."

Annabelle resisted applauding, but Coleman winked over the duke's head.

Sambridge made the perfunctory greetings with little ceremony and picked the armchair to Annabelle's left, while Silvia sat on the settee across from her. An awkward conversation followed with Sambridge appearing more interested in the display of porcelain figurines than in conversation.

"Your Grace, it was good of you to call," Silvia said, breaking the silence.

He cleared his throat, then shifted in his seat. "I had hoped to speak with Viscount Oakmont."

Silvia chirped with glee, but Annabelle felt the entire room shift beneath her slippers. If the duke wished to speak to her cousin during calling hours that implied the desire to strengthen their current acquaintance, possibly even extending to courtship. Surely one dance was not enough to encourage the stodgy duke.

"I must apologize. My cousin is still on his Grand Tour." Annabelle felt the heat behind Silvia's glare.

"Yes, we are a house of only women at the moment." Silvia waved a fan and smiled widely. "If there is perhaps something you would like to address with me as Miss Greene's relative, I would be happy to speak with you in the morning room."

Winston, curious about the newcomer, rose from its basket. It snaked around the duke's ankles. Sambridge tried pushing the cat away with his polished boot, but it was more persistent than usual.

Silvia gasped when the duke reached down, coming away with orange and white hairs covering his gloved hands, but much to their relief, not sporting a fresh round of scratches.

Annabelle released a puff of air. "Your Grace, I had no idea you had such a way with animals. Winston is normally disagreeable to anyone, especially those brave enough to pet him."

Sambridge shook his hand and brushed it against his trouser leg. "I am more inclined to befriend horses, Miss Greene. But if your feline wishes for companionship, I have no objection."

Annabelle's heart dipped at the sight of Sambridge scratching Winston's notched ear. The cat purred. Perhaps it was meant to be, this duke and Annabelle. The cat certainly found him an agreeable sort.

The knocker thumped loudly. Winston withdrew from the affectionate newcomer, opting to curl upon one of the other armchairs.

"Who could that be?" Silvia asked no one in particular.

Sambridge glanced at his pocket watch. "Will you be at Almack's tomorrow, Miss Greene?"

Before Annabelle could answer, the butler entered followed

by a group of welcomed faces. It was Cissy along with her brother and another man, whose face was obscured by a bouquet of posies.

Nigel was the first to speak. "My dearest Miss Greene. My sister insisted we stop by to introduce our friend, Viscount Linscott."

The man lowered the bouquet, revealing a face she had never thought she would see again. Perhaps in a dream, but not here in the middle of her parlor.

He was more striking than she remembered with the dimples being the giveaway. On a darkened terrace or a bright afternoon, his was a face impossible to forget. If Sambridge made her heart dip, this Linscott made her soul take flight.

"My lord, please allow me to introduce you to my aunt, Lady Brighton."

Silvia's face pinched with disapproval. She would not cut the newcomers directly, but she would make it uncomfortable enough for them to leave. "Yes, Lord Linscott. I am well acquainted with your father. How is he?"

"He fairs well."

The Hammonds took the available seats in the room impervious to the matron's grumbles. The only chair that remained held the snoozing Winston. Annabelle opened her mouth to issue a warning, but the duke repeated his question about Almack's.

Linscott handed the posies to Coleman and reached for Winston.

Coleman leapt forward, trying to snatch the cat before Linscott. The flowers scattered across the carpeting. "My lord, that might not be..."

The warning came too late. The sleeping feline was not to be disturbed and released a displeased yowl while swatting without regard with his claws fully extended. Before Annabelle or Coleman could save the viscount, the cat had scratched the man's face and sunk its claws in through the layers of fabric covering his arms. In a puff of orange fur, it fled the scene.

"Wise," Coleman said as the last clump settled in the mayhem that was the parlor.

No one moved. They waited. Nigel's face twisted in what could only be a weak attempt to stifle laughter. Cissy covered her mouth, her eyes dancing wildly. Sambridge froze halfway between entering the fray and self-preservation. Silvia paled to a sickly shade of white.

"My lord, I apologize for my niece's ill-behaved pet. He shall be destroyed. We cannot allow for such behavior from our animals." Silvia had made the threat many times before, but she had never followed through. That was when it was only Coleman and an odd housemaid who suffered the vicious swipes from Winston's claws.

Annabelle feared this time the threat had heart. "You cannot hurt him," she cried.

"If you will escort me, my lord. The cook has an excellent salve for cat scratches." Bless Coleman for trying to intercede in the way a butler could. He gave a sympathetic tilt to his head, one that tried to say *do not worry*.

Linscott squeezed Annabelle's shoulder. She should have shrugged away the familiar gesture but was too distraught to think.

"Fear not," he said. Removing a handkerchief and dabbing at an oozing scratch, he flashed his dimpled smile at her aunt. "The fault lay entirely on me. I am fine. Nothing worse than what His Grace has done to me in the pugilism ring. Now, I will see about this salve and when I return, I would love to taste some of those biscuits on the table." He pointed to the refreshment tray left for visitors and winked at Annabelle.

She felt a flutter in her chest. Conversation carried on in

the room, swirling around her, but her attention remained focused on the missing viscount. She finally had a formal introduction, and it only made the night on the terrace more magical.

CHAPTER NINE
DINNER AND INTRIGUE

The drawing room of Lady Sinclair's townhome overflowed with guests from the fringe members of the fashionable *haute ton* and the rising stars of the middle class. Sea captains conversed with earls, vicars with whisky distillers, and sprinkled among them were eligible misses on the hunt for a husband.

The Ladies Sinclair and Brighton had known one another since before they were debutantes when Louis XVI still had a head. Similar to Silvia's long line of matrimonial disasters, Lady Sinclair outlived all three of her husbands. Though fortunately for her, each subsequent marriage provided more wealth and prestige than the previous. Her current Mayfair address was the prime example of the splendor a husband's deep pockets provided.

Walls covered in paintings from Renaissance masters. Imported Italian marble. Carved cherubs extended limbs from crown molding. Dotted throughout was an abundance of servants dressed in purple and gold liveries. Overabundance in every corner.

Before dining, the attendants mingled as apéritifs, and conversation floated around the room. Silvia flirted with a pair of septuagenarians while Annabelle found a quiet corner in which to hide from a particularly amorous Army colonel. A man who seemed far more interested in her bosom than any words she uttered.

She could not help but hope for the appearance of one particular gentleman—the dimpled viscount with lips of sin. Each glimpse of a newcomer stirred anticipation within her breast, only to be quickly dashed by the sight of older men. The ones who tended to wear a corset to hide their ever-expanding waistlines or too much pomade to disguise their thin hair.

At that moment, Lord Stalworth had Annabelle cornered while he sang his praises for her aunt. She listened with half an ear and sipped the overly tart lemonade. Was the mere thought of a person enough to conjure their presence?

By nine o'clock, Annabelle's stomach rumbled in protest of the late hour. Lady Sinclair was disinclined to end her flirtations so everyone could move into the dining room. It was only a matter of time before Annabelle succumbed to her hunger pains, as her body released yet another audible grumble of frustration. She was ready to make her excuses to Lord Stalworth. Perhaps she could complain of a megrim. That might encourage Aunt Silvia to make an expeditious exit. They might be able to catch the cook before she retired for the evening.

She snatched another glass of lemonade. The fourth since she arrived.

The gathered crowd parted. Their hostess twittered and fluttered around her newest arrival like a hummingbird that fed on gossip instead of sugar. And there he stood. Tall. Dimpled. Dangerous.

Annabelle expected him to swat away the pest, but instead, he was genial to the point of perfection. As he conversed, he searched the room until he acknowledged Annabelle with a slight tilt of his head. Even with the distance between them, she felt the heat of his scrutiny. A burn so intense every molecule of her body burst as if two stars collided. Her skin came alive at the mere sight of him. Tingles and quivers. An awareness of her body she never knew before. The way the fabric of her chemise rubbed against her bare skin. Her breasts pressed against the confines of her corset. An itch she could not scratch. Unsettled. Terrified. Intrigued. She averted her eyes and hoped to regain control of her senses.

Linscott stalked across the room like a wolf. Prowled around the perimeter while she cowered in a corner, trapped in conversation between a lord and vicar. The lecherous colonel had spotted her once again, and now loomed to block her exit. Two hunters and only one prey.

Too late, firmly ensnared in the trap. Even his canines gleamed in the candlelight as he sensed his victory. "Lord Stalworth and Vicar Carter." The wolf bowed his head. "My lord, I hear you recently acquired a new mare from Tattershall."

"I am hoping to breed her with Pirate's Booty. He has had a good run, but it is time to put him to stud." Lord Stalworth's belly jiggled as he elbowed both the vicar and Linscott. "We should all have to suffer a similar fate, eh, Vicar?"

The man's face suffused crimson as he stared at his empty glass. "Apologies, Miss Greene, I believe I am out of refreshment."

He patted her arm and made his excuses. Thus, she was minus one virtuous man. Perhaps the only virtuous man present.

"Annabelle Greene, it is my pleasure to present Viscount Linscott. His father and I are old hunting buddies." Stalworth's avuncular tone betrayed a particular fondness for the man on his right, while his voice dripped with disdain when he turned to the other. "And this is Colonel Burton."

"A pleasure." She dipped into a polite curtsy to both men. "I hope the evening is enjoyable."

"Rather intolerable if you ask me. I am famished." The colonel patted his round belly.

Annabelle winced at the crudeness of the gesture.

"Perhaps if you speak with Lady Sinclair, she will hurry and announce dinner." Linscott's suggestion surprised Annabelle with its obvious intent of luring at least one of the men away.

"A capital idea!" Before Lord Stalworth escorted the colonel away from Annabelle, he whispered, "Since I have saved you, make sure you put in a good word to your aunt, the charming little vixen."

"Absolutely." She squeezed his hand, certain to extol his virtues tomorrow, yet terrified to be left alone in the clutches of a wolf. Or man. Or manwolf? Wolfman? Being in a room with thirty other people should mean Annabelle was protected, but why did she feel like a fluffy little lamb about to be gobbled up by a ravenous predator?

"My dear Annie." Linscott's face dimpled as he spoke with blatant familiarity.

"Do not call me that." Annabelle pressed against the wall. She wished for a priest hole to fall through and disappear, even though she had waited all night for him to appear. Now she grew shy. She could not understand her desire to both be near him and run for the hills. Self-preservation. The only explanation.

"Why ever not?" He moved closer as if he sensed her desire to flee. A classic wolf move.

"Only my friends call me that. You may call me Miss Greene. Besides, I am not even aware of your Christian name."

She gasped, realizing her mistake too late to take back the words.

"It is Jack." His voice rumbled, laced with invitation. Invitation to sin most likely, but an invitation, nonetheless. "Miss Greene is far too formal for us, my little Butterfly. After all, we already…"

Her gasp caused a few heads to turn in their direction. She flicked the fan on her wrist open to hide her pinkening cheeks. The action caused a smirk to tug at his full lips. Great, now she stared at those lips again. She remembered far too clearly their shape against hers. Desire hovered in the air around him.

His breath wafted over her face, a pleasant aroma tinged with the sweetness of red wine. "Find any creatures in need of rescue today? Perhaps other creepy crawlies hidden up your glove or down…"

With the edge of her fan, she smacked his broad chest. "Alas, I am afraid I am the one currently in need of rescue."

"From what?" His feigned innocence irked her further.

The way his gaze raked over her body left heated tendrils behind. Yet, the colonel's similar regard only provoked her irritation. She understood none of this inexplicable draw to one man and repulsion for another. Nothing made sense.

"A wolf and a colonel," she replied.

His nostrils flared. His voice thickened. "A wolf can be a dangerous predator."

"I know." She watched his close study of her every move. Calculated. Burned. Lord, but she was intrigued. Lambs should not willingly approach wolves. But here she was, gleefully lying down. Practically screaming—*take me!* Stupid fluff brain.

"A wolf's prey often does not realize it is an intended victim until it is far too late. Until it is trapped." His words became a threat, or a promise, or something else capable of stealing one's breath.

"I fear there is little chance to abscond at this point," she said. Heat pooled in her stomach. She wanted to move away, but movement was impossible.

"Perhaps then it is better to be caught. Face the inevitability of fate." He took a long sip of wine.

"But I could never capitulate so easily. I must fight until the end." She straightened her back and lifted her chin in defiance, yet knew he won.

"Challenge accepted."

The gong sounded, which sloshed the moment with icy water as their hostess announced dinner. Jack crooked his elbow for Annabelle to take, but Lady Sinclair shooed him away. Their hostess placed him on the arm of an elderly matron and her debutante daughter. Colonel Burton escorted Annabelle. Blast the luck.

Jack shot her a commiserating glance over his shoulder. The feathers in the matron's hair smacked him twice in the face. Annabelle stifled a giggle behind her gloved fingers.

Amusement danced in his eyes. Ready to chastise the woman on his arm, the feathers tickled his nose again. He sneezed twice.

"My dear Lady Croswait, perhaps if we kept our focus on the people in front of us, we could enter the dining room more quickly. I am eager to enjoy the first course."

The woman appeared irritated until he flashed his dimples, her ire quickly dissolved.

Colonel Burton sat on Annabelle's left, Mr. Stanley to her right. Linscott, unfortunately, sat much closer to the head of the table, between the ladies he escorted. An accidental brush of the colonel's arm against Annabelle earned him a glower from Linscott. By the time the meal finished, the viscount's fork was bent in half. The wolf had a second victim in mind. This one would be afforded no mercy.

Annabelle bit back a grin, then shook her head.

Jack winked, but before he could take a bite of his roast filet of sole, a pair of feathers knocked the fish from his fork. He plucked the offending accouterments from the lady's hair to stuff them under the table before she even noticed. Annabelle's cheeks puffed, then released with an unladylike snort. The madam glared daggers with her coiffure listing to the side. Jack grinned triumphantly.

The meal lasted five courses before the women retired to the parlor and left the men to their port and cigars. Annabelle once again wished to escape, but Silvia never left before Lady Sinclair's parlor games.

Before the men returned, Annabelle slipped unnoticed onto the terrace. The night had turned pleasant after the heat of the day faded. The clouds left behind a clear moonlit night and the solitude she craved. She moved along the slick stones to find a bench out of direct sight of the windows and lecherous colonels who might peek through parted curtains. In the blissful quiet, she sat and listened to crickets chirp and frogs croak.

She felt the heat from a body brush against her arm. She nearly shrieked until she discovered the source. "Hello, Mr. Wolf."

"You still have not learned your lesson about stalking."

"Perhaps this time, I hoped to be caught."

He tugged at one of the loose ringlets framing her face. "Caught by me or perhaps by your Colonel Burton?"

She wrinkled her nose, which caused Jack to tremble with laughter. "I need to burn this gown."

Jack pulled at the sheer silk sleeve. "I rather like you in this color."

She smoothed out the skirts and lifted the fabric a little to inspect the cream and gold trim. "You flatter me."

"I find myself more and more mesmerized by you. Eyes of gold, hair of browned sugar, skin iced with pink."

Annabelle swallowed. She tried to regain her bearings, but she no longer remained moored to shore. She was adrift on the waves of an ocean, drawn to Jack like a siren's song. His fingers danced along her arms, tugged gently at the gloves. They said nothing, instead they tried to digest the flurry of thoughts that sailed through their brains.

"I am sorry," he whispered before his mouth descended to hers. The kiss was gentle. His lips suckled against hers.

She reached up. Brushed through the curls along the collar of his jacket. Threaded her fingers through his hair. She gently tugged, eliciting a moan.

His tongue traced along the seam of her lips prying them apart. She obeyed the silent command and was rewarded with his hand wrapping around her nape to guide her mouth into position as their tongues explored each other's flavor. He tasted of forbidden port blended with a spice uniquely his own.

Forbidden. The word described Jack perfectly. The taste of him was so foreign, yet her body yearned to learn more. Of the texture of his lips against her own. Her body craved the feel of his. She wished no space remained between them.

Candlelight from the uncovered windows filtered through the gap between their bodies. It cast golden sparkles along the simmering fabric of her gown. Like magical fairies who dance on a midsummer's night.

Jack's hands rested on her shoulder as he pulled back, breaking the kiss. With him, the fairies abandoned their stages, shadows replaced the glittering lights. He leaned in for a nip—or two, or three—before he ended it all with a sigh. "I could do this all night, but if we continue, we risk being caught."

Annabelle pressed her lips against the pad of his thumb.

She nodded in understanding. "Perhaps I should slip back inside."

"I will take my leave from here." With a final press of his lips against hers, he cupped her cheeks with both hands and nuzzled his nose against hers. "Until the next time." With those parting words, he rose and disappeared into the night as silently as he arrived.

She remained on the bench. The laughter from the open terrace doors swirled around in the air, but the sweet press of Jack's lips lingered like the last sip from a mug of chocolate. The way his hand cradled her face so lovingly. The scent of port and musk remained infused in her gloves. On her gown.

Thoughts of future terrace encounters appealed far more than reputations and her life pre-Viscount Linscott. If only he could have stayed, if only the night on a terrace could continue. Never fond of terraces before, now she could not wait until her next interlude. Hopefully, it too included an all too amorous wolf. Silly, woolly lamb, the allure of the big bad wolf grew irresistible with each chance encounter.

CHAPTER TEN
SOCIETIES

"Now, tell me why I am here at a dingy building on the corner of... Where the hell are we?" Nigel glared at the building covered in a thick layer of grime and soot.

Jack straightened his beaver pelt top hat, pointing to the sign over the front door. "I explained to you in the hackney. We are attending a meeting of The Society Against the Inhumane Treatment of God's Creatures in the hopes of earning favor with a certain Miss Greene."

"Annabelle? That's who you are wanting to pursue? What happened to Gladys Fitzherbert?"

"She called Khali a nag." Insulting a man's prized stallion truly was an unforgivable offense. "Then mocked my choice of waistcoat, followed by a remark regarding my preference for Scottish whisky over French brandy."

"How unpatriotic," Nigel said. "What about Isabel Howard?"

"Beautiful, but cannot dance if her life depended on it."

"Francine MacKinnon."

"There are newborn colts with more grace."

A footman dressed in the Duchess of Whitewater's livery directed them to a large space, which had previously served as a ballroom in a once grand mansion. Now, it boasted a makeshift stage at one end with rows of wooden chairs lining the sparsely furnished room. Nigel and Jack opted to sit in the rear, hoping for anonymity.

Jack scanned the patrons, drawn almost by instinct to the slight stature of Annabelle, talking animatedly with the Duchess of Whitewater.

"Vivian Stratham?"

"Who?" Jack forgot their previous conversation, distracted by his charming quarry.

Nigel elbowed him in the ribs. "Remember we were discussing the candidates for your potential bride-to-be. What of Vivian Stratham?"

"Simply because you wish to be rid of her advances does not mean you can foist the virago onto me."

The duchess pointed to a basket in the far corner. Anabelle's face lit. She clapped her hands together, earning a swat from her aunt's fan. Jack's fingers gripped the edge of his chair. He resisted the urge to rip the cheap papered fan from her aunt's wrist and break it into pieces.

"Can you blame a man for trying?"

"Can you?" Jack spotted another newcomer to the meeting. They glared at one another from across the room. "What is he doing here?"

"Sambridge?" They watched as the duke greeted both the Duchess of Whitewater and Miss Greene. "Perhaps he has a tendre for verbose octogenarians?"

Annabelle pointed to the far box, bouncing on her heels as she included the duke in the conversation. Sambridge grimaced over her head, before he offered his elbow to escort

Annabelle to a seat at the front of the audience. He stared down a man occupying one of the available chairs, who scurried to the back row muttering an apology as he went.

While the Duchess of Whitewater introduced their guest speaker, a man Jack paid absolutely no attention to, the viscount stared at the couple six rows in front of him.

Sambridge appeared even less interested in the society or animals than Jack. Instead, he feigned interest to garner Annabelle's attention, using the same clever ruse Jack had planned: show up to a charity event, appear concerned about the ill-treatment of animals, win fair maiden's heart. It should not have been a surprise to be bested by Sambridge. Or at least beaten to the punch. Nevertheless, it stuck in Jack's craw like a piece of fetid meat that the duke sat next to the alluring young woman, while Jack was at the rear of the room and left to throw metaphorical darts at the back of the other man's dark head.

At least the weather had finally cleared, though he would rather be out of doors than confined to this dusty, dull room. Too bad his internal thoughts failed to mimic the serenity Annabelle possessed, sitting with her hands demurely folded in her lap. She leaned forward to hang onto every word the pompous blowhard espoused from his pulpit. Inwardly for Jack, a tempest brewed with gale force winds threatening to topple the final remnants of his dissolute existence—and all because of a diminutive debutante and her confounding lips.

Twice now they kissed. Once could be blamed on being carried away by the moment, but the second? Terraces must be avoided at all costs, else he might find himself facing the wrong side of a gun barrel.

"What's in the box?" Jack nudged his companion as he snored.

"What?" Nigel blinked blearily, wiping away a trail of drool from the corner of his mouth. "The box? I do not know. What might make a young woman giddy and a duke green at the gills?"

"My guess, a creature in need of a loving home."

A yip from the box drew Annabelle's attention away from the speaker. She positively vibrated with excitement when a tiny brown head popped into view, its tongue lolling to the side.

By the end of the hour-long sermon about inane gobbledygook regarding the treatment of animals by specialized physicians, Jack determined Sambridge needed to be warned away. How dare the man presume to encroach on his territory? Had Linscott not made it abundantly clear to everyone in a ten-mile radius—Annabelle Greene belonged to him?

Not enough, apparently.

At the end of the meeting, a liveried footman belonging to the Duchess of Whitewater approached asking for donations. Jack threw a shilling into a tin the footman carried.

"Very generous, my lord." The footman walked away, leaving Jack with the impression his donation was not well received.

Annabelle arrived at the box by the stage at the same time as Jack, with Nigel conveniently staged to waylay both the duke and her aunt.

Three puppies climbed over each other, yipping. Their tiny hindquarters swayed from the momentum of wagging tails. Cooing, she reached for the most vocal of the trio and cradled it to her chest.

She rubbed the velvet softness of its nose and giggled. "Aunt Silvia says I can keep one."

Jack reached out to scratch the flea-covered mutt behind its ears. He earned an affectionate swipe of a tongue. "How many rescues does this make?"

"I've lost count," she confessed. "We currently only have Winston. Though, I fear Aunt Silvia is not particularly fond of him."

"I can imagine." There it was again, the flutter deep in his gut. The feeling he dreaded naming. Contentment. Could marriage to Annabelle bring him to such a state? Jack had not been contented a day in his life, how could things be any different with an artless debutante by his side?

She nuzzled against the puppy's snout; Jack felt the gesture against his chest. An ache stung, a need to feel the same affectionate regard directed towards him.

Her gloved hand wiped a bit of puppy slobber away from her chin. "Would you like to hold one?"

He scooped up a darker version of the same mutt, one with eyes the exact color as Annabelle's. It brushed its head against his palm, demanding affection. Perhaps a puppy might be the cure for what was missing from his life. Certainly easier to manage than a wife. Tiny needle-sharp teeth gnawed at the fingertip of his glove. Then again, perhaps not.

Setting the pup in the box, he pointed to the one cradled in Annabelle's arms. "What will you name your new dog?"

She stroked its ears lovingly. Jack found himself jealous of a puppy. Jealous of other men. This obsession of his had to stop.

"By chance do you have a suggestion?"

It took Jack a moment to focus on her question, he was too busy imagining Annabelle's fingers gently plucking his hair while he laid his head in her lap. "Perhaps Lancelot?"

"I believe the puppy is a little girl. Guinevere, perhaps?"

"Ginny. Guinevere is too much of a mouth full for such a tiny thing." Now he imagined naming his own children, this was too much. He had to leave. A visit to a brothel should cure his ardor, satisfy these indecent urges for a virginal miss. Yes, Madam Lafitte's would cure his seething lust.

"Ginny, it is perfect." Annabelle practically sparkled with radiance and affection.

He took in the whole of her. Her gown of yellow sprigged muslin with flowers printed along the hem. A sparkle in her voice. The possessive hold of the pup. "You are a summer's day."

The air around her brightened with the compliment. He immediately wished for a hundred clever words to forever inspire such unadulterated joy.

"Thank you." Her voice stirred feelings deep within his chest. Those emotions he dared not name.

Before he could bid her farewell, Sambridge intruded on the moment. "Linscott, what brings you to such an event? I was not aware of your regard for unfortunate creatures."

Jack resisted the urge to smash the man's face. "The welfare of animals is one of my greatest concerns. Is it not, Crayfield?"

Nigel currently held the third puppy, scratching its belly, causing the hind leg to thump in appreciation. "Hmm? Should I get one for Cissy?"

"What a splendid idea!" Annabelle cheered.

"Unfortunately, it is already spoken for. I am taking the other two. I am in need of a few new hunting hounds." Sambridge picked up the box, gesturing to Nigel to set the dog down.

The Countess of Brighton appeared. She shooed Annabelle towards the door with an abrupt farewell to Jack and Nigel. Sambridge smirked while he discussed names and the proper care of his new dogs. So engaged in conversation was Annabelle, she failed to bid Jack adieu as they strolled outside to wait for the carriage to reappear, leaving the viscount and his friend behind.

"Tough break." Nigel slapped Jack's shoulder. They followed the couple.

Jack shielded his eyes from the bright sun. At least something good would come of this day. Perhaps a hard ride in the park on Khali. After the week-long deluge, the purely azure sky was a welcome reprieve.

Traffic on the crowded street stalled, while a horse struggled to pull a cart ladened with heavy machinery up a small incline. The driver whipped the creature once, twice, thrice... Each slash of the whip against the burdened beast caused it to whimper, to lower its head in defeat. By the second lash, Jack was in motion. By the third, the driver tumbled to the ground. The whip clattered against the cobbled street.

"Unhand me, you wretch," the man bellowed, struggling against Jack's hold.

Jack tightened his grip, telling himself to resist the temptation to throttle the man like he deserved. "How dare you beat your horse! You force him to carry a load meant for a team of four, not a lone swayback gelding with one foot in the grave."

"It is my horse, you bloody nob!" That did it. Conversation over.

Jack punched. He relished the feel of the man's bulbous nose breaking beneath his knuckles. A second punch landed on the man's chin as he screamed for help.

Nigel appeared at Jack's side. "Carry your own damn load."

The viscount pushed the sniveling lump onto the curbstone before he approached the gelding with care. Calmly, he stroked its gray withers. Once Nigel had unhooked the harness tethering the horse to the cart, it leapt forward. It took little to regain control of the dappled gray.

Jack spoke in a hushed whisper, hoping the emotions would translate into equine comprehension.

The man clutched his nose, sputtering in protest. "Yer stealing my horse."

Sambridge stepped away from the gathered crowd to stand between Jack and Nigel. Throwing a wad of pound notes against the man's chest, he managed to diffuse the explosive situation. "No, he is not. You have been paid more than enough to purchase another unfortunate soul."

Jack stroked the white blaze on the gelding's muzzle. It whinnied and pushed against him.

"It is a beautiful horse." Annabelle reached out a shaky hand to brush the forelock. "Though I am partial to swayback ponies ready for a life of luxury in a meadow."

Jack turned to her, finally remembering she was there. There to witness his brutality against another human. But she did not appear frightened. She did not cower. Or shake. Instead, she moved closer to him, her arm grazed his sleeve. He wanted to reach out, but no... That would be foolish.

"I apologize if my anger distressed you."

"The only distress was my inability to inflict pain upon such a man. How can anyone be so heartless? Its haunches are covered in scars." She bit her trembling lip.

The horse was as bothered by her tears as Jack was, but lucky for the beast, he could nuzzle its muzzle against her face. Jack could only watch, jealous of the affection the horse could freely give. He wished the world would disappear, so he could grab Annabelle by her face and crash his lips against hers. How he needed to have her in his arms.

She reached over, squeezing his hand. "How can I thank you for saving this horse?"

Her touch singed his skin. A heat flooded within, burning away doubt and recrimination.

"No thanks is necessary. I needed a new horse."

She wiped tears from her cheeks. "You needed an old gelding? For what, pray tell?"

"A gift for my father."

How she stroked with such loving hands. Jack felt the touch against his skin. Silencing the tempest of his mind. "I am sure he will love him."

"Of that, I have no doubt."

"Annabelle!" her aunt admonished, holding the squirming puppy in her hands. "Come here. Our driver awaits." She climbed into the landau and waved to her niece to hurry. "Brawling on the street like common thugs, what is the world coming to?"

Sambridge gave a curt nod, a flash of gratitude washed over his all too handsome features. "Come, Miss Greene. Let me see you to your vehicle."

She reluctantly accepted his hand. "Farewell, my lord," she said to Jack.

Her words, so full of compassion, were a soothing balm to his soul. "Miss Greene."

"Linscott, well done. If you have need of a stable..." Sambridge tipped his hat with the rounded knob of his cane.

"My father has a ready stall." He extended his hand to the duke, who shook it firmly.

As they walked away, Nigel whistled low. "Did I witness a truce between Linscott and Sambridge? This must be a magic pony, else I am suffering from a fever dream."

"Nigel?"

"Yes?" he asked.

"Shut up."

CHAPTER ELEVEN
FATHER KNOWS BEST

"If you hoped to bribe me with a half-dead horse, I am afraid you are out of luck," his father said by way of a greeting.

"He is mine. You are only stabling him until I have enough funds to take him to Morefield Hall."

Jack rubbed salve over the wounds on the gelding's flank while it munched on the groom's special blend of mashed oats. The horse's ears twitched, the only recognition it gave to the newcomer.

"How did you come by this old gray?" The earl picked up a brush to rub down the horse's coat.

Jack retold the story. He made sure to leave in the gorier details, knowing his father detested Jack's tendency to use his fists to settle any dispute.

Silence settled between them as they cared for the horse while the groom hovered in the background. "I do hope you bested the man."

An interesting turn, not an immediate lecture against the

use of violence. "He crawled away with his tail between his fat little legs."

"Unfortunately, he can purchase another and abuse it."

Jack's fist tightened. "Too bad there is not a registry of sorts."

"The world is full of far too many unscrupulous people. At least this horse will live out its remaining years in comfort. Assuming Khali approves."

On cue, Jack's stallion whinnied in recognition of his name. "Kahli will approve. The groom is readying it for a ride. I need to clear my mind."

"Women have a way of making us feel that way."

Jack stumbled backwards. "What part of this discussion involves a woman?"

"Why else would you be at the Society Against the Inhumane Treatment of God's Creatures?" Maitland set the brush on the shelf. "I believe the Duchess of Whitewater sponsors the charity."

Great. In a matter of another day, his father will manage to discover Annabelle's identity and begin making assumptions. As much as it rankled Jack to have his father's interference, the thought did not bother him nearly as much as it once would have. Instead, her face. Her honeyed voice filtered in his ears. All Jack wanted to do was find a way to be near her again. He would endure any number of charitable functions in order to see her smile. Hear her laugh. What a fool he was becoming.

"I've invited Miss Greene and her aunt, the Countess of Brighton, to accompany me to the theater tomorrow."

So, the old man already knew her identity. He worked fast.

"What gave you the idea to invite Miss Greene?"

His father merely shrugged, retrieving a sugar cube from his waistcoat. The action earned a snort of displeasure from

Khali as the gelding munched greedily until he pulled out a second cube. The groom threw up his hands in defeat.

"Did I ever tell you about when I rescued a squirrel?" the earl asked.

"Whyever would you rescue a rodent?"

Maitland's face glowed. "A woman, your mother, in fact. When I had my heart set on fair Clara, we were riding in a phaeton through Hyde Park. Without warning, a squirrel darted out. The wheel rolled over it. She was hysterical, so I wrapped the creature in my coat, promising to nurse it back to health."

It did not surprise Jack. His mother was inordinately fond of squirrels. He remembered climbing a tree one spring to peer into a nest with two babies asleep next to their mother. "I am surprised she did not make you keep it."

"She did." His father stroked the gelding's muzzle. "But you are getting ahead of the story. Before I even arrived home, the creature died. I buried it in the backyard." He walked with Jack to a rhododendron bush blooming bright pink in the spring sun. "However, I could not bear to tell your mother it died. Instead, I spent the next six days trying to trap one, so I could claim it miraculously healed."

"Did you succeed?"

"In trapping one? Yes. In fooling your mother, no. I had forgotten the poor creature lost its foot in the accident. However, the new squirrel grew accustomed to eating from my hand, so for the next six years the little red lady visited our house almost weekly. Eventually, her children started coming. And her children's children." His father laid a pile of nuts on a table, then whistled. A minute later, a tiny redhead popped into view. It scurried across the smooth wooden surface, before it stuffed its mouth with nuts.

"The things we do for those we love." His father chuckled, then turned on his heel to walk inside without a goodbye.

Jack watched as several more squirrels joined the feast on the table. George Davenport—savior of squirrels. Jack Davenport—rescuer of horses. What a strange day it turned out to be.

CHAPTER TWELVE
THE THEATER

At last—the theater! The lantern flames danced in the heated air, welcoming all to the revelry inside. The air suffused with boundless energy. A fizzing fuse of excitement, ready to explode like fireworks.

Annabelle leaned out the carriage window. A daring move she normally avoided due to her fear of moving vehicles, but it was the theater! She only ever dreamed of coming here.

Annabelle inhaled deeply, the atmosphere filled her soul with tingles. Her blood flowed in waves, tightened her chest with the glee that was surely about to bubble in a gush of incoherent exclamations.

How lucky they were to receive an invitation from the Earl of Maitland! A chance to attend a Drury Lane play—a Gothic one at that! *The Vampire* promised a bit of everything: romance, murder, a ghost. Annabelle enjoyed Polidori's tale *The Vampyre*. An adaptation for the stage only made the night more enticing.

With the help of a liveried footman, the two women located the earl's private balcony. They slipped through the heavy curtains. Before them, a prime view of the stage yawned unobstructed. Giddy, Annabelle nearly brushed past the waiting earl in order to lean far over the edge to the view below. At the last moment, she restrained herself. The skirts of her gown swished like a bell against her satin slippers, reminding her how customs must be followed despite one's glee.

"My lord," she said, dipping into a curtsey with her aunt.

His amiable face broke into a wide smile, dimpling much the same as his son's. So alike did they appear in the moment, Annabelle felt like she stared into a magical orb, spying Jack Davenport five-and-twenty years in the future.

"I am pleased you both made it safely through the madhouse below. The play is quite popular. I despaired you might not make it through the traffic on Covent Garden."

"Our coachman is rather proficient," Silvia sniffed, being so bold as to loop her arm through Maitland's. "My niece has never been to the theater before."

"Ah," he hummed. "How splendid. Come, my dear. Indulge this old man. Allow me to be your guide until my son appears." With skillful ease, Maitland extracted his arm from Silvia's. "Countess Brighton, the Ladies Sinclair and LeDoux are anxious to speak with you on some matter of import. I would be happy to keep your darling niece company whilst you attend to their concerns."

Silvia's eyes grew large, as they always did when sniffing gossip. The Comtesse LeDoux never failed to supply ample tales of titillation. "Yes, quite. I will return in a moment."

A whirlwind of satin fluttered past Annabelle as her aunt rushed away.

"I hope you do not mind entertaining an old codger like me, but it has been far too long since I've been in the company of such a cheerful young woman."

They gazed onto the stage and the gathering crowd below.

The earl made passing observations about updates to the theater and his patronage of the arts. Annabelle tried absorbing every word he said, but the spectacle distracted her. What a spectacle it was!

"I must thank you again for the invitation. I am not sure how to appropriately express my gratitude."

"No need, my dear. I must confess my own ulterior motives." He turned towards Annabelle, drawing her away from the theater below. "It has come to my attention that you have garnered my son's affection."

"Oh." She shrank back against the chair. Disappointment weighted her breast. She should have known this invitation came with ulterior motives. Any moment, she expected to hear admonishments against her character and name. It would serve her right, believing this invitation was anything other than a kindness. "I assure you, any regard your son may or may not have, has not been encouraged by me."

His smile vanished. "You are not receptive to his advances?"

"I, ah... Well, that is to say..." Was the Earl of Maitland encouraging his son's infatuation? After all, she was a debutante with few connections and even less income. "I am not sure."

"Not sure?" His head tilted to the side.

"Rather, I am unaware of his advances. Er, rather any regard he might have for me." *Kissed twice and rescued a gelding, but who was counting?*

His silent contemplation left Annabelle unsettled. She wanted to speak, but what could she say? Could he read her mind, did he know about the kisses? Oh, heaven forbid! Perhaps she was wanton after all.

"What about..." he paused.

Please do not ask about the kisses, she pleaded to the gods of mercy. The question lingered as he checked mental notes.

"...Lady Sinclair's affair? A close friend informed me that he introduced you to my son. Had you not met prior to the event?"

Lord Stalworth! Drat the man. "Yes, my lord. Lord Crayfield and his sister brought your son to my aunt's home."

He did not appear to believe her. "Tell me about the dog."

"Ginny?" Her voice squeaked, then she cleared her throat.

"Yes, I believe he mentioned you acquired an animal, shortly before the incident with the gelding. Something about your fondness for animals in need."

An earl asked Annabelle about one of her beloved creatures! She could hardly believe it. When she told Cissy about the puppy, her friend groaned: *Not another one!*

"The Duchess of Whitewater's butler happened upon a litter of pups. She brought them to her charity. My aunt graciously agreed that I could keep one." By the end of the story, her voice almost reached its normal octave.

The earl's lips pursed. "According to a friend, there was a beastly man abusing a horse, a dangerous and gruesome occurrence happened right in front of you. You might have been injured."

"Your source exaggerates, my lord. I was in no immediate harm."

"Hmph," he said without argument. He gazed at her intently, before he smiled once again. "Tell me about the dog. How did you come up with the name?"

"I suggested Guinevere, but your son preferred Ginny. The name fits her rather well."

He schooled his features. "He named the dog. Interesting."

From behind, a voice interrupted the quiet conversation. "What is so interesting?"

Jack leaned against Annabelle's chair. One hand rested on

the high back close enough to brush her hair if he chose. He was the picture of an elegant male with his thick mane of nut-brown hair parted smoothly on one side.

"Ah, late as usual," Maitland said in greeting, flipping open his pocket watch. He tsked at the hands on the face.

Jack's eyes trailed over her before crinkling with approval. There was no friendly regard in his gaze, but it did not lack warmth. No, his stare was an inferno, stoking flames in her belly.

"You are lovely," he whispered as he kissed the air above her gloved fingers. Even through two layers of gloves, the heat of his skin burned.

Maitland guided her to the back of the balcony when her aunt reappeared. The viscount followed them.

"Linscott, it is good of you to come," the earl said with warmth lacing through his words.

"Maitland, thank you for the invitation."

"I leave this delightful young lady in your care. I confess I have an interest in speaking with her aunt. I trust she will be well cared for."

Heat radiated from Jack's hand as it brushed against Annabelle's arm. Even hotter when it accidentally rubbed against the bodice of her gown when he looped their arms together.

"Naturally," Jack said.

The candlelight dimmed as music played. Jack motioned to the set of velvet upholstered chairs behind them, offering her the first pick. She sat. The curtains opened. Her heartbeat accelerated. She could scarcely contain her excitement, inching forward to hold both sides of her seat in an unbreakable grip. Jack's voice broke through the fog of anticipation with the only words capable of drawing her attention away from the parting curtains.

"You are stunning tonight. Green is the perfect shade for you."

She gawked in disbelief at her gown. The dress was beautiful, but his words thrilled in a way she could not explain. She admired the stunning emerald-shot silk gown with a banded empire waist, feeling at once pretty.

"Thank you," she whispered, undone by his quiet regard. The narrowing of his focus on her, only her. The theater around them dissolved.

Reaching across the space between their chairs, his hand clasped her wrist. He unhooked her taut fingers to slowly draw the silk glove free of her hand. Then he removed his white glove. He enveloped her bare hand with his own. The touch of unbound flesh—naughty and delicious. Like the decadent bite of Belgium chocolate melting over the tongue.

A liberty she should never allow, a dangerous familiarity. Yet, she could not retract her hand, no matter how much the logical portion of her brain railed against the definitive ruin of her reputation should they be spotted. She consented simply because she was unable to resist his allure.

In order to fill her lungs, she breathed deeply from her abdomen. His hand clasped hers in the billowing pile of emerald skirts.

So much was written in the shape of his hand. Long, elegant fingers dusted faintly with fine hair. His fist dwarfed hers but cradled her snugly within his palm. Her other hand all but itched with the desire to trace over the lines covering the back of his hand, the scar across two knuckles. A hand of strength. Of power. Such beauty in this ordinary part of him.

Annabelle lifted her eyes to the stage as ghostly spirits warned Lady Margaret of the dangers lurking in the cave. Jack's fingers moved against hers. They traced the length of her fingers to the manicured nails, then back to the tender skin webbed between. She imitated his gesture, releasing a sigh. She failed to notice his triumphant grin.

Shortly before intermission, Jack removed his hand from hers, placing her glove in her lap and pulling his back on. A loss so familiar, so stark, pounded at her chest. *No, please do not let go.* The plea formed upon her lips, but was swallowed as the candles illuminated the theater, erasing all evidence of the transformative experience of the touch of a man's skin.

Maitland and Linscott both begged their pardon to search for refreshment and reprieve from the confining box. Silvia dozed with her head lolling to the side. Her feathers nodded along with her snores.

Annabelle reclined in her seat with bemused wonderment. She stared without direction across the building to the balconies opposite the earl's. A flash of gold from a lorgnette caught her attention. She spied a woman studying her from a balcony left of center.

The woman wore a diaphanous gown of scarlet layered in satins and gauze with gleaming raven hair piled upon her head. Ropes of pearls draped around her thin neck highlighted the woman's elegance. Annabelle recognized the gentleman seated next to her, his face pinched in disapproval—the Duke of Sambridge.

Annabelle tilted her head in acknowledgement; however, he turned and directed his attention towards the stage. Perhaps it was a cut, perhaps he did not see her. Either way, her stomach recoiled from his angry gesture. His lady companion did not shift her keen regard, instead keeping the lorgnette focused solely on Annabelle.

Annabelle turned her head in any direction but toward the unhappy couple. She crept forward on the balcony to occupy the seat next to her aunt. Leaning down, as if to adjust her slipper, she poked her aunt's side.

The woman startled awake with a snort. "Wha... what's happening?" she asked. She used her gloved hand to wipe at the drool gathered in the corner of her mouth.

"You nodded off, Aunt."

"I would never!" she protested in a hushed whisper. "Is it intermission already?"

"Yes." Annabelle pointed discretely to the woman in red. "Aunt Silvia, by chance do you know her?"

She inhaled sharply. "I do, but you should stay clear of such a person. She has a terrible reputation, sullied by her tendency to surround herself with the demi-monde."

"Is that Sambridge next to her?"

Her aunt fished a lorgnette from her reticule, holding it to her nose as she peered across the space between them. "How odd, it is in fact the duke. She must be his newest paramour. You must abandon any notion of his affectionate regard toward you if he is embroiled in an affair with the likes of the Countess of Anworth."

"Anworth?" The name prickled in the recesses of her mind. "Did her husband pass away recently?"

"Indeed. According to the Comtesse, Anworth's death is considered suspicious. Bow Street even investigated but discovered nothing to substantiate the claims." She folded her glasses and stuffed them back into her reticule. "Regardless of whether or not the woman is a murderess, she has a horrible reputation. Anyone associated with her will be tarnished by default."

"Even a duke?"

Silvia scoffed. "Men are, as always, secure when they associate with such creatures as long as they are not foolish enough to consider her marriageable. A duke can do as he chooses."

Annabelle witnessed the duke's slow withdrawal from the

woman to his right. She placed her hand on his frock coat, only for him to drop it unceremoniously onto her lap. The woman glared pointedly across the ever-shrinking expanse. Annabelle knew exactly who the woman blamed for the duke's reaction. Even though hundreds of people occupied the seats on the floor below them, Annabelle felt the icy stare as if they sat no more than a foot apart.

She shuddered, only to have the shivers stilled by a gloved hand on her shoulder.

"I hope lemonade might quench your thirst." Jack offered her a glass cup.

Annabelle drank it greedily, grateful to turn her attention away from the pinched-face disapproval of a woman she did not know. "The play is about to restart."

Once the lanterns dimmed for the second time, Jack leaned over. "Whatever made you upset? You were happy when I left. Are you angry about how long it took?"

"It is nothing, please do not worry." She flashed a wavering smile.

Jack's quiet command sent shivers over her body. "No, my Butterfly. Tell me, why are you upset?"

She coyly peeked over her shoulder, giving a delicate shrug.

"Oh, so now we are going to play games?" he growled, the words dripped with sensual promise. "You do not want to play games with me, my pet. I always win."

"Do you? Maybe you have not met your match?" She masked her concern with a playful lilt to her voice. "We are being watched by a friend of yours." With a slight nod of her head, she indicated Lady Anworth.

He followed the direction of the head tilt, and she closely observed his reaction. Mostly, he remained unchanged, except for the tightening of his posture and a twitch at his jaw. The rest of the performance, they sat rigidly in their seats, neither leaning in to whisper in each other's ears. A gulf separated their hands.

The play faded into the background. How could a man, at first so desirous, morph so quickly? Did the countess still hold his affections? Whoever Lady Anworth was, she could not be ignored. If another woman held Jack's regard, Annabelle was a fool to believe she meant anything at all to the viscount.

CHAPTER THIRTEEN
THE PICNIC

Annabelle balanced her reticule, plate with cucumber sandwiches, cup of punch, and Ginny's lead, praying her ankle did not find a gopher hole on the way to the blanket and cushions the footman had spread across the lawn. Over a hundred more steps to go without a droplet of ruby liquid tumbling down the snow-white walking gown embroidered with lavender flowers.

She managed a sudden stop when Gladys Fitzherbert gestured wildly behind her, narrowly missing a collision with a wayward wrist. A quick how-do-you-do and Annabelle was on her way again. Weaving around waving parasols and strolling couples. Children running free from Nannies. And other potential picnic disasters.

This was the Dowager Duchess of Sambridge's annual picnic. It was a practical coup to have received an invitation. Aunt Silvia had dragged Annabelle to the modiste the second after a footman delivered the embossed vellum, then held court for three consecutive days, bragging to any caller about their luck. Annabelle had garnered the Duke of Sambridge's attention.

If anyone had bothered to ask Silvia's niece for her opinion, they might have discovered an alternative explanation for the fortuitous invitation. Seeing as how every available debutante dotted the verdant lawn in a dazzling display of pastel muslins and silks, Annabelle suspected she was correct. She was simply a fluke in a sea of fishes.

"Made it," Annabelle said with a heap of relief.

Aunt Silvia was busy playing coy with Lord Stalworth, batting his sleeve with her fan. As long as she was occupied, Annabelle could enjoy the quiet peace beneath a drooping willow tree before she would be thrust into the role of a husband-hunting debutante.

Ever so carefully, she sat without using her hands. Success. Not a smudge on the white gown. Ginny plopped on a cushion wagging her tail.

"You can have a bite if you are a good girl." This statement translated into dog as: snatch a sandwich directly off the plate. Annabelle stood, trying to free herself from Ginny's eager pawing. But as circumstances played, Annabelle lost control of the punch cup, fumbling to keep it and the contents upright.

The cup sailed through her fingertips and splashed against the broad, cream-covered chest belonging to none other than the Duke of Sambridge.

"Twice," he said, flicking the excess droplets off his fingertips. "You would think I'd be more cautious around food and Miss Greene."

Annabelle felt the color leach from her face. His waistcoat looked like it had been slaughtered. Utterly soaked in ruby-colored punch. And he was not alone. No, her mortification was witnessed by the Countess Anworth. She wished she had found that gopher hole and slipped right inside.

"Ginny," she scolded, but the dog had already devoured the sandwiches and was currently scratching at its ear and paying no attention to the disaster it caused. "My sincerest apologies, your Grace." She offered a handkerchief. Little good it would do.

"What a terrible faux paus," the countess clucked, dabbing the handkerchief against the stain covering Sambridge.

The duke waved her away. "It was an accident, though I might need to ban hounds from attending future picnics."

It took a moment for Annabelle to detect the subtle twinkle in his gaze. "You are not upset?"

"Why should I be? I was never a fan of this waistcoat. But please refrain from telling my valet." He winked.

The action was both a relief and unsettling. She always felt she was on the wrong foot whenever she was near the duke. Wobbling as the earth shifted rapidly in the opposite direction was the best descriptor. Wringing her hands together, she bit back a tear threatening to fall.

"Nevertheless, please accept my apology." With her half boot, she kept the snuffling Ginny from venturing too close to the duke's polished boots. Lest the dog lifted its leg to relieve itself on the man.

"Miss Greene, there is nothing to apologize for. I happen to like punch." He handed her the soaked handkerchief. "Though, I prefer to drink it and not to wear it."

She dropped it onto the blanket with a heavy splat. "I would not advise trying to absorb liquid through the skin," she said.

"Might I introduce to you the Countess of Anworth. This is Miss Greene."

The pinched-faced countess extended her gloved hand, bending it at the wrist. "It is my pleasure. I have heard so much about you and have been anxious to make your acquaintance."

Annabelle dropped into a short courtesy and returned the greeting. "It is nice to meet you." She tried not to swallow, but her mouth felt alarmingly devoid of moisture. The clutch of the countess's fingers sent a tremble of shivers up her arms.

There was no denying the attractiveness of the woman with almond-shaped eyes and glossy raven curls pinned beneath a fetching velvet and ribbon bonnet. She held all the grace that Annabelle aspired to have. If only.

Sambridge opened his mouth to speak, but the words stilled as a shadow eclipsed his face. "Linscott," the duke ground out.

"That is an interesting fashion choice," the viscount greeted. "What would you call that particular pattern?"

Ginny waddled to Linscott, pawing and whining at his boots. He scooped up the puppy and scratched its ears. "Are you responsible for this picnic disaster? If this continues Sambridge might ban all dogs from the whole of England."

The duke rolled his eyes. "That is preposterous. I do not believe you were invited to this picnic."

"I received a last-minute, hand-delivered invitation from your mother on behalf of my father."

"How fortuitous for all of us to be gifted with your presence." The duke sneered.

Annabelle retrieved Ginny, hoping for an escape should the opportunity present itself. She never understood the posturing of men. It felt like they were two stallions pawing at the dirt and establishing dominance. How silly.

She smiled at the countess, hoping to share a bit of her humorous observation. Judging the glare directed at Annabelle, perhaps it was not only the men who felt their territories needed protecting. Where was a gopher hole when you needed it?

She stepped back, trying to skirt around the repartees

being tossed between Sambridge and Linscott. Instead of finding freedom, she bumped into the viscount. His hand settled at her waist.

She shrieked.

The countess morphed into a disturbing shade of purple.

The duke cleared his throat and pointed to the far house. "I must change my waistcoat. Linscott, we have much to discuss over a glass of brandy. Come with me."

The men abandoned the two women with hardly a word of farewell. She clutched Ginny to her chest, which the puppy delighted in with a swipe of its pink tongue against her cheek.

The countess stepped closer, backing Annabelle against the willow's rough bark. "Miss Greene. How fortunate it is to be alone with you. I have been needing to speak with you for some time. It is important that we clear the air and any potential for misunderstanding."

"Mis-under-standing?" Annabelle tried to still the tremble in her lips. "I do not know what you are talking about."

Anworth rested her hand on her hip with a sly smile curling her mouth. "My dear. Do not play coy debutante games with me."

Annabelle felt the unspoken threat in her stare. "Have I done something to displease you?"

"The fact you are here displeases me."

Oh, dear. "To refuse an invitation by a Duchess..." She channeled her aunt, wishing the woman would look up from her flirtations for a few seconds and rescue her niece. She could use the help. Even Ginny whimpered.

"Why did Lord Linscott sniff you out the moment he arrived? Is there an understanding between you?" She reached out, caressing the lavender satin ribbon tied beneath Annabelle's chin.

Never had a bonnet felt like a noose before. "You have no right to ask such a question," Annabelle squeaked.

"I have every right. The man belongs to me." The ribbon crinkled in the countess's hand.

Annabelle tried to remember how to swallow. It was incredibly difficult given the confrontation. She did not enjoy being cornered and feeling threatened. Now she understood why Francine preferred to cower in corners during *ton* affairs. "So, you have an understanding?"

"Oh poppet, we have more than an understanding." She dropped the ribbon and clapped her hands together. "Now if you excuse me." With a dismissive swish of her skirts, the countess disappeared into the crush of party revelers, leaving Annabelle in stunned silence.

CHAPTER FOURTEEN

BRANDY WITH A DUKE

"That is an improvement," Jack said, waving the brandy snifter in the general area of Sambridge's navy blue waistcoat. "The dark hides stains, which is the primary color palate for my valet."

Sambridge twirled the brandy, long legs sliding down the sides of the crystal. They sat in his study beneath the watchful gaze of his late father snarling above the mantle. Ironic to think Jack had won the lottery on fathers. The 5th Duke of Sambridge made the Earl of Maitland into a positive milquetoast by comparison.

"This is fine brandy." Jack drew the snifter beneath his nose, savoring the subtle hints of leather and oak in the aged Armagnac. Allowing the liquid to wash over his tongue before swallowing, he noted the flavor of dried cherries. Those frogs knew liquor. He would grant them that victory.

"Winthorpe offered me a case in exchange for a Gainsborough I had hanging in the dining room. As pleasant as the painting was, this brandy is by far a more enjoyable exchange."

Sambridge did not sit, instead leaned a hip against a sturdy desk angled in the corner.

Jack reclined in a comfortable tufted leather chair, enjoying the liquor but detesting the company. If he had to suffer with the duke, he might as well enjoy the finer offerings. "Enough chatting. Why did you summon me, your Grace?" Needling him with the obsequious address earned him a pinched scowl.

"Miss Greene. Is there an understanding between you?" Sambridge set down the crystal and crossed his arms over his chest.

"What is it to you?"

"Answer my question." Sambridge quirked his brow in challenge.

One Jack dismissed with a similar gesture.

"She is one of a few potential future viscountesses." Jack knew a decision needed to be made. The deadline was fast approaching, and he had yet to propose, let alone wed. If he was not careful, by the end of the month, he would be a pauper, and brandy would be a memory keeping him warm in the gutter.

"Anworth informed me yesterday that our little arrangement was never an arrangement. Merely I was a pawn in her grand scheme." The light shifted in the duke's green gaze. Softening like it was when they were boys and not the hard cynics they had become.

"Who is the target of this supposed scheme?"

The duke tilted his chin. "Who do you think?"

The liquor fell like a rock into Jack's gut. It was no longer sweet but bitter and tainted. "So, her quick dismissal of me was a game."

"She believes she will be your wife by the week's end and Miss Greene will be ruined." The duke pushed off the chair and stepped forward. "So, I ask you once again, what are your intentions regarding Annabelle? She needs the protection of a name."

CHAPTER FIFTEEN
A LADDER AND A PLAN

"Tell me again why I am risking the hangman's noose?" Thomas adjusted the ladder, aligning it with the fourth window above and to the left of the front door.

"It is the third," Viscount Linscott bit out. Whereas a clandestine mission with his batman-turned-valet was not entirely a new experience, the seven years between had left them both a little rusty. Perhaps they should have planned more than: *Get a ladder, I have a plan.*

The valet tilted his head and rubbed his square jaw. "You sure? I know you said it was the third window, but if you adjust for the hallway and the two that belong to her aunt's bedroom... Maybe you fancy busty ladies with four dead husbands, but I do not think marriage to a woman twenty years past her prime is what your father had in mind."

Linscott glared at the row of darkened windows lining the second floor and buried his retort under the reluctant admission that Thomas might have a point. About the windows, not Lady Silvia Brighton. His testicles retracted at the mere thought of catching the woman in anything less than layers and layers of clothing.

"Give me that," he snapped, grabbing the ladder. His shoe slid across a glob of mud, at least he hoped it was mud. In all likelihood it was excrement. There was a particular odor permeating the area.

"If you were not so impatient, I could have warned you about the dog shit."

"Tell me you are joking." Linscott lifted his boot, and a glob of muck splattered against the ground. "You are the one who has to clean my boots."

"Breathe in a little. That will tell you if I am joking or not." Thomas's face twitched. Running his hand over his mouth, he tried to rub away his smirk.

Linscott struggled with two incompatible urges–rip his valet's throat or join with self-deprecating ha-has. This night was a disaster by every measure. "Can we get on with this?"

"Yes, I am ever so eager to assist in the crime of the century if you explain one final point of confusion." Thomas held the ladder steady, meeting Linscott's gaze with one far too serious to ignore—the one he saved for moments of crisis and not humor.

"If you must." Linscott tested a few of the rungs, not entirely certain that the ladder would hold his weight. Not after the day he had.

A much-needed confrontation with the Countess of Anworth only confirmed his worst suspicions. She was not through with Jack, despite his lack of wealth. For reasons he could not articulate, she wanted him. More than likely, it was revenge. The Duke of Sambridge had dismissed her after the incident at the theater and there was one person she blamed for it all–Miss Greene.

He could no longer carry on with a courtship. He needed a

plan. Probably a better one than a rickety ladder and a reluctant valet, but a man had to work with what he had.

"I want to understand why you are choosing to hide away during the middle of the night with a woman you lamented was an animal-obsessed mouse with unfortunate relations and a meager purse." Thomas never did hold his punches. Not when being direct could clearly illustrate his point.

"She is no mouse." It was a weak defense, but Linscott was not ready to explain his why. Not to his valet. Certainly not to himself, because even he could not adequately explain their connection. How it began over a stupid spider and an unoccupied terrace, but he felt it, instantly. Other women faded by comparison. Yet, there was something unique about Annabelle Greene. An ability to soothe the beast raging within him when others piqued his ire. She was his balance. His peace.

Thomas stared blankly, his mouth a straight slash across his face. "And?"

"Listen. I had three weeks to choose a bride. I am a month away from losing it all. So, I am picking the one least likely to turn down my proposal." If he was not careful, his valet might replace his conscience. He could not afford that.

"Two of which you spent bemoaning your unfortunate set of circumstances."

Linscott started climbing. "I am a procrastinator."

"Only when you are not properly motivated."

That was a fair point. One would think losing one's income was a proper motivator, but it was not in this case. It was the loneliness that started creeping in and the prospect of being saddled with a paramour who had plans that did not include his consent. "Napoleon's army is no more. It is difficult to find motivation in dreary London."

"Lack of fortune normally inspired quick action. But you are avoiding the question, my lord."

His valet only used the proper form of address when he wanted to needle him. It worked. "She is pretty."

"So are half the debutantes who are out this season."

"Fine. You want to know the truth? It is…"

A carriage approached, the click on wheels and the clop of hooves echoing too close for comfort. Linscott slid down the ladder. They removed it in time to catch the Duke of Whitewater's carriage turning the bend and coming into view. Linscott and Thomas darted down the townhouse steps leading downstairs and out of view.

Once the carriage passed, they waited for a moment before hurrying back to where they had hidden the ladder.

"Explain this to me again, Lord Linscott." The valet scratched his whiskered chin, staring up at the brick facade and releasing a long whistle.

Thomas was the worst of skeptics. Linscott was not sure why he tolerated the man for so long, but at this moment, he needed someone to hold the ladder.

"For the last time. Keep it steady. Then meet me in the mews."

"Not that. It is pretty obvious what I am doing here holding a ladder. I mean, why are you sneaking around the outskirts of Mayfair at half past three on a Tuesday morning? Why not propose?"

"I am sorry. Did you have other plans?" Linscott's jaw twitched, holding back the litany of curses he refrained from saying. Not out of respect. Rather, at any moment, more carriages would come tumbling down the road as some *ton* fête emptied out and the guests headed home.

"Seriously, Linscott. I know you have reached dire straits, but be real with me." Thomas crossed his arms and waited.

There was no way Linscott could outlast him. Mules took

lessons on stubbornness from Thomas Dale. His intractability was legendary.

"She has another suitor." Jack's confession tasted bitter. A bit like the floor of a pugilism ring after a bout with *the other man*. Why *Sambridge*? But Linscott was not about to lose her to a Duke, even if they were better suited.

"Miss Greene? The mousy deb with no dowry and far too old to be in her first season? I find that difficult to believe."

Linscott's face morphed. He felt the anger tightening his fists and lips.

Thomas smirked. "So that's the suitor. The man who has bested you at every turn. Yes. This all makes sense." He patted the wooden rungs, lining it up. "Hop on board, my lord. Let us secure you a bride in traditional barbarian style. Toss her over your shoulder and carry her off in the night."

"Fuck you," Linscott said.

"Nah, save that for your bride-to-be."

Linscott smacked his valet's shoulder and started climbing.

"My lord?"

"What!?" he hissed through clenched teeth. His jaw was beginning to ache. If he wasn't careful, he might break a tooth.

"Is it not the fourth window from the left?" Thomas did not bother to conceal his laughter this time. If it were not for a ladder he was holding, he would have been bent in half, doubled over.

Linscott stared at the second floor. He was halfway to the third window to the left. Climbing down, he swore a litany of curses so inventive that Thomas whistled his approval.

"Well said. Can you explain what a weeping pustule on a doxy's cunny is?" The valet cackled.

"Shut up. You will wake the entire neighborhood."

Thomas bit his lip, but his eyes continued dancing a drunken waltz. Linscott would have fired him on the spot, but what was the use? He had fired his valet fifteen times since he had hired the man, but he never left. And why would he? They were once brothers in arms, now they were conspirators in a kidnapping. The latest of a long list of exploits.

The ladder was situated correctly this time. Leaning against the red brick and aligned with the correct window. Thankfully, the lord of the house remained on his Grand Tour or else this scheme would have ended twenty minutes ago. The aggressive butler with a neck tattoo would be occupied as long as Nigel's coin held out.

The liquid courage Linscott guzzled in the carriage did little good. He needed another. Or six.

He made it. Wedging his shoulder against the window, it protested with a horrendous squeak, then raised enough for him to work his fingers between the sill and the frame. The altered angle helped him to apply enough pressure to lift it wide enough to crawl through. Unfortunately, his toe caught on the rung.

Thump! Linscott pitched through the window onto the floor, landing more on his face than his feet. He paused and waited for footsteps to come thundering up the stairs after the calamitous cacophony he just made. A muffled snore was the only sound to greet him. He moved his arm out from under him.

First to pull up the rope looped around the ladder, then to wake sleeping beauty. His curiosity about what she wore to bed nearly derailed him. Whatever it was, it would be nothing like his recent light o'love.

Ginny waddled from a basket on the floor, snuffling his boots and whimpering. He scratched its ears, before pushing off the floor. He removed a flint from his pocket and used it to light a candle sitting in a holder on a circular table near the window. A small flame sprang to life and illuminated enough of the room so that he did not fear tripping over anything. Or rather, anything else.

The rope was easy enough to coil onto the floor. He picked up Ginny to kiss the puppy's soft head, then approached the bed.

Did he find the correct room? Bed curtains shielded the sleeping occupant from view. If this was her Aunt Silvia's bedroom and he glimpsed her in a negligee, he would swear off women for eternity. Rendered impotent at the mere sight of that creature and her bosoms freed to wander. He shuddered, fighting back the vivid image creeping forward in his brain. Now if this was Annabelle's room and she wore a diaphanous nightrail made of translucent tulle and satin...

A whistle sounded below. He leaned out the window.

"Linscott!" Thomas shouted.

"Stop using my name." Linscott wanted to rip his valet in two.

"Your Majesty."

Oh, much better. Jack rolled his eyes and gave his valet a sign of his disapproval. He could see Thomas' teeth flash in the amber haze of the gas street lamp.

"Perhaps, I should away to the carriage." He snapped to attention with a salute, then withdrew the ladder.

He was efficient. Linscott would grant the man that much. And the cool head one needed in battle. But one had to endure the endless quips and provocations that were characteristic of his personality.

Now to search the room. Heavy rose and peach brocade curtains surrounded the bed. Linscott tiptoed, approaching the side nearest the window. This, he hoped, should be enough to conceal him if the bedroom door opened for any reason. He gripped the curtain in his hand and counted one... two... three... He tugged it to the side... *Oh, shit.*

CHAPTER SIXTEEN
THROUGH THE WINDOW

"Merr-row! Hiss!" An orange and furious blob launched at his face. Jack knocked into the candle, the flame blew out. Surrounded in mostly darkness, he tried to dislodge the harassed feline from his waistcoat, but its claws sunk deeper.

He crashed against a chair. Smashing the flimsy piece of furniture and landing hard. A bit of debris scratched through his breeches. Had he worn the buckskin it would not have mattered. But in the attempt to disguise himself with dark layers, the thinner material was no match for the jagged wood.

"Blasted creature! Be gone!" He flung the cat off of him and it scurried beneath the bed. But not before it protested with a hiss.

Using the glowing embers in the fireplace to orient himself in the darkness, he expected to see a sleeping occupant in the bed. It was empty. He shook away the sting from his hands and lifted his gaze. There she was, silhouetted in the silvery light that cast an ethereal glow over her pale skin. She wore a demure nightrail, buttoned to her chin, but through the thin material, he made out each and every one of her rounded curves. His fingers flinched reflexively, wanting to mold his hands over her shapely body.

She held a statue in her hands, ready to bash in his skull, he presumed.

So, he deflected her anger with humor. "Funny meeting like this. Me down here. You up there." He grinned.

She sputtered, dropping the objet d'art.

"Come give me a kiss hello, Annabelle."

"Lord Linscott. I believe I instructed you to call me Miss Greene."

Damn, how he loved it when she sounded all prim. The nightrail clinched his fantasy. It would not take much to have her writhing in his arms, while he taught her the very worst of vulgarities. She must have sensed the direction of his thoughts, yanking the ruffled collar to conceal the scant inch of flesh below her chin.

"Miss Greene," he purred.

She huffed indignantly, but he had her right where he wanted her. He began uncoiling the rope.

"Did you throw my cat?" she hissed as angrily as the feline cowering under the bed.

"A gentle toss." He could not resist her tempting lure. With measured steps, he approached in hopes of drawing her into the cradle of his arms. One kiss before he trussed her up like a Christmas goose.

"A gentle toss, my foot! You threw my cat!"

"I did not expect to encounter a guard cat. He would not release himself from my person." Jack held up his hands, so she could inspect the numerous scratch marks. "I am bleeding."

Annabelle rolled her lovely topaz eyes and placed her hands on those delightfully rounded hips. Inadvertently, the gesture caused her gown to pull enticingly across her substantial breasts, giving Jack the faintest glimpse of dusky, pink-tipped nipples. His mouth watered.

"Am I expected to feel sorry for you?" she asked.

Jack shrugged a shoulder, then the corner of his mouth turned up. "I am the injured party."

"My *cat* is the injured party."

He captured her hand, bringing it to his lips.

Her eyelashes fluttered so quickly, he thought she might take flight. Breaking his hold, she took a step back, bumping against the bedside table.

"Do you mind explaining why you are in my room, dressed all in black with a length of rope coiled around your hands?"

"Certainly," he replied. "We are going on a little adventure."

Her tone reeked of skepticism. "In the middle of the night? This is no adventure, my lord. Tell me where are we going?"

Her saucy tone would be his breaking point if he did not hurry her along. Waiting would only end in one of two outcomes, neither of which would accomplish his ultimate goal. Engage in sexual congress or be delayed enough for the butler to come home. That would most certainly end with Jack being skewered alive. Best to move her along.

"Hurry, little Butterfly. We do not want to be caught."

She crossed her arms with her fingers tapping against the crook of her elbow. "The blasted cacophony of you falling into my room will bring the footmen running. Any minute."

He knew better. "They sleep two floors above. They would have heard nothing."

"You have woken Silvia." She lifted her chin and sniffed.

"I barely woke your cat." He pointed to Winston, who was currently attacking the frayed end of the rope. Ginny was pawing at his boots, trying to get his attention. "Besides, I have it on good authority that your aunt cannot be roused before noon."

Her eyes narrowed. "Whose authority?"

He knew he had her. "Yours."

"Oh." She visibly deflated. "Coleman then. He will be here at any moment. I do not know why you are not currently dangling from a pike, but you will be." She shook her finger like a nanny scolding a child. "He must be delayed. Mark my words, he will be here to rescue me."

He leaned against the bedpost with his legs crossed. Might as well be comfortable and let her tie the threads together. "But he is not home. It is Tuesday. His day off. As of right now, he is at the Boatswain's Whistle tossing back a bottle of their finest whisky."

"I highly doubt that. He drinks gin." A comment for everything. She was frightened, might as well give her a bit more time. Then he would use the rope.

"Not if Lord Crayfield is plying the man with a bottle. My friend is rather a fair study of men. Knowing the right mix of words with the ideal amount of liquor. Your butler will be lucky if he can stand on his own by the end of the night."

"Baron Crayfield? Surely you jest. Why would he help you..."

He watched the realization play across her face. While the baron's sister was her closest friend, Nigel and Jack went back at least a decade before Annabelle was even born. In order to commit a crime, one needed trustworthy accomplices. There was none more capable than Lord Crayfield. Jack had always been the brawn, but Nigel had been the brains.

"I needed a guarantee that your butler would not be home at an inopportune moment. By the time he returns to sleep off a monster of a headache, we will already be well on our way."

"I see you thought of everything," she said with more venom than he expected.

"Naturally, my dear. Now gather your things and let's be away." He stepped forward with the rope.

She paled and pointed. "And what is that?"

"Insurance, my sweet. Quickly now!" He went to her wardrobe and extracted a carpeted valise. When she failed to spring into action, he pulled out a few gowns and stuffed them into the bag. "If you do not help, who knows what I will pack."

He had the gall to rifle through drawers, finding a pair of stockings, garters, and a few underthings. Her underthings! He pawed through her private clothes like they belonged to him!

Motioning to her nightrail he added, "You will want to change quickly."

She crossed her arms and stared mutely at him. His eyes did not meet hers, they dropped a degree or two. He cleared his throat.

"Sweets, you will want to wear a dress." He held one up. "Else you will be leaving in what you are wearing, and people will see you in your night things."

"I refuse to move an inch until you tell me what you have planned." This was ludicrous and needed to be stopped. Leave with him in the middle of the night. To where? He was mad. Absolutely balmy!

"Annabelle," he warned.

She refused to kowtow to a bully. "Linscott." She imitated his tone, drawing out all the letters in his name and marching over to him to knock some sense into his brick head.

Straightening to his full height, over a foot taller than her, he dangled the rope. "Do not force me to use this."

If he thought to use intimidation, he was barking up the wrong tree. She batted his hand away. "Tell me of your plans. Then I will decide on my own what I choose to do or not. Otherwise, you have no choice."

They stood measuring each other's resolve, neither flinched nor uttered a single syllable. When the clock in the grand entry rang, it snapped Linscott into action. He wrapped a handkerchief around her mouth, tying a knot at the nape of her neck that included a great hunk of hair. With deft movements, he turned her around to secure her wrists behind her back.

She did not fight him. She could not exactly say why. Maybe it was part curiosity. Maybe, though she could only admit this in the quiet of her head, she wanted this man. To no longer wonder what waited at the end of this season when her father would demand that she return to Hampshire to live out her days as a spinster caring for an aging father.

If Aunt Silvia had a choice, Annabelle would wed the Duke of Sambridge or worse Lord Welsham. But the man currently trying to appear as the strong and capable mastermind of a criminal undertaking was the one she would choose and the reason she did not struggle. Though his reasons for kidnapping her rather than approaching on bended knee did send a shiver of trepidation through her spine.

"You've left me with no choice," he said, grabbing the bag and her wrapper from the end of the bed before tossing her over his shoulder.

Impressive. He lifted her as if she weighed no more than the carpet valise in his hand. This thought sent a different kind of shiver cascading through her body. One that was much more pleasant and a bit heated.

The door was locked when he approached it. Flipping the latch, he opened it quietly, keeping her perched on his hard shoulder. Somehow, he knew the layout of the house, finding the servant's stairs at the back.

Winding down the back staircase, Linscott carried Annabelle like a precious bundle. Not once did he bump her against a wall or stumble as he descended the tight stairs.

Once in the kitchen, he paused to look around the corner presumably for servants, but the house was as still as a tomb. He approached the door to the back garden. There he reached for the knob when a hiss froze him in place.

Annabelle stiffened. Near the larder, a pair of glowing orbs peered out of the darkness. *Winston!* With a curled back and a poofy tail, the cat hissed.

Annabelle tried speaking through the gag, but the cloth stifled the words. She gestured with her foot, her knee coming too close to his center. Wrapping his arms around her legs, he lowered her to the floor before he freed her mouth.

"Bring the cat," she commanded. If she was going to endure this trip to wherever, she was not about to go alone. Especially since she strongly suspected the destination was Scotland. Why else would he bring a bag? If he wanted to seduce her, they had just left the bedroom. Surely his intention was to marry her. He was not the murderous sort. Was he?

"Are you out of your mind? No!" He secured the gag back in place, a bit tighter this time. Then he picked her up again.

She groaned in frustration. He gripped her legs tightly. Shoving the cat to the side with a foot, he hurried through the door.

Annabelle's muffled protests were the only sound as he navigated the tenebrous pathway through the garden. They arrived at a plain carriage without incident. A coachman sat with the reins in hand. A second man held open the door.

"My lord, Miss Annabelle," he greeted. "Lovely weather we are having."

"Shove it, Thomas," Linscott bit out.

The servant laughed.

Linscott settled her on the bench across from him before Thomas shut the door. Taking a moment to breathe, Linscott wiped his brow, then pounded on the roof. The coach jolted forward, and they were off.

"I am sorry," he said.

Her face flamed what she assumed was a brilliant shade of red. Her torso shimmied as she struggled against the restraint binding her wrists. She muttered a litany of expletives through the gag that even had her captor blushing, but she remained in this uncomfortable position while he reclined against the squabs. He did not appear the least bit concerned with her state, even going so far as to pick at a hangnail as the carriage rumbled through the night.

Perhaps she read the situation incorrectly. Perhaps he was not the man she believed him to be. Once freed of this gag, she would give him every last bit on her mind. One thing was certain, this was going to be a long night for the two of them.

CHAPTER SEVENTEEN

THE JOURNEY NORTH

The carriage rattled over cobbled streets. Jack wished he rode between the coachman and Thomas even with the drizzle falling from the sky. Anything to avoid Annabelle, who currently vibrated with anger.

He debated removing the gag and freeing her mouth, even though a blistering lecture was sure to follow. Perhaps another five minutes to help her anger simmer instead of seethe. She sat rigid with eyes narrowed to tiny pinpricks.

Ten might be better. An hour? *Let's not get carried away,* he reminded himself.

He needed to admit this plan might not have been the greatest. Perhaps he should ask the coachman to turn around, but who was he kidding? The plan had to move forward, there was no going back. Not after he stole her from her chambers in the middle of the night.

He braced himself for the flurry of stinging barbs as he removed her bindings. His knuckles lingered along her jaw. She flinched and pushed herself into the corner farthest from him.

Her breaths slowed to a more normal rate; at least she was not going to expire from lack of air.

He waited. She glowered. He smiled. Her lips twisted, nearly disappearing into her pinched face. Jack shifted, distributing his weight unevenly as half the carriage dipped into a rut before tilting in the opposite direction.

"Say something," he pleaded.

"I am counting," she said through clenched teeth.

"You should have reached ten by now," he joked but stopped abruptly on only the second ha. "What number are you counting to?"

"A thousand." The muscle in her jaw twitched.

"That high? A little ridiculous to... Ow!"

She kicked his shin, then counted aloud, "678... 679... 680." The numbers faded, Jack could only assume she resumed her countdown.

Properly chastised, he sat back and waited. She refused to meet his gaze, instead, he was met by stony silence. He watched as her hand tightened into balls, then stretched out flat. She bit her bottom lip until it turned white. Then released it, the berry-red returning. Minutes became hours.

A lone tear trickled down her pale cheek. *God, I am an ass,* he thought watching the drop splash onto her nightrail. He reached out to wipe the tear away, but she recoiled from his touch, breaking the silence as she stuttered.

"Wh-where..." She swallowed deeply before continuing. "Where are we going?"

"Gretna Green."

Annabelle nodded and fell silent once again.

He wanted to beg her to talk, to say anything to him. Words of anger were preferable to unrelenting silence. When her tears faded to hiccups, he tried again.

Her fists bunched the sides of her nightrail, wrinkling the

fabric. Her breaths stuttered, while her skin glowed a sickly pale in the faint light.

During the war, there was a soldier with her exact pallor standing frozen among the lines ready to charge while the battle roared in the distance. It did not take long to figure out that the boy was frightened out of his wits, but Jack was able to bring him about and help him return as the soldier he was destined to be. Jack tried not to picture his face later that day when he found him among the dead.

"Annabelle?" He placed his hands on her knees, seeming to pull her out of a trance. "Speak to me."

Her lips trembled. "I... I do not like riding in carriages. Especially at night."

Despite the tight confines of the vehicle, he shifted his bulk and sat next to her. "Talk to me," he encouraged, clasping her hands between his. "Let me help."

"It has been this way ever since there was an accident when I was young. My mother... she died." A tiny hiccup of a sob gummed up her sentence.

He did not know what to say, letting instinct take over, stroking her hands until her fingers released their death hold on her clothing.

"I cannot bear being in a carriage. It brings back memories, I would rather not remember." The wheels hit a deep rut, and she gasped, but he refused to release her.

A soft pink began to creep into her cheeks. The warmth of the skin cradled between his hands gave him the promise that this too might ease.

She sighed heavily, then withdrew. "Thank you."

"Are you feeling better?" Part of him wanted to stay as they were. Not sure exactly why, only that it felt right.

Her lips curled in a wry grin. "About the means of transport, yes. You, not so much."

That was fair. "Perhaps, I should move back to where I was." He shifted, the carriage wobbled on its axles until he settled onto the opposite bench.

He witnessed a calm settle over her features. The tension eased from her face. At least she was not afraid of the means of conveyance, but she was still put out with him.

The carriage rolled over miles of roads, leaving London behind. The drizzle changed to a steady rain, then disappeared as violet and magenta streaked the navy sky.

Morning. Her servants would soon discover her empty bed and the search for Annabelle Greene would begin.

Finally, her voice broke through his self-recriminations and scoldings. "Why did you not ask for my hand?"

The question landed like a blow, momentarily forcing clever deflections into retreat before he answered. "I could not risk you saying no."

"So you left me with no choice." Her voice was flat, but her gaze caused him to flinch.

When he did not respond, she continued.

"I'm ruined. How will my reputation ever recover? The *ton* will assume I went willingly. Or worse, that you..." Her eyes darted around the confines of the carriage. Despite the din of carriage wheels rolling over roads, she still whispered, forcing Jack to lean closer. "That you seduced me."

He bit back a laugh. It was not a funny situation, rather her innocence amused him. So pure when all he knew was the opposite. "Would you have preferred seduction?"

He studied her reaction. Pink bloomed along her cheeks. Her pupils swallowed the golden rings of her eyes. The idea intrigued her, giving him a modicum of hope for the future.

She never answered his question. Instead, she squeaked once, closed her eyes, and appeared to drift off. This was going to be a lengthy journey indeed.

CHAPTER EIGHTEEN
THE COCK AND HEN

J ack could not say exactly when the carriage rolled to a stop at a coaching inn called The Cock and Hen during the third night on the road. Thomas opened the door and yawned, covering his mouth with an embarrassed apology.

"Begging your pardon, my lord," he said.

"There is no need. She passed out an hour ago." Linscott pointed to Annabelle slumped against the side of the carriage with her head back and mouth agape.

"Bertie and I both need sleep. Even if we change horses, we are bone tired. Mind if we catch a few hours before the mad dash continues?" His valet's eyes watered as he yawned a second time.

Jack alighted, stretching his long frame and hearing half his joints creak a protest after days confined in one position. As much as he wanted to lie horizontal for a few hours, they needed to continue. "Stopping is not part of the plan, Thomas."

"Our brilliant coachman went off the North Road a few hours ago." Sensing Linscott's protest, Thomas rushed to finish his explanation. "This plan is ingenious, hear me out. His family owns the Cock and Hen. This detour cuts fifty miles and has us away from the main road for several hours. Long enough for anyone who might be following to lose our trail."

"Clever." Jack stared at the inn.

It was best described as a hovel with a sign that hung from one metal loop while the other had long since disintegrated. Paint curled and peeled away from window panes, while the eaves sported at least three holes. The stables would fall in a strong breeze.

"I fear if we stay here, we will wake to find our carriage and purse gone." Jack voiced his fears.

Bertie paused on his way back from the well, carrying the first of several buckets for the horses. "You are right fine here, my lord. Me mam's kin owns the place. They'll take good care of you and the missus. Already arranged it with little Tom. He's fixing you up with the best room in the place and a bath if you want it." He set down the bucket and wiped his brow with a dusty cloth. "But I wouldn't leave your lady fair alone. While your horses are safe with me, there is no telling what wastrel might have stumbled into the place. Best keep her close."

The word bath made his knees go weak along with the prospect of spending the night with Annabelle under his protection. A rough crowd was nothing new. A standard night at the Obsidian Club. "If a hair on those horses is touched, it is your hide that will suffer the consequences. Five hours and then we must be off."

"Six," Thomas pleaded, rubbing his buttocks. "Please. My ass cannot handle that wooden bench for at least six hours. Give me that and no complaints."

"And if her family catches us?"

Thomas waved away his concern. "We are days ahead of anyone who might have noticed. Think about it. Her aunt will run around directionless until Lord Stalworth comes to her rescue. Chances are, they assume she went home and are waiting for news of her arrival."

He left no note, though Nigel knew. The question was, would he inform Annabelle's aunt? "What about the butler?"

Thomas sucked air through his teeth. "If he is on our trail, I suggest you disappear to the continent under an assumed name."

"Very helpful."

"What are you worried about? During our journey, it was only you or I who showed ourselves to the proprietors. Not to mention the obvious." He clasped Linscott's shoulder.

"Enlighten me." Jack would not rest easy until he said his vows over an anvil. Until that time, constant vigilance was the only way to see this through.

"You left nothing. Not the faintest clue that you hied off with a penniless debutante. They have reason to be far more suspicious of Sambridge than you. Trust me, my old friend. And give me six bloody hours of peace." He did not wait for a reply, marching into the coaching inn and disappearing from view.

"Here's your key." Bertie dropped it into his palm. "Room six. The inn is filled up, but Little Tom promised you will find the accommodations more than adequate. They always leave the best room for the desperate." Off he went, a third bucket of water sloshing against his legs as he returned to the stable.

The solitary key burned his fist. Being alone in the carriage was one thing. The confines of the space limited movement and buried all thoughts of seduction. But a room, with a single bed and a tub filled with water gave unscrupulous men ideas. He was the worst sort of rake because the kiss on the terrace on the night they met only served to whet his appetite. Avoiding temptation might be near impossible. A single bed. A woman in need of claiming. Perhaps he should sleep in the carriage. He had to convince his body to leave comfort for the sake of the sleeping beauty he intended to leave in peace.

CHAPTER NINETEEN
THE INN

Annabelle stirred, waking on a snort and the realization the carriage was no longer moving. "Where are we?" she asked, wiping the corner of her mouth.

Linscott hovered over her, his face a few inches from hers. "Somewhere between London and Scotland."

"Helpful," she said.

His lips were close. Moist and beckoning. That night on the terrace swam before her. The memory of his mouth. His tongue. Oh heavens, his tongue as it brushed along hers while his hand cradled her cheek. What would it be like to kiss him once again? She found herself drifting closer and he remained steady. The air around them stilled, yet felt weighted with anticipation, like the calm before a thunderclap and the deluge of a rainstorm.

The moment broke when he shifted away, holding out his hand for her to take. She shook off the feeling, unfolding from her position in the carriage and nearly tumbling to the ground as she missed the step down. He was there, catching her before she tumbled into a heap at his feet. With no effort, not even a grunt, he righted her. His hands cupped her elbows.

"Careful" He pressed his cheek against her temple.

She felt the words curl in the air, dropping the letters like drops of sugar. How did he always manage to unsettle and yet also calm her mind? "Apologies, my lord. It seems that I have developed a bit of a cramp in my, erm..." She almost said buttocks. In front of a man! Mortified that she even started the sentence, she averted her gaze and stared up at the coaching inn.

Or what might be by sheer definition called such a name, but for lack of an alternative, it proclaimed itself as a destination for travelers. Personally, sleeping in an open field might be a much more appealing alternative. At least she would not be a feast for whatever bugs lurked in the mattress. The stuffing was more than likely wet, and she might catch her death.

"Are we staying here?" she asked. Her hands twisted together in a knot as trepidation settled in her belly.

"Naturally. Fear not, Miss Greene." Proffering his arm, he led her inside and up a winding staircase to the next floor. "You will have the finest accommodations. The best room five shillings can buy."

His eyes did not meet hers. That a lie could tumble so easily from such a finely formed mouth was beyond her. Then again, charlatans often came in pretty packages. It helped solidify the ruse. Her beautiful, conniving mother taught her that.

He opened the door of a surprisingly well-appointed room. Large and clean. A hidden treasure in a pigsty. Perhaps this was part of the appeal. Lure away all but those desperate enough to stay here and surprise them with their own piece of heaven.

Their two valises sat on the floor already carried in by Thomas. Little luxuries in the form of steaming water in a hip tub and a vase full of white flowers elevated the room to quaint. A patterned quilt was rolled down, inviting Annabelle to luxuriate the way she dreamed of for the past three days. The urge to rub her sore backside was nearly overwhelming as was the urge to stick her head in steam curling above the tub's rim.

"Is this my room?" Annabelle bounced on the balls of her feet. If he said yes, she might just kiss him. She was that excited to be out of the carriage and on solid ground.

"About that," he started.

She did not pay attention to his answer; instead, she picked up her bag and searched for a brush and her nightrail. Finding both, she laid them out. "We are staying the night, am I correct? I am grateful for the bath, though I am afraid I haven't the energy for a long soak. Long enough to wash off the grime and to crawl between the covers before I am out again. Who knew sitting could be tiresome." Gathering her towel and bar of soap against her chest, she turned, ready for him to leave.

And waited. His mouth worked, but no sound left. Until he closed the door, turning the skeleton key and locking them both inside.

"You are first for the bath. Then it will be my turn," he said, loosening the cravat from around his throat.

The entire room shifted. She had to take a step, lest she collapsed onto the ground. Her jaw hung open. Had Aunt Silvia been there, she would have felt the sharp sting of her fan to remind her to close it. As it was, she snapped it shut again. When he finished unwrapping the cravat, she finally settled on one response.

"Out!" She pointed a shaking finger at the door.

He worked on the buttons of his waistcoat. If she did not hurry him through the door, there was no saving her reputation. Or her sanity. She was at the end of her tether. How dare he presume it was acceptable to undress in front of her? How dare he dream of sharing her room when he could have his own? When he could be anywhere but here with her.

Reputation. Forget about her damn reputation. She was not going to be coerced. She would refuse to comply with whatever scheme he concocted.

"I am afraid this is the only room available. Either you stay here or sleep outside." His waistcoat gaped wide. The man was practically naked!

"But... what? Have you taken leave of your senses? You cannot possibly plan to sleep here. With me. When we are not wed." Her voice rose with each sentence until it ended with a squeak. "Leave, my lord."

"We do not have a choice in accommodations other than the cold, cramped carriage. So if you prefer to sleep there, I will not stop you. Even though it is my money paying for this room, I have been kind enough to give you the first chance at the bath, but my generosity only extends for the next five minutes. Make up your mind, Miss Greene." Linscott shucked his waistcoat to the side. His shirt clung to him, soaked with sweat after hours inside a sweltering carriage.

Miss Greene. Indeed. He called her that simply to get the best of her. She did not want to admit how much it worked.

"No! You cannot. My lord, this is untenable." She clutched the soap tighter against her chest but contemplated how hard to throw it at his head. Or perhaps his chest might be a better target. It was certainly wide enough.

His exasperated sigh filled the room. "Jack. Call me Jack. Everyone else calls me my lord. Or Linscott. Or other names too detestable to utter. But once in my life, I want someone to call me by my Christian name. So call me Jack, for the love of God. Then give me the soap because I am rank, woman. All I have dreamed of since this nightmare started was a bucket to submerge my head into and I am not about to waste this water."

"Nightmare! How dare you call this abduction a nightmare? You do not get to complain when you are the perpetrator, my lord. That is for me to do. Have you forgotten who the victim is?" She sounded like a shrew, screeching loud enough to wake the entire coaching inn.

He stomped across the room, snatching the bar of soap and towel from her hands. "I told you. Call me Jack!"

"My lord." She added the courtesy to rankle him. Judging by the tick in his eye it worked.

"Jack," he bit out.

"I would never be so bold as to use your given name. I shall address you as my lord. If you insist on carrying out this forced marriage, then you shall be addressed as is fitting. Which is by your title." Crossing her arms, she lifted her chin in challenge. It was not perhaps as effective as she hoped, considering he towered over her. But she could be brave. She would be brave.

"Fine." He took the tiniest step back. "Have it your way. However, I am going to bathe." He did not wait for her to protest, drawing his shirt over his head and tossing it to the side.

Swallow. She had to remind herself to swallow, else she might begin drooling. Statues did not do a man justice. The way his muscles flexed and rippled. Dark, curling hair across his chest. Soft. Inviting. Flat coppery nipples. She found herself wondering what they might feel like. Smooth or with tiny bumps like her own.

"But you will be naked!" Why her mind did not recoil and feel the least bit horrified, but rather sparkled, confused her. Why she tingled along the lines of titillation she dared not speculate. She needed him to leave, so she could think.

He had the gall to roll his eyes. "That is the way one generally takes a bath."

"With me in the room?" Alone with a naked man! What would her friends think? What would her cousin say? There was no coming back from seeing a man in the nude. Unless she desired a life living in the service of men.

"There is always waiting outside." His offer was anything but accommodating.

She took a step forward and imagined running as fast as she could. She might manage to make it most of the way back to London. Perhaps a post-chaise would feel sympathy and pick her up. Or she could encounter a band of highwaymen. Or worse. What was worse, she did not want to contemplate.

"But... No. It would not be safe for me to do so. Of course, you knew that already. It was more than likely part of your plan all along. So, you are not bathing. Neither am I. It would be indecent."

He tugged on the enclosure of his breeches. She squeaked. He laughed.

"Soon enough, you will be my wife. Until then you can play the innocent debutante, but we both know you are already picturing me without my clothes."

The curiosity about where the trail of hair below his navel led occupied most of her thoughts. "I would do no such thing! How dare you imply I would have any sort of knowledge of the male anatomy." Except for the statues in the British Museum. And that drawing Cissy showed her from a smuggled book. Or the time she happened upon her cousin swimming in the pond on his country estate.

Good thing Linscott could not read her mind.

He morphed into the wolf once again. She, the wee lamb in his sights.

"I know what books Cecilia Hammond has hidden between

her mattresses," he said. It did not sound like a scold, but gooey and filled with a promise of things to come.

She shook off the feeling. He was a master of confusion. Of confusing her.

"Why! I... You..." She felt her face flush, knowing that it skipped through all shades of red, flushing a scalding purplish hue. She had seen the color a few times in a mirror.

"I only guessed about the book, but you should see your face." He chuckled, reaching out to stroke the flat of his nails against her cheek.

She tagged him with the brush and tried to storm out of the room, but the door would not open.

"Needing something?" he asked with the key dangling from his fingertips.

Taking a breath, she mentally counted to five before she stomped over to the brut. Standing on tiptoes, she yanked the leather thong and key from his grip.

His laughter followed her through the door after she slammed it shut on a curse. How she wanted to rail against him and to feed him a piece of her mind, but knew it was fruitless. That all protests would fall on deaf ears because this man was a different breed of stubborn.

What happened to the rogue on the terrace, the one who helped her release the spider onto the bush? Where was the man who held her hand while watching a Drury Lane theater production? She did not like this side of Linscott. Not at all.

CHAPTER TWENTY
BART

For a generous moment, the hallway granted Annabelle a reprieve from the inward struggle between interest and disgust. How could one man both titillate and evoke feverous rage? She wanted to feed him a piece of her mind but not while he bathed. Of all the outrageous suggestions.

A door at the end of the hall opened, then slammed shut. Slurring the lyrics to a bawdy tune, a bearded man stumbled down the hall toward Annabelle. She tried blending into the darkness. The small window facing the courtyard offered a scant bit of light. Enough to illuminate shapes within shadows but nothing more. He continued past her, using the wall as support until he stopped mid-step. Twirling around, he doffed his hat in a flourish and wobbled upright. Following a puff of gin-soaked breath, he grinned.

"Whasa pretty lady like you doing all alone?" Had the wall not been there for him to rest his elbow, he would have fallen on his face.

"You will address me as my lady as is befitting my station."

One little lie should not hurt. Though the boast did nothing to dissuade the man. It actually appeared to encourage him.

"Milady, where is milord?" His tone was more taunt than question.

She wanted to shoo him away. Or disappear. Perhaps she might dart downstairs at a speed too quick for him to follow. Though, she would be outside with no one to protect her. If lecherous drunkards like this with a gut rolling over their trousers and a mouth full of rotted teeth frequented this establishment, there was no telling who might be on the outside. She shivered. Staying put felt like the safer choice.

"He is seeing to a matter of some import. Now, leave me be, my good sir." There. Curt but polite. It should encourage the vagabond to carry on in another direction.

He leaned closer. "I would never leave a lady so fair as yourself alone. Without the protection of a strong male like meself."

His belch hung in the air, coating her nostrils with the aromas of gin, fish, and a third smell her nose refused to identify.

"Be gone." She waved down the hall.

His head followed her hand. He faltered but managed to catch himself before taking a header onto the floor. Wide eyes blinked up at her with a question in mind but just as quickly forgotten.

"Not without a kiss." He smacked his lips and tugged on the sleeve of her gown.

Annabelle tried the knob, rattling it to no avail. "Leave," she commanded.

"Na. I think you want my kiss." He grabbed her arms with both hands, pulling her against his sweat-stained clothes.

"Unhand me you detestable swine."

Leveraging her foot between them, she managed to shove

him to the side. However, drunkards were an impossible lot. He found his footing, righting himself with a tug on his waist-coat and wiping his hand across his fleshly lips.

"Bart!" a woman's voice called from the floor below.

"Your woman is calling for you."

"Let her call. You're pretty. She's a shrew." His puckered lips made a beeline for her mouth.

She darted to the side, then dodged the other direction. He tottered on unsteady feet like a toddler reaching for his nanny. If she called for Linscott, he would come running. She was positive of that fact, but she could not bring herself to do so. Instead, she tried to fend off Bart and his gin-soaked intentions. Around and around he chased her like a duck with one wing swimming in circles. He would lunge, she would leap to the side. A drunkard's dance that she was in danger of losing.

The door swung open behind her. *Womp*! She fell into a pair of warm, firm arms. Her elbow shot back. She was not about to be caught off guard. Not by two derelicts. Until she recognized his voice. The laugh that wedged against her heart and made its beat accelerate irrationally every time.

"Who is your new friend, Butterfly?"

Bart paled. "Good day, milord. Milady," he slurred and stumbled away without another word.

She was never so glad to see Linscott. Freshly washed, he smelled of rose-scented soap and clean linen. His voice was honied with his old affection and not colored by irritation.

"Your bath certainly took long enough."

The chastisement came from a place of frustration. One he must have recognized because he did not scold her for the bite in her tone.

"After such a long journey, the hot water felt wonderful. Which is why I left you plenty to enjoy. Be quick. Hop into the tub and I will return shortly."

She bunched the neckline of her dress together as if it might conceal some of her flesh from his ogling. Yet, it was a futile gesture considering he did not look in her direction. He stared at the hall window, his fist hitting his thigh.

"Are you going somewhere?" she asked.

"Yes, to stretch my legs," he said with a shrug and his back still turned towards her.

"When will you be back?" Her hands twisted around and around. How did she admit that she wanted him to stay now that she knew men of Bart's caliber were lurking about the inn.

"I will sleep in the carriage."

His offer caused her no amount of guilt. Not that it should. That was what was proper. But she knew the carriage was cramped and he struggled to sleep.

"Jack." The name tingled her lips, while the quiet whisper forced him to turn around. "Please come back. I... This place frightens me." Not entirely true. It was a bit unsettling, but in truth, it was Jack who caused her the most worry. Yet, he was a comfort. This was a conundrum.

He shoved her inside the room before she could issue another protest.

"What do you mean?"

"While I was waiting for you a man came down the hall. He spoke rudely and would not be deterred." She averted her eyes and tested the temperature of the water with the tips of her fingers.

His jaw twitched and his fist clenched, but his words came out smooth as glass. "If you lock the door, he cannot hurt you."

His lack of concern was worrisome. Was she truly just a means to an end? Whatever end that was?

"I may have implied that you were my husband."

He smirked. Drat the man.

"Did you now? What else did you say?"

"Nothing. Enjoy your stay in the carriage." She tried to shove him out of the room, but his foot would not budge.

He was not easily deterred. "I could. But you said you wanted me here."

"Perhaps I did."

"Which is it, Annabelle? I do not enjoy guessing games." He leaned against the doorjamb and waited.

She wanted to tell him to get lost, but thought better of it. Perhaps there was an advantage to having him near. Better than facing drunkards in the hallway.

"Please stay." It was the truth. She did not want to risk another stumbling around the inn and into her room. At least Linscott was the rogue she knew.

"Gladly. But there is something I must take care of. If you will excuse me." He bowed to her, turning on his heel.

This was unacceptable. She admitted that she was frightened and now he was abandoning her. This would not do. Running to catch him, she reached out for his coat and came away with a fistful of air. He must have sensed the movement because he turned around and lifted his brow in question.

"You said you would stay. With people like Bart wandering around..."

"Who's Bart?"

She said too much, or perhaps not enough. Never did she believe a man could offer such comfort. Such security. "Please stay."

"You need to bathe. Worry not, you will be fine. I'll post Thomas outside the door, but as I said, there is something that needs attending." He dangled the key between them, then shut the door. Through the paneling, he reassured her once again, twisting the key in the lock before he left.

Thomas rapped on the door as she slipped into the tub.

"Miss, er, my lady. It is I, Thomas. My lord will return shortly. Call out if you need me."

Annabelle added more water to the tub. It was still warm, sitting near the fire the entire time. It was not the hot water she preferred, but it still felt wonderful after the long ride. She cleansed her body of the accumulation of filth and rinsed off with a pitcher of warm water.

She dried off quickly, not wanting to be caught au naturel when Linscott returned from wherever he went. The inn was silent, and it left her wondering where he could possibly have gone. There were no pubs in the area to drink away the night. There was a coachman to see to the horses. Where in heaven's name had he gone?

CHAPTER TWENTY-ONE
A FIGHT IN THE YARD

Jack was on a mission: find the man who dared to touch his bride-to-be. When Annabelle fell into his arms, her pleading eyes and tightened mouth said all he needed to understand. Bart needed to suffer.

Despite the minutes that had passed, it was easy to follow the stench of gin and unwashed skin. These so-called men all had a type, and that type stank. En route, he ran into Thomas, who was busy flirting with a buxom bit of muslin.

"I thought you needed to rest," Linscott said, dismissing the woman with a toss of a coin and a shoo of his hand.

"I was intrigued by an offer to help warm her bed as I am set to sleep in the carriage. You cannot blame me for pursuing areas of comfort." She had not gone far, hiding around the corner. Thomas whistled and she waved back at him. "Do not tarry, my fair one. I shan't be long."

"Laying it on awfully thick. You are not bloody Shakespeare." Linscott rolled his eyes. He scanned the halls, but Bart was nowhere to be seen. "By chance did a drunkard stumble through here?"

"I am afraid I will need a bit more to go on. Because yes, there have been at least five."

"Man with a thick beard who had not seen a bar of soap since Napoleon was Emperor. Stunk of horse and pig shite?" *A dead man* Jack wanted to add but restrained himself.

"About shoulder height? Wearing an emerald-colored waistcoat?" After Jack nodded, Thomas continued. "Missed him by a minute. I think he is outside trying to negotiate with his light o' love a means of conveyance."

"Do me a favor and stand outside my room while Annabelle bathes." Jack was halfway into the courtyard before Thomas called him back.

"What idiotic idea are you pursuing at the moment, Jack?"

He marched up to his valet. "Do not use my given name."

"When you act like a child, you should be addressed as one, my lord. You cannot possibly be planning to punch the lights out of some drunkard for insulting Annabelle."

"He dared to touch her." When that did not seem to impress his valet, he dropped the final blow. "He frightened her."

"Then do as you must. Who am I to stop you? But send the lady over yonder back in my direction when you finish. I have need of her services."

"You will end up riddled with French pox." The disease all men with their sexual appetites feared the most.

"I have no intention of bedding the Haymarket ware. Some flirting will get me into her bed and then I will be fast on my way to dreamland. I am smarter than you give me credit for. Besides, the brandy we shared a moment ago should be hitting her shortly. So do me a favor and hurry up. Else it will be the flea-ridden barn where I lay my head. And I will be one grumpy servant come morning." Issuing his final demand, Thomas whistled along his way inside.

It was a minor relief to know his best man would guard his bride. Now he set his sight on another. Near the road, he found his quarry. Bart was blowing kisses to a mule that was far more interested in the hay it munched than the man trying to mount its saddle. When Bart, by an indescribable feat, managed to hook his foot in one of the stirrups, the mule moved. It stepped to the side and dropped the drunk onto the dusty ground.

"Bart, is it?" Linscott called out.

The man froze, turning wearily in his direction.

"Pardon, but can I be of service?" He took off his cap revealing matted dull brown hair slicked with grease.

"We need to have a discussion." Linscott folded his hands together, then stretched them before him. Every knuckle cracked. "You seemed to be under the impression that my wife was a person you could address without repercussions."

"Now, that is not what happened."

Linscott stepped closer to the sniveling lump. "I believe that is exactly what happened. Then you had the temerity to proposition my lady wife." Another step.

Bart pulled on the mule's reins. It sensed his desperation and took off without its rider. "Come back," he hollered but his piteous plea fell on ears immune to his charm.

The mule stopped at a clover field in the far distance and resumed its midnight snack dragging the reins along its sides.

Linscott flashed a smile. The one that left bigger men quaking in their boots. The effect was not lost on Bart. He visibly swallowed and put up his hands.

"You have the wrong man."

"I saw you. So you will have to try again." Linscott punched his open palm with a fist. The sound echoed in the courtyard.

"She came on to me."

The claim was so outrageous that it stunned the viscount. He faltered but regained his composure. "Wrong."

His left hook connected with Bart's nose, releasing a brilliant spray of crimson arching in the air.

Bart held a hand to his nose and whimpered. "I did not mean to insult her, my lord."

"It was worse than an insult. You frightened her. I cannot—I will not abide any man believing he has a right to terrify an innocent woman."

He delivered two swift blows to the lump's gut.

Bart doubled over. Linscott took a step back, waiting for the attack. It came in sloppy form with the drunkard rushing forward and shoving his shoulder into the viscount's stomach. Jack had anticipated the move, tossing the man onto his backside using his own momentum.

The fight was over before it had actually begun. Bart covered his face and wept. Wetness seeped between his legs, darkening his trousers.

"Did you try to kiss her?" This was what Jack wanted. What he needed. To hear either weak excuses or a bald-faced lie.

"Yes," he sobbed. "I did not know."

"I don't believe you. Now stand up. Face your punishment like a man should and perhaps I will go easy on you."

"I am a lover, not a fighter." He sat on his knees, holding up his hands in surrender.

The viscount was not fooled. He knew this ruse well and anticipated the counter move. "Well, I am a right bastard who never learned to hold back. Take your punishment like a man."

Grabbing the drunkard by his collar, he stood him up and dragged him across the courtyard.

At the trough for the horse, he dropped the stinking pile into the water with a great splash. He sputtered, clawing to sit upright. Jack obliged, yanking Bart to his feet, only to let him drop once more into the water trough.

"We will do this over and over again until you can be

honest with me. Can you do that Bart? Are you capable of telling the truth?" With his hands on his hips, Linscott waited for the shite pile to cease his flailing and face off.

"Yes. I did it. I tried to kiss your woman." He fell out of the trough, landing on his knees. He begged in a way that made Linscott furious.

He whimpered like a child. The sound grated on Jack's nerves. Anger rose. Anger he wanted to flay wide and pound into oblivion until he thought of her. He took a step back. Then another. He left the whimpering mess of Bart on his knees because what would Annabelle say if she saw Jack attacking one so much weaker than himself? He was no better than a man who abused animals.

Disgust. He felt it rising in his chest and cooling his temper. He reached into his pocket and pulled out a coin. He flicked it at Bart. "Leave. Tonight. I do not want to see you anywhere near my wife again."

Quicker than Linscott thought possible, Bart fled, leaving a trail of wet earth behind him as he ran after the reluctant mule.

Then his thoughts returned to his woman upstairs. He made it to their room in record time, bursting through the door with an amused Thomas stepping to the side.

"You look a little worse for wear," she greeted. She clutched a wrapper tightly to her chest.

The bath was empty. A damp towel lay near the fire to dry. The bed was turned down and waiting while one candle flickered in the breeze coming from the open window.

"What were you doing outside?" she asked.

He wondered what she knew. If she had heard the fight, but the window faced the back of the inn while the fight was out front. He shrugged away her question.

"Where am I sleeping? I am fine with almost anywhere, assuming I do not have to sleep in the tub."

The sight of her turned his brain. She was calm in a raging storm.

She pointed to the floor. "There should be comfortable enough."

"A moth-eaten rug on a hard wooden floor? Heaven." He was so relieved to be near her, he would gladly sleep at the foot of the bed like one of her rescued pets.

"Yes. There are two quilts and two pillows. You shall be able to make a bed and rest." She smiled sweetly at him, and it all felt right.

Perhaps his father was onto something with his demands to wed. Jack felt the rightness in this moment. The need to keep her close. His paramours had been one misfortunate tryst after another. They wanted a share of his fortune. The advantages of his title. They wanted nothing of him. But even with a makeshift bed on the floor, he felt a fundamental difference between Annabelle and all the other women in his acquaintance. He might get used to this entire marriage thing after all.

He picked up a pillow and quilt, arranging them on a rug close to the bed. He laid down, tugging his boots off of his feet and loosening his cravat and waistcoat. Though he normally slept in the nude, perhaps tonight he should be more considerate of the company with whom he shared a room.

The frame squeaked as she crawled in. Then she blew out the candle on the nightstand. "Goodnight."

He heard her muttering beneath her breath, imagining they were prayers but for whom and to whom left him curious. Did his name grace her lips?

"Do you always say prayers?"

"It is what a good and pious Christian does." Her answer had a defensive bite.

"Is it a problem that I do not pray?" Cupping his hands together, he cradled his head and stared at the ceiling.

Her eyes swam into view. He could stare at those expressive golden orbs and get lost in them.

"Do you not believe in God?" Her question sounded hurt, but how was he to answer it?

He turned onto his side and pulled the blanket up to his chest. He was not entirely sure the reason, but that it did not feel right to be seen so openly in front of her. To be so unguarded.

"That is a difficult question. Yes, I guess there is a creator. How else do you explain all of this?" he asked, waving his hand around the room. "But that he answers your prayers and pays attention to the requests of his creations? That I do not know. Living through war taught me that nothing will ever make sense. Those who are good die. Those who are evil die. There is no reason why some survive, and others do not. Prayers felt like the desperate pleas of the frightened. And I am never frightened."

"Truly?" she asked, the word expressing so much doubt for two syllables.

Even he found himself skeptical. He could be frightened, but he would never admit it. Not here with her able to hear his thoughts. Even if they were voiced within the confines of his brain. Davenport men did not show weakness. And Jack Davenport, the sixth Viscount Linscott was not a weak man.

"Did you enjoy the bath?" He tried to stifle his yawn, but it rang against the walls.

"I did. Thank you for leaving me some warm water." There was an echo of a tease in her voice.

"You could have had first dibs, but you were being stubborn."

"You have been the most stubborn. Not I." She sounded certain for a woman who chose to stand in the hallway, unprotected.

"When you next refuse to bathe when I give you the opportunity, I might just empty the entire tub and leave you with nothing more than a dampened towel." Now that was an image he wanted to see. Annabelle, nude, sitting on the lip of a tub, and toweling herself off.

She hurled a pillow at him.

"Thank you. I could use more cushioning." He tucked it behind his head with a triumphant sigh.

She leaned over. "Give it back. And don't flash those dimples at me, my lord. They have no power here."

So, she liked his dimples? That was probably the worst thing she could have mentioned. They felled harder women than Annabelle Greene. With a flash, she would be putty. He was sure of it. "Did your mother not teach you the importance of restraint and to not throw objects at innocent, young men?"

"You are neither young nor innocent," she quipped, snatching the pillow back and shoving it beneath her head. "And no, my mother died before she taught me anything at all except for how much she despised my father."

He sat up, tugging on the quilt. She batted his hand away, facing the wall and not him. There was no way he would let such a telling statement lie. To ignore a glimpse into the woman that was Annabelle Greene.

He crawled onto the mattress, feeling it dip beneath his weight. The action caused her to roll closer, even though she clamored to get back across the tiny expanse of the bed.

Sleeping with a woman. Not sex with a woman, but actually to lie in bed and drift off into dreamland was such a foreign feeling, he actually felt giddy with excitement at the mere prospect of sharing a bed.

"Move over. I decided I want to sleep here." What he said did not match the gentleness of his movements. Gingerly, he laid down, keeping enough of a distance that their bodies did not touch. Even though his cock sang *touch her* louder and louder with each passing second.

"Unhand me." She put very little feeling behind the scold.

Surely after the night journey and most of the two days in the carriage, sleep was about to claim her. The emotional toll alone must have worn her out. It certainly was ready to do him in.

He was not entirely sure why he did it, rather it felt right. He scooted to where he could bury his nose in her curls and inhale her scent deep into his lungs. The heat of her body radiated in waves, warming the air beneath their blankets to a comfortable temperature.

She yawned and nestled into the mattress like a kitten in a pile of blankets. He lifted his hand, smoothing out a curl that teased his nose.

A soft *oh* came from her side of the bed. A protest or a curiosity, he was not certain. The room was still. Peaceful. Content.

In a moment Jack started to snore with thoughts of complacency racing through his brain.

CHAPTER TWENTY-TWO
A NOT SO RESTFUL SLEEP

T hough it did not take long for sleep to claim him, Jack woke during the small hours of the morning after a recurring dream that taunted him too many times. The ache in his shoulder was the reminder of what blind rage awarded him. In the darkness he focused on the ceiling, trying to smother the memories that came alive at night. The sounds of horses and his men in the throes of agony. The rattle of death. The acrid smell of gunpowder permeated the air, clinging to the wisps of dreams. The sticky ooze of blood. Some his. Most not.

Seven years. Would the past ever leave him in peace?

On an exhale, he drew a breath, filling his lungs with faint hints of rose and lavender. Then he heard her. Sifting through unfamiliar sounds from outside and in the hallway, from the only other occupant in the room. There were tiny sniffles. Tears smothered into a pillow. No more than a whispered hiccup. It nearly broke him.

This was his fault. This sorrow was because of him, his

plan to rescue himself from dire straits. She was the victim, and he was the perpetrator. And for what? Money. It was always about money.

"Annabelle," he said, drawing her closer with the guilt that he had caused this. To the one person who did not look at him with the same disdain and distrust of too many to even count.

She turned, swiping her face with the back of her hands. Sticky tears tracked down her cheeks. "I did not mean to wake you."

"I do not sleep well. Too many thoughts battling in my head to keep them all quiet." How easy was it to talk with her. To say thoughts he normally locked away. Never daring to admit that he had the slightest weakness. Unless it was to Thomas.

It was nights like this he needed his valet and former batman as they both sought comfort in the form of a bottle. Conversations that contained scant words but shared meaning. It was a bond he never thought to have, but it was unshakeable.

"I did not give you leave to use my Christian name." She shoved her palm halfheartedly against his chest.

Pain disguised as anger he could handle. He squeezed her against him. "Do not be like that. You call me Jack, so I can call you…"

"Miss Greene." Her lips turned to a mulish pout, but a lone finger brushed strokes against his chest hair peeking through a gap in his shirt.

A few more minutes like this, and she would be putty. The distraction was exactly what he needed to remove his mind from memories of battlefields. From death.

"Fine. Miss Greene. Have it your way." Her huff meant a victory he allowed her to have and one step closer to her ultimate defeat. "Why are you awake and not asleep?" He added a knead of his fingers across her back. The tension melted from her muscles.

"They were silly thoughts." A dismissive statement, one that masked a reality: what she believed did not matter. "Besides, I am your captive. What do you care about my feelings?"

She had a bite to her, he would grant her that. Feisty was a good quality in a wife. To a certain point.

"I care because..." Why did he care? If his paramours cried, he left. More often than not, he would only return to drop off a parting gift. Then again. The parting gift was usually Thomas's department. "Because you will be my wife." Huh, the reason did not gum up his mouth as much as he thought.

"Touching," she said.

Defensive and sarcastic. He could do without the latter. Perhaps both. "I am trying, Annabelle."

"I know, my lord. Jack," she corrected. "I am not used to people asking about my tears. Certainly not men."

"Not your Aunt Silvia?"

She chuckled. A wet ha-ha that sounded more painful than humorous. "Definitely not."

"Your father."

She stiffened and said nothing.

"Your cousin, Viscount Oakmont." He barely knew the lord as years separated them during school. He was currently on his grand tour. Jack missed his own because the continent was too busy fighting a madman.

"No, he is like most of your breed and does not know how to handle tears. He would awkwardly pat my back and then offer to buy me an ice from Gunter's." The tension left.

"Oh. My idea was to buy you a pony." He knew animals were her soft spot.

Now she giggled. Though there was the sheen of tears on

her cheeks in the faint moonlight, he detected the flash of a smile. "I do not need a pony."

"But I made you smile." His lips tingled with the desire to kiss her. To distract her from unhappy thoughts and to make the night a bit less lonely.

"Yes, you did." She tried to conceal it with her hand hovering over her upturned lips.

He pulled her hand away, clasping it with his. There was no reason to hide. Not from him. "Then I have a request. I want to hear more about your mother."

"No." Her smile faded into a straight line. "She is not up for discussion."

"Fine. Let me tell you about my father," he began.

Like a kitten he once tried to hold, she pushed against him until his force broke her reluctance. She allowed his arms to stay where they were, but the minute he loosened his grip, she would flee. He could not say exactly what his reasoning was for pursuing this line of questions, but after a few hints about her family, he needed answers. The importance of building a foundation for a true marriage was compelling. An overwhelming desire to be more than a husband and wife who only shared space together in order to procreate and then go on living separate lives. He needed to be different from the rest of the *ton* or else he would go mad. He was certain of it.

"Most of my life it was simply my father and I. My mother died shortly after she gave birth to my brother Charlie. He lived six days and twenty-two hours. So, since the age of four, it was just the two of us and a handful of nannies in between. I was lucky if he spoke to me at all." Thoughts he never shared with anyone, not even Thomas, flowed easily from his lips to fall upon her ears. She did that to him. Somehow it was easy to talk whenever Annabelle was near.

"I am sure he was grieving." Her tone was dismissive, but her body language spoke of concern.

He heard that excuse before from nannies. From teachers. It did not ease the concerns of a boy too young to understand. "I am positive he was. It is only now as a man of nine-and-twenty–"

She interrupted him. "I thought you were thirty."

"I have five more days," he qualified.

"I think you are quantifying the inevitable. Round up, my lord." She was no longer fighting his hold. This was promising.

"How old are you, then?"

His fingers twisted in the long tendrils cascading down her back. She released a sound halfway between a moan and a purr.

"One-and-twenty. I am young, where you are positively ancient."

This was a side of Annabelle he had not witnessed. "You are purposefully being rude. This is not like you."

The laughter in her eyes faded. "Perhaps it is."

"Yet, I remember you differently." He tugged her curls. "You are not rude. You are infinitely kind and compassionate." He meant it. It was a compliment to be regarded as different from himself.

"I am weak," she admitted quietly.

"Annabelle, no. You are not. Compassion is not a trait to dismiss. I adore you for it." It was one of the most compelling reasons to choose her.

She leaned closer, studying his face. Her fingers danced along his brow and down the edge of his nose to lay across his lips. "Adoration is a strong word."

"I would not have taken just anyone to be my bride. You also did not fight me. So, tell me why?"

Going along with his plan willingly confused him a bit. It boded well, but he expected more of a struggle; instead, she did not fight. A willing captive was better than one who fought him the entire way, but it left him with a heap of unanswered questions.

"There is something more to you, Jack Davenport, and I am determined to figure you out."

That sounded vaguely like a threat. "Am I one of your rescues?"

"Perhaps you are."

He felt like one. He was ready to pant in her lap like Ginny, the mutt. "The Davenport men have a tendency to find women with savior complexes."

Now she flipped his question back to him. "Was that your mother?"

"Most definitely."

"Is that why you are afraid?" she asked.

Her question stunned him. Afraid? There was nothing to fear, not even during the war. Not death. Yet maybe that held a kernel of the truth. He was afraid. "I fear nothing."

"Those are prophetic words."

"Perhaps they are. But tell me, Annabelle. What is it you are afraid of?"

"Loneliness." That was her answer.

A word he did not expect to hear, but it struck such a deep chord it physically hurt. That was why she came so willingly.

"Where would you be without me?" she asked.

"Utterly lost, I am afraid." He found himself admitting his inner thoughts to the darkness. Stirred on by a bravery he did not feel.

"But we just met."

He had the same thought. "I am not here to question it. I am simply following the stars."

"So, what do they say?" she asked with a sleepy yawn.

He waited to answer until he was positive she had drifted back asleep. Then he allowed himself his final admission. "I am in trouble. Deep trouble."

CHAPTER TWENTY-THREE
ARGUMENTS

The next day did not start in the way Annabelle had hoped. Perhaps if she had woken when the sun was rising and a fresh gown was laid out for her to wear, she might have been more accommodating. As it was, she woke with a knee in her ribs and a palm smacking her shoulder.

The rest of the morning went as roughly, from Linscott shooing her out the door with barely time to put her night clothes back into the valise. Then there was the basket of stale bread for breakfast. Once the rain started to fall, it went from bad to horrendous.

Linscott shoved against the carriage squabs and released a distasteful curse.

"I will ask you to kindly watch your language in my presence. This is not your gentleman's club." She sounded like a shrew, but damp had crept beneath her gown causing her skin to itch and crawl. She felt very uncharitable.

"Oh, that it was the Obsidian Club and not a carriage filled with Prudence McComplains-a-lot and her holier than thou proclamations."

"Pardon me. I had not realized I was disturbing you." She kicked her valise, shoving it across the carriage to rest beneath his feet.

He tossed it into the corner with the addition of yet another curse. This one was more vile than the last. Pustules indeed.

"The least you could have done was pack a book. Or my needle point. Then I would have something to entertain myself on this journey other than to stare out at trees." She lifted the leather shade from the window only for a splash of gunk to strike her cheek.

He had the temerity to laugh.

"You are the worst sort of brute." Her chin snapped upward.

"And you are the worst sort of dried-up spinster." He appeared far too pleased with himself. His lips curled in that irritating way of his, all smug and self-assured.

"I assure you, while my reputation might teeter on the plain and ordinary, yours is detestable." That ought to hush him up.

What happened to the man from last night? The kind, gentle protector.

"Enlighten me, your highness." He sprawled across his seat, teasing the hem of her dress with the toe of his polished boot.

"While I might not be the most sought-after guest at *ton* functions, I am at least a welcomed one. You received an invitation to Lady Sinclair's affair due to your repute as a rogue. She only invites the worst sort of men. Colonel Burton for example." Her fingers tapped the inside of her elbow, waiting for his retort and bracing for a stinging barb. It felt good to spar with him, though she hoped she was up for the challenge.

"Oh, little Butterfly. You do not know what you are getting yourself into. Do you really think your tiny insults stand a chance against me?"

"It is for you to examine your own deficiencies. Here you are a man of thirty and yet, you remain unwed. That is your own personality flaw. Not mine."

His jaw flexed. "Even if your father had a dowry of sufficient funds, do you think you would have had an offer? Already past your prime, Miss Greene. Not one interested party. Why do you think that was the case?"

Money. That was what everyone saw in a debutante. Money or breeding. She had neither and Linscott knew that. He had done his research, and she was the candidate most lacking appeal for any other suitor.

Except, there was one. His nemesis.

"I had a very interested party, or have you forgotten the attentions of Sambridge? He expressed a very keen interest in courtship." She made sure to drag out the word courtship, while Linscott's actions around her fell very short of that important and formal distinction. Occasional meetings, a few odd dances, and one occasion when he stopped in during calling hours was by no means a formal declaration.

"Yet, here you are with me."

He had a fair point. She did not struggle when he was there in her room. The truth was, Linscott intrigued her. Even when he was argumentative and being a frankly disagreeable sort.

"You stole me in the middle of the night. Otherwise... Is it Friday? Yes, it is. I should be enjoying a ride through Hyde Park as we speak." She hated rides through the park. If he remembered what she told him the first night, he might catch her in a hollow boast.

His eyes narrowed for a scant moment. As if he was weighing what she said before volleying his next attack. Instead of catching her, he replied with a mundane response. "How unfortunate you are not there."

"How unfortunate indeed."

She did not expect him to zero in on her doubt, but he seemed to know her thoughts better than she did. What he asked next hurt in a way she had not anticipated.

"Do you honestly believe you would be a suitable duchess?"

A sob lodged in her throat. She cleared it away. He would not get the better of her. Not today. "I do not see why not. You obviously think I am a suitable future countess. Though it must hurt your tender ego that the duke is more amenable not only to your paramour but the woman you are forcing to be your wife." There. That ought to have done it.

He straightened to his full height. The additional space between them evaporated leaving behind a steaming and very angry male. "Do not threaten me. I could leave you at the next coaching inn for whatever family member believes you are worth enough to journey all this way to retrieve."

She did not wallow in sadness. She struck hot. By her calculations, Coleman would be dashing up to rescue her any second. Surely. Then again, how would he know where to find her? "Do you not believe I have value?"

He hesitated. The wait burrowed into her chest, the words sticking themselves to her heart. He warned her not to challenge him. Coleman was on his way. He had to be.

"Every person has value."

That bothered her to hear because she had diminished him as much as he had degraded her. "But what is mine if the dowry is too low and my looks so unappealing?" She gave voice to the seeds of doubt he had planted.

But he came back assured with kindness instead of hate. "I already told you. Though this argument has filled my head with doubts, you are compassionate and kind." His posture changed, shrinking back against the squabs and taking his threats with him.

"Yet, you manage to bring out the worst in me."

He shrugged and lifted his chin towards the window. "This damnable weather brings out the worst in everyone."

"Do you really find me lacking?" she asked, barely hearing the question tumble from her mouth.

"No," he said with such certainty it rang in the small confines of the carriage.

"Then why the cruelty?"

"When shots are fired, I fire back without prejudice."

"I do not want to marry you." That was not entirely true. Given a choice, she would have followed Linscott over any other.

"You have no choice."

Though the way he said it made her pause and think that perhaps she did have a choice.

So she asked him, after all this time together, the one most important question. "And still not a reason for why I should marry you. I have to give my consent, after all. You cannot force me into a marriage. That is not the way it works. I must say yes, or the marriage will not be valid. So, tell me, Lord Linscott. Why me?"

The clatter of wheels droned on for miles, and still he had not answered. He remained still with his attention directed elsewhere. She stared at the passing scenery dripping after days of rain.

"You do not fear me," he finally said. "It is a stupid reason, but it is my reason." He twisted a button on the tufted seat. "Happy now?"

"I guess that is a start."

"It seems to be."

She gave him a wobbly smile that he returned with only a hint of dimple showing. An unexpressed truce. It was better than fighting at least. She was sick of the arguments. So, to Scotland they would travel and after that remained to be seen.

CHAPTER TWENTY-FOUR
ANVILS

The rest of the journey to Gretna Green was tedious but uneventful. The tension between Jack and Annabelle reached the pinnacle on the fifth day when a jolt in the carriage sent Annabelle sprawling onto his lap. The awkward angle hindered an easy extraction and forced her to rub against his groin. A hard pole beneath the fall front of his trousers stiffened and heated.

Annabelle froze, unsure of what to do. Jack remained equally so. Their mouths opened inches away from each other. She tasted his breath—sweetened by berries from their luncheon meal. Saw the inky black of his pupils dilate. The flare of his nostrils. He swallowed. So did she. And waited…

The carriage lurched to a stop. Annabelle jerked free from his embrace, falling against the bench. The spell broke.

"Perhaps I will ride the rest of the way with the coachman and Thomas," was the last Jack said before he left her alone with only her wandering mind for company.

She could not comprehend these feelings that stirred within her breast. His inexplicable draw.

After a few days locked together in the same carriage with no one else to impress or fool, Annabelle grew more curious about the man behind the roguish visage. It was moments like now when she suspected his true nature revealed itself. After he momentarily retreated to the top of the carriage, a downpour forced him back inside. She guessed that being dry and enduring Annabelle's company was preferential to being sopping wet.

Weary from sitting in a confined space, Annabelle could not find a comfortable position. Though she said nothing and tried to keep her discomfort to herself, Jack perceived what ailed her. Grasping her lower legs, he lifted them onto his lap, kneading her sore calf and ankle. She tried to pull back, but he tightened his grip.

"Hush, no one will know. Let me do this for you." He turned his head as if to help her maintain a hint of modesty. He made passing observances about the scenery as his fingers dug into the muscles to loosen the knots from prolonged sitting.

Tension melted away like chocolate on a hot summer's day. Her sigh of contentment echoed in his smile. When he stretched, rotated, then flexed her ankles, she made a sound suspiciously like a purr. Heaven.

"Jack, if you do this once a month, I have a feeling we will have a joyful marriage indeed."

"It takes so little to keep you happy?"

"Oh my," she sighed, "please do not ever stop."

"Like all good things, this too must end, as we have almost reached our destination. But I promise you, there will be more of this." He wiggled his fingers in front of her. "Whenever you desire."

She pouted. Searching around the floor of the carriage with her stocking toes, she managed to locate her half boots. Jack leaned forward to tie up the laces.

"No need for such a long face. Today is your wedding day," he said.

Wedding. As if she needed a reminder. A swarm of hummingbirds took flight in her gut. She was at once dizzy and hot.

The carriage pulled into the yard of a coaching inn in the village of Gretna Green, shortly after crossing the border into Scotland.

Thomas snagged Jack's arm, while the coachman saw to the care of the horses. Annabelle paused to admire a planter with a rainbow of colors.

"I know it is your wedding day, my lord. Perhaps you feel generous to spare my company for a few hours." The valet yawned and ran his hand across his face.

Jack had spent many sleepless nights with Thomas, but he had never looked as exhausted as he did at this moment. "Rest. I think I can handle this on my own."

"If I am not too premature, I offer you my congratulations," Thomas said before disappearing around the corner.

Jack profited his arm to Annabelle. They ventured inside.

It was a new building that smelled of freshly baked bread and other aromatic delights. Maybe breakfast might calm her nerves. The death grip on her reticule was not helping.

Inside the door, they were greeted by a giant, barrel-chested man with a vibrant red beard and a smooth head. His face broke into a wide grin as he flipped open the registry.

"Welcome to the Gretna Green Inn."

"We require a room for the night and directions to the nearest blacksmith." Jack pulled a few coins from his waistcoat pocket.

The man rubbed his beard. "Fancy a quick wedding, aye?"

"We are too impatient to wait." Jack looped his arm through Annabelle's, tugging her closer to his side.

"The wife and I felt the same. Married going on sixteen years." He scratched a bit of information in his book, then pointed to where Jack should sign. "For an extra three shillings, we will include a special wedding dinner."

"Oh, that sounds lovely," Annabelle cooed.

The innkeeper cupped his hand and leaned in towards Jack. "An extra shilling will buy you a hot bath for the missus after the ceremony. It is important for the ladies to feel refreshed after a long journey."

Before Jack could pay the extra coin, the innkeeper started to describe a third additional service.

"How much for the complete wedding package?"

The man's mustache twitched. "Two pounds, eight shillings."

Annabelle choked at the exorbitant price, but Jack did not equivocate, instead, he dropped the money on the registry book.

"Martha!" the man called, stopping a stout woman carrying a stack of linens up the staircase. "This couple has bought the exclusive wedding package."

"Why, it must be true love." She set the stack on the counter, whispering to her husband. He nodded. "Keith and I have been married nigh sixteen years. We wish you a multitude of blessings."

"Now, if you could show us the way to the nearest blacksmith." Jack appeared anxious to move the ceremony along.

Annabelle assumed she could dress properly after a bath. Instead, he gripped her hand, tugging her towards the exit.

"Dougal McGuire does the best ceremony in town. He is across the street. Tell him Keith Ferguson sent you. You will get the best deal."

She had to run to keep up with Jack's gait as he tore across the street to the blacksmith's shop. The clang of metal against metal reverberated through the air. The molten iron and slag combined with the oppressive heat was a far cry from the romance found in the splendor of a church.

But Annabelle refused to allow the atmosphere to set the scene. This was her wedding day after all. Such as it was. A little voice of doubt ran laps in her brain. Should she say yes? Or should she say no and find her way home again?

Jack called out. A young girl in a woolen dress peeked around the corner, rushing forward to greet them with a giddy bubble of laughter.

"How may I help you, sir?" she asked, rubbing at a spot of dirt on her nose.

"We were told Dougal McGuire could perform a wedding ceremony."

She clapped her hands excitedly, then yelled behind her. "Pa! There's an English gent wantin' your services."

A tall, lanky man with hair tied into a queue at the back of his neck appeared, rubbing his hands on his leather apron. He appraised the couple.

Jack leaned over, whispering into Annabelle's ear. "He is assessing the size of my purse."

"Hush," she hissed and prodded his arm, so he would turn around.

"The license is ten pounds." His shrewd brown eyes gleamed.

The cost of this entire wedding was outrageous. A church wedding and paying for her trousseau would have cost significantly less.

As if sensing her concern, he patted her hand. "Not to worry. We have plenty." He then addressed the blacksmith. "Keith Ferguson sent me."

"Ah, good man Keith. I can give you the wedding flowers for two pence."

"That's not necessary, we will only take the license."

Dougal harrumphed. "No flowers for a wedding? Tis bad luck." He turned to his daughter. "Whatever would your poor minnie think of a wedding with no flowers?"

She shook her head, her strawberry curls bouncing left and right. "You must have flowers!" His daughter held out a bouquet of dried heather wrapped with a violet ribbon. "It would not be proper without them."

"And a ring." Dougal pulled out a tray with a variety of gold and silver bands. "I make them myself. Now this top row..."

Jack interrupted, "I have the ring, but we will take the flowers."

This was becoming real. Entirely too real. A ring. Flowers. The ceremony. She twisted, trying to run through the door. Jack's grip on her hand tightened.

"And a song," piped his daughter.

"And the song," Jack agreed.

The heat from the furnace was overwhelming. Sweat dripped from her brow. Darkness swam before her eyes.

"Then, stand over here and we will begin."

CHAPTER TWENTY-FIVE
A WEDDING

The blacksmith situated the couple before the anvil. "Are ye willing to have this woman as yer wedded wife?"

"Yes," Jack said. Marriage. If he had to commit to another whether by force or choice, he would do so without hesitation.

The blacksmith addressed Annabelle. "Are ye willing to have this man as yer wedded husband?"

Her eyes swallowed half her face, darting from the exit to Jack, to the blacksmith, then back around again. "I...I..."

Her palm was clammy.

Jack knew she needed to find her courage, and she would make the right decision for the two of them. His index finger drew circles around her wrist, calming her rapid pulse. She looked at him, searching for an answer. Whatever she found, must have assured her, because she finally said...

"Yes, I am."

Relief washed over him. He wanted to kiss her, but the ceremony was not over. The blacksmith used a ribbon to bind their hands together and reiterated that Annabelle had one year and a day to change her mind. Jack absorbed nothing but her.

A tentative smile tugged the corner of her mouth while the daughter sang. The ceremony was simple. He preferred it that way. If they were in London, it would have been a drawing-room affair with Thomas and the Hammond family present.

The clanging of the hammer against the anvil shook Jack out of this trance. He was married. To a woman he barely knew. A woman so shy and timid, he was positive he would inevitably hurt her tender feelings.

"May yer home be filled with babies and happiness." The daughter strewed dried petals in their path.

Babies? Tiny humans. Fragile beings with feelings. He never thought of children until this moment. How spectacularly he would fuck them up. His chest tightened. He could not breathe. The shop began to spin around and around. Tilting from side to side. He needed air. There was not an ounce of it in this confounding space.

The blacksmith clapped his shoulder. "I know that look, son." He walked Jack through the doorway. "You had your reason for marrying her, tell me about it."

Jack stared at his hands, wondering where the urge to slug this Scotsman fled to. "I had to marry a woman, or I would lose everything."

"That might be why ye started looking, but there is a reason ye dragged that bonnie lass all the way here. Find it before you break the little filly's heart. She is a sweet one—can tell that easily enough by the way she treats my daughter. But I have learned a thing or two over these many years of wedding yer ilk. I ken a bit about people. Ye get yer head screwed on right, ye will find yer answer."

What was a short distance between the inn and blacksmith had to be miles across the street. Each step was a hundred before he walked past the front vestibule. Keith Ferguson congratulated the couple, but Jack was in no mood for small talk. He needed to escape. To think alone and find enough oxygen before he expired.

After depositing Annabelle in their room Jack found the common room. There was a table by a window and away from the few patrons consuming their midday meal. No one gave him a second glance as he sat down and lit a cheroot. In a blink, he was nursing his fifth mug of ale.

Married. Now he had to worry about the tender feelings of another person. About needs other than his own. Children. He clutched the mug in his hand. Though he secured his income and satisfied his father's demands, that was only a means to an end. Now what? What was next?

Consummation. There was a silver lining. Sex. Yet, this would involve a virginal woman. His lady wife, not a courtesan. He had no idea how to bed an untried woman. Gentle and slow were not his modus operandi. No, they were fast and hard.

He dragged his hands over his face and stared into his emptying mug. Thomas pulled back a chair and sat down.

"Do you mind?" his valet asked.

"Yes." Jack did not want company.

Thomas did not leave, not that it was surprising. He ordered another round. "Solving your problems with liquor?"

"At least it is watered-down ale. I am not even tipsy." Jack shoved away the mug and stared at the scratches covering the wooden tabletop. How many men had agonized over these same thoughts in this exact spot?

"Be careful with this tavern stuff. It has a way of sneaking up on you." The valet's warning fell on deaf ears.

Jack wanted to be numb. Then the guilt eating his insides

would disappear. "What was I thinking by hauling my ass up here and forcing Annabelle into marriage?"

"Besides the obvious: I need money, so I do not have to live in a gutter?" He tapped his fingers on the polished table. "You do not want to hear it."

The barmaid arrived, dropping off two new tankards and removing the old.

"Try me," Jack said. For once he was interested in Thomas's theories.

"It is simple. Miss Greene..."

"Lady Linscott." It was the first occasion he strung those two words together and it felt remarkable. Lady Linscott. It had a nice ring. She belonged to him—once the night together was over.

"Yes, Lady Linscott challenges you. You have to accept the challenge and learn from it or a lifetime of misery." He took a swig of ale and hummed his approval. "You lucked into the success of this entire scheme. You bested Sambridge. She was a willing partner. No one chased you down. Now you are wed, so what will you do? The answer is simple: make her your wife."

CHAPTER TWENTY-SIX

A NIGHT TO REMEMBER

After a delectable dinner of steak and ale pie with sides of mash and mushy peas, Annabelle was ready to retire. But retiring to bed meant more than sleep. This was the reason she insisted on a dessert she did not need. Anything to prolong the inevitable.

Jack ordered clootie dumplings. A brief reprieve in the form of surgery delight. It astounded her how she managed to eat not one, but three. As she reached for a fourth, Jack snatched the plate away.

"Perhaps later we can enjoy the rest. For now, my sweet, we must retire."

Her eyes glazed over. Groaning, she pushed herself away from the table and shook the crumbs from her dress. "I ate too much. I should go straight to bed."

"A wise choice," Jack whispered, his sensual tone causing the little hairs on her neck to stand on end.

At the door to their bedroom, he turned the key. It swung wide. Slowly releasing Jack's arm, she folded her hands across her belly to still the nervous typhoon stirring in her stomach.

It appeared much smaller than she remembered. The bed enveloped the entire room, yet could not possibly be large enough to fit two grown bodies. She swallowed hard. A rickety chair, dressing screen, wooden washstand, and tarnished mirror were the only other objects, aside from their two small valises. Hurrying to her bag, she unlatched it, snatching up her nightrail and wrapper.

"Excuse me." She hurried behind the screen to dress, hoping against hope that she could find another way to delay the inevitable. He had consumed vast quantities of ale before dinner. Surely, he was tired enough to fall asleep the minute his head hit the pillow.

While she unclasped her gown with shaky fingers, her husband moved throughout the cramped room. The muffled thuds of clothing and boots landing on a chair. The sloshing of water into a bowl. Splashing as he washed his face and other body parts she dared not name. The crackle of sheets being pulled back. The shifting of stuffing as the mattress settled.

With each sound, her heartbeat accelerated repeating... I. Must. Share. A. Bed. Over and over. She struggled to undress further. By the time he lay in bed, she was only halfway through the buttons on her gown. How was she ever going to get through this night?

She managed to don the white nightrail, even though it took three attempts to sort out the sleeves from the neck. She could not imagine a less romantic piece of clothing. This old gown, though infinitely more comfortable due to its age, was worn in places. The hem—dirty from the nighttime sojourn to the carriage. She always imagined wearing an elegant negligee for her wedding night, not creeping along a room, hoping her husband did not notice the chocolate stain down the front.

She walked around the screen. The light from a single candle cast a yellow-orange glow. There was her husband. He reclined in bed, with—*dear God*—no shirt! She tripped on the edge of the screen. Her arms flailed in front of her. As she sailed through the air, the bed shifted, then his hand enveloped hers.

His ankles appeared in her line of vision. Then came the rest of him unbounded before her. Every inch of a glorious male body displayed in full, unobstructed view. And all she could say was: "You are naked!"

Not a more brilliant exclamation or praise. A bland statement of fact tumbled from her unworldly mouth.

"And you are not." Jack's devious dimples puckered his face.

Damned dimples.

Jack was splendid. Fit and lean, with defined muscles throughout his torso rippling as he bent to help her stand. Crisp, curly hair covered the expanse of his arms, legs, and chest. Hair begging for her to stroke and pet. A hairy beast for her to tame. She sniggered, then she caught sight of another distinctly male part of his anatomy.

An intriguing trail of hair led from his navel to his... She could not divert her gaze. *Lud*, she thought, her mouth watered for some inexplicable reason.

Inside she felt—how could she explain it? Hot and cold. Tingles and shivers. And wet. *Wet! There!* The distinct dampness between her thighs demanded that she retreat behind the screen. Instead, Jack scooped her into his arms, carrying her over to the bed without allowing her a moment of protest.

He settled them both, but she leapt back up. "What is it, my little fraidy cat?"

His long legs stretched out in front of him, crossed at his ankles. His hands clasped behind his head. Annabelle could not stop staring at all the hair that covered his limbs. So soft. So inviting. Her fingers twitched. The desire to touch was nearly too great to resist.

Gah! The wetness again! She scrambled to the opposite side of the bed. "I must use the necessary."

"There is a chamber pot by the bed, sweets."

Was he mocking her? "I cannot do *that* with you in the room. I will go outside." A roll of thunder and a crack of lightning disturbed the silence, followed by pounding rain.

He merely quirked a brow, motioning to the pot, knowing she would never venture out in this weather.

"Never mind." She shook her head in defeat and crawled under the covers. She yanked on the end until it covered every part of her, up to her quivering chin.

Jack lounged against the bed frame and unfolded his arms. "You have nothing to fear." He reached for the little wisp of hair that had fallen from her chignon.

His heat soothed a bit of her nerves. Annabelle leaned against the palm, smiling at him. Perhaps this would not be at all what she feared. From the dark nest of hair at the juncture of his thighs, she noticed his male part bobbing. Its length was considerably longer than she remembered.

"It moves?" she asked in barely veiled horror.

It took Jack a moment to understand what she had asked. He followed the gesture of her hand and chuckled. "Yes, as I get aroused, it changes."

"Does it hurt?" She reached toward it, as if to give him comfort, but snatched her hand backward and shoved it beneath the blankets.

"Yes and no." He shrugged his shoulders, then moved closer. "It craves attention. When it finally gets it," he sighed, "it feels amazing."

Jack plucked the pins from her hair, setting them on the

chair next to the bed. He hoped to infuse Annabelle with a sense of calm. It was a little unnerving to watch his doe-eyed bride clutching the blanket to her chin as if he intended to do her bodily harm.

After the final pin clattered on the chair, Jack threaded his fingers through the long, honey locks. He combed out tangles and knots, smoothing the strands until they flowed like silk through his fingers. Without saying a word, he massaged her scalp and neck, until the tension eased from her body. Her throaty moans inflated his cock.

"You need to release the blankets. Let me see you, love."

"No," she groaned.

"Please," he begged.

"My nightrail is dirty."

"Take it off," was his helpful suggestion.

Annabelle gripped the blankets tighter.

"I will even blow out the candle. But we cannot do this with me here and you in there."

"Are you sure?" she asked.

"Timid little butterfly. Move out from under the blanket." He gently pried the counterpane loose from her fingers. "Much better." Jack had to bite his lip to hide his humor. "I do not want to hurt you."

Her mouth was set as a thin, straight, white line. "But it does hurt?"

Annabelle's watery question nearly did him in. He was a monster to want this final act of the wedding night, but his conscience would not get the better of him. All his ruminations about his virginal wife fed a ferocious hunger. He had to claim her.

Jack's fingers stroked her arms in soothing passes. "In the future, it will not hurt. Only this once, and I promise you, I will make you feel so good, you will not even mind the pain."

"It feels good?" Color crept back into her lips.

The corner of his mouth raised in a sly grin. "Stupendous. I promise."

The pads of his fingers skated beneath the hem of her nightrail, drawing circles along her knees to her thighs, inching closer to the magical spot that would have her quivering in his arms. Annabelle sank further into the mattress.

"Keep talking," she moaned.

"You are lovely. So smooth. I want to taste every part of you." Emphasizing his desire, he traced his tongue from her ear to the hollow of her throat.

His fingers worked at the many buttons lining the front of her nightrail. While he moved over her, he kissed every inch of her exposed flesh. She was no longer tightly wound. Tension ebbed away from her muscles.

Finally, she lay before him, her gown gaping open to her waist. "Glorious." He skated his palms down her chest, lifting the heavy weight of each breast in his hands.

"Annabelle, tell me you want this. Tell me you need me."

She had to feel the same yearning he did, this could not be all one-sided, could it?

Her lips parted. She nodded and threaded her hands through his hair, pulling him closer. Jack came undone.

ANNABELLE WANTED to open her eyes, but she was afraid to. Afraid it would chase away the enchantment of this moment. The spell he cast with his words, his touch so insubstantial, her skin ached for more. His mouth, his fingers, his tongue. She felt wicked.

Jack's lips brushed across hers. Fleeting passes. Once. Twice. Thrice. Then he pressed his mouth against hers, nipping, tasting, devouring. Placing gentle pressure against her chin with his thumb, he coaxed her to open for him. His tongue invaded, a gentle marauder exploring its new territory.

Her body hummed with a hunger she did not understand but wanted desperately to sate. Her hands cupped both sides of his face, holding him to her. The guttural groan emitting from Jack's throat encouraged her. She lifted her hips against his, wanting to feel every inch of his skin against her body.

His mouth moved, his tongue licking a heated trail down her throat to the center of her chest. This was where she needed him. This was what she surely missed because her body cried out with need and want.

Jack kneaded her breasts, plumping them with his hands as he feasted on her. His fingers danced close to those stiffened peaks, but he teased her with tiny retreats. Annabelle growled in protest, but he gave her no relief until his mouth descended to her chest. His tongue traced the outline of her areola, then brought the tip into his lips. She was a tangle of sensations as his mouth laved her breasts. Suckling, while his hands pushed her nightrail further over her hips until she was completely bare.

Annabelle welcomed the cool air, dousing the internal flames he stoked as his body worked hers into a heated frenzy. His hands glided over her skin, switching from the pads of his fingers to the tips of his nails, confusing her body with varied sensations. She never felt so alive. Then he brushed past her dewy curls, finding the essence of her heat. Parting her flesh, a single finger dipped inside.

"Annie, you are so wet, and it is all for me," he growled in a voice rough with desire.

"I am supposed to be wet?" she asked, torn between embarrassment and excitement.

"Yes," came his reply, as his second finger joined the first.

"So wet, so tight. Your body is pulling me deeper. I am not sure how much longer I can wait."

He brought his hand to his mouth and licked her essence from his fingers. Suckling them as he did the pastry not many days before. So naughty. She should feel disgusted, but how might he taste?

It nearly frightened her how much Jack understood her body, how he could evoke such sensations from within.

She caught his wicked grin. He lowered his head to the other breast, repeating every tantalizing moment from before.

She did not want him to stop. Four words repeated in a circle in her mind: *do not stop, more.* Perhaps she was wanton to cry such things, but it was all she thought: *do not stop, more!* And he knew what occupied her thoughts because he did not stop. He gave her more.

Jack released the nipple with a pop while Annabelle growled in protest. He chuckled, then throwing her hands above her head, pressed his body against hers, fitting his hard member within the cradle of her thighs. His fingers gripped her wrists, holding her in place while his lips teased hers mercilessly.

"Do not move," he commanded before he explored more of her body.

It was all so much. Sensations built on sensations. Annabelle floated above a precipice. Waiting. Wanting. *Do not stop, more!*

She could no longer think. It was overwhelming. His hand released one wrist to invade her private space, sweeping across her fleece.

"Here is where I will take you, my sweet." A second finger slipped inside while Jack nudged his steel-hard member against her thigh. "You are almost ready."

Jack lowered his mouth again to her breasts, bathing her

nipples with his liquid heat. He suckled in rhythm with the plunging of his fingers. In and out, over and over again. A knot tightened low in Annabelle's belly. Standing again at the precipice, she transformed into a butterfly. Soaring through the sky, weightless on a wave of ecstasy she never knew existed but rode with unrestrained enthusiasm. Flying apart in his arms. Crying out. Shuddering until she floated back to Earth.

Jack gripped her hips, pulling her against him. Pressing his member against her silky entrance. "Let me in."

She nodded into the cup of his shoulder. His tumescent member prodded where Jack brought her to such exquisite heights. He pushed himself inside. She wanted this. She needed the release as his member slid forward until it pinched and burned.

Whimpering, she struggled against his shoulders, confused by the aftermath of liquid satisfaction and the resistance of her body to his invasion. It could not possibly hurt. Not when it felt so right earlier. But as he pressed forward the pinch became unbearable.

JACK PAUSED as he met resistance, her body clenching around him. "Do you want me to stop?"

"No," Annabelle caressed the pucker between his brows. "I want you to feel as tremendous as I do."

Jack's heart skipped a beat. Two beats. Before he pressed forward, hating himself for the pain washing across her face. For her groans of discomfort. Hated himself even more for how much his body thrilled at the feel of hers wrapping around him. The way her body cradled him. How her muscles pulled him deeper and deeper inside of her. Her heat bathing his cock.

Loving it. Pulsing around it. Exquisite torture. Absolute ecstasy.

He whispered incoherent words of praise and encouragement until he finally breached her barrier. Then, and only then, did he pause to give her a reprieve. Her nails no longer gripped his shoulders.

She shifted, nudging him inside further than he thought he could go. This was all the encouragement he needed as he began a rhythm as old as time. He plunged forward, then withdrew. Over and over.

Sweat prickled his brow. A few drops dripped from his face onto hers as his moans deepened, his pace quickened. By the tightening of her inner walls, he knew she was close again, dragging him to the edge along with her. His spine tingled, but he wanted to resist. To prolong this other-worldly pleasure. How could a virgin feel sublime? It was almost as if... as if their bodies were designed only to be filled by each other. As if every woman before her was like a shoe that did not exactly fit.

Exquisite perfection. "Yes," he said, his voice encouraging when words failed to possess his tongue.

She gripped his buttocks, holding on as she threw her head back, lifting her hips to meet him. The angle she created allowed him to slip further inside. Impossibly deep.

"Fly with me," Anabelle begged, her muscles contracting along his member, gripping him deep inside her. "Fly, Jack, fly."

Jack yelled her name. He did not take flight, instead, his body exploded within her, bathing her womb with his essence. The only woman to ever have all of him. His wife.

Collapsing on top of her, Jack buried his nose in her hair. A heady mixture of scents filled his nostrils and the one he sought the most was uniquely hers. Lavender. Feminine Musk. A hint of clootie dumplings.

"Does it always feel like that?" she asked.

"My God, I hope so." Jack tried to roll off Annabelle, but she wrapped her legs around him, tethering him in place. He relaxed further in her arms, allowing her ministrations to calm the rapid beat of his heart.

"Do you expect me to believe it has never felt like that before? You are a notorious rake." Annabelle playfully swatted his backside.

Jack grunted, then extended his arms, rising to look into her eyes. "No, it has not. It has never been like this."

Jack rolled to his side and brought Annabelle with him. Her fingers swirled the hair of his chest.

"Now that we've finished, will you throw me over for another?"

"What kind of question is that?" That she asked, insulted and frustrated him.

"But is that not what happens to all couples? Aunt Silvia said not one of her husbands stayed loyal to her after they were wed. She found two different husbands in bed with housemaids, one with a friend of hers, one in bed with his valet."

Jack could not hold back his shocked laughter. "I can assure you, I am not the type to chase after the household staff, especially the male members. Your closest female friend is Cissy. She would flay me alive if I even imagined another woman in your place."

"She is terribly loyal and protective." Annabelle snuggled closer, toying with the planes of his chest.

Jack captured her wrists. "You need to stop, or I will not be held responsible for what happens next."

Annabelle tried to reach lower, but he tightened his grip. "Please! I did not get to touch it. I am ever so curious."

He half groaned and half whimpered before shaking his head. "No, I hurt you enough tonight. Even though you want more, it will only cause you more pain. Go to sleep now." The command was gentle, followed by a tap of his finger on the tip of her nose. He pulled the coverlet over both of them, then turned her to face away from him, his body spooning against hers.

"What do you call it?"

"What do I call what?"

She wriggled her bottom against his groin. He clamped his hand against her waist. "Stop it."

"Well, answer me. What do you call your, um, male thing?"

Jack thought about which word to teach her. Something respectable or perhaps common, but the idea of hearing the dirtiest spill from her innocent mouth was too exciting to resist. "There are many names, but I prefer my cock."

"Cock," Annabelle said.

His groin heated. This might have been a mistake.

"Yes," Jack whispered, his teeth pulling against the lobe of her ear. He needed to distract her, or else she would find herself flipped onto her back before she was ready again. "Sleep."

"I have more questions."

"Absolutely not. Save them for later."

The weight of the day seeped from Jack's shoulders into mattress stuffing. What a revelation was this new species of woman now sprawled across the naked length of his body. A rather curious creature—wife. Reaching down, his hand cupped her fleshy derriere eliciting a delighted purr as she wriggled her hips against him—the saucy minx.

The storm outside raged, blowing rain against the glass panes. The thunder rolled from a distance, lulling him into a deep slumber. He floated on waves to distant shores. Contented. Pleasured.

Jᴇʀᴋᴇᴅ ᴀᴡᴀᴋᴇ, Annabelle blinked owlishly above him. A cacophony of pounding fists reverberated through the heavy door. Confusion etched her lovely brow.

With a huff of irritation, Jack rolled Annabelle away. Nothing less than the interloper's head skewered on a pike would bring him satisfaction. Revenge for disturbing the first, of hopefully innumerable, trysts with his sweet and no longer innocent viscountess.

From the pile of clothing, he extracted his trousers but forwent his shirt. Let whoever dared to bang on the door glory in his bare chest. Indecent or not, his priority lay in bed, cowering under the covers, redressed in that infernal nightrail.

He swung open the door. A fist connected with his nose. *What in the actual fuck?* His responding punch connected with flesh and answered with a pop. Served the bastard right for breaking his nose without so much as a word of introduction.

CHAPTER TWENTY-SEVEN
VISCOUNTS ARE TROUBLE

"Y ou broke my nose!" Jack cupped his hand, feeling the blood pool in his palm. It was not the first time Jack's nose had been broken, probably would not be the last. With his thumb against the bone, he applied enough pressure to feel it snap into place.

All he saw when he opened the door was the glint of a signet ring, followed by an explosion of lights behind his eyelids. Annabelle, fumbling with her wrapper, breezed past him to confront the fist and whomever said fist belonged. Reaching out the hand not currently bloodied, he pulled Annabelle back behind him, wanting to keep her away from the melee that was sure to follow. No one punched Jack Davenport and walked away. He straightened to his full menacing height and faced his assailant.

"You have two seconds to explain who the bloody hell you are." Jack sized up the fair-haired man, debating the merits of waiting for an answer.

"Marcus! How could you?" Wagging her slender finger up at the interloper, she railed against the injustice done. "You punched my husband! I cannot believe you would do something so cruel!"

"Who is Marcus?" Jack was furious. Annabelle addressed this lump like lovers, using his Christian name. He was duped by an innocent face. What a fool he was.

"He is my cousin, Viscount Oakmont." Annabelle tugged at the back of Jack's trousers, yanking him back into the room.

Her efforts were in vain. No amount of pressure could induce either opponent to slacken their stance. Down the hallway, a few doors opened, curious faces peeking out.

"Come, Annabelle, we are going home." Marcus tried grabbing her shoulder.

"She stays." Jack sliced his hand downward, cracking it against Marcus's wrist.

Marcus shook off the sting and growled his threat. "Marriages can be annulled."

"She is my wife in word and in *deed*."

Jack's posturing did not dissuade. Oakmont lunged, attempting to extract his cousin from behind her husband. Jack slapped his hand back. Marcus reacted by punching with his left, then right fist. Blocking both hits with his forearms, Jack maneuvered around, keeping Annabelle to his back. If she would move, he could end this quickly, but as it was, there was no direct punch Jack could throw without endangering her. That was one risk he was not willing to take. Finally, he managed to push her back far enough to launch at his quarry.

Grunts. The dull smack of flesh against flesh. Fists flew, but neither effectively managed to gain the upper hand. They were heedless to Annabelle's cries of distress. To the cheering of onlookers.

"Hey, Davy, wake up! You are missing two nobs going at it!" cried one of the spectators.

What happened to her sweet-tempered cousin and her good-humored husband? Both had been replaced by absolute barbarians. She had to stop this before someone was seriously hurt!

"I am betting on the brown-haired one. He fights dirty. Fists flying this way and that. Oof!" A man exclaimed. "He kneed the other in his bollocks. Double my bet!"

"The blonde is defending his kin. Counts for more. Atta boy, give him a left and right!"

Money exchanged hands in the growing crowd. One shouted odds, another provided a blow-by-blow accounting for those unable to see. More spectators came from the tavern below, dividing into factions to cheer on the men.

"Enough!" Annabelle jerked at Marcus's greatcoat.

He shoved her back. The momentary distraction allowed Jack to land a punch against Marcus's jaw.

"That's right, dearie. Hold 'em back so the brown-haired one can win," chortled an elderly matron.

Annabelle glared at the woman, hoping the look would wither her to a tiny nub. Instead, the action included more cheers, and bets were placed against her.

"Enough!" Annabelle screamed. She shouldered between the two of them, heedless of the furious jabs being tossed.

She turned just as a fist meant for Jack crunched against her cheek. Lights burst behind her eyes as arms banded around her waist to keep her vertical. *At least the fighting stopped*, she thought wearily through a wave of nausea and blinking away spots.

"Annabelle!" Both men cried in unison.

"Get her something," Marcus yelled over his shoulder.

A young barmaid who had been watching the spectacle, curtsied and hurried down the stairs.

Jack scooped his wife into his arms and carried her to the bed. He wrapped around her, a steady male warmth. When he pressed a handkerchief to her cheek, she caught the faint tremble in his hand.

"You two are nothing but a pair of heathens," Annabelle scolded.

Jack told her to hush while Marcus poured water into a bowl and dampened a few towels. Giving all but one to Jack, he pulled up a chair near the bed. He yelped and leapt to his feet. There, scattered across the seat of the chair, were her forgotten hairpins. He glared at the other man smirking at his obvious discomfort.

"Oh, Annabelle. I am sorry." Marcus tried to apologize, extending his hand.

Jack refused to yield, clutching her against his shoulder. "You will not touch her."

Annabelle tried to speak, but the sound was muffled against his skin. He needed to ease his hold unless he planned on suffocating her.

"I had no intention of harming my cousin," Marcus snapped.

Annabelle patted Marcus's hand, even with the awkwardness of her face pressed against her husband.

Jack tightened his hold. "You barge in here, hell-bent on doing damage with no regard to her safety. Or her modesty. You've embarrassed Annabelle and made an enemy of me."

The chair skidded, then clattered to the floor as Marcus thrust himself upright. "Enemy! You stole my cousin from her bed in the middle of the night with no regard for her personal welfare. You forced her into marriage like a coward, then assured the legality of the union by seducing her. You are my enemy."

Before Jack could speak again, Annabelle sunk her teeth into his shoulder. "Ow, what the devil was that for?"

"You were smothering me, you big oaf." Annabelle struggled against Jack before he relented. "You are the two biggest idiots I have ever met."

"You steal me in the middle of the night with no thought to the consequences of your actions." She thumped a fist against Jack's chest. "I told you, you simply had to ask. They would have accepted our marriage if they realized it was what I actually wanted!"

"And you!" She poked Marcus in his chest. "Barging into our room on our wedding night. Opening the door so God and the whole of Scotland could see me in nothing more than my nightrail and wrapper. You smashed my husband's nose. Then you do not stop until you punch me in the face." Annabelle pointed to her swollen cheek. "How am I going to explain an injury without people assuming the worst of my husband? I will not stand for such rumors to be bandied about."

"You could explain the story," he offered. "People will understand when they realize I was fighting for your honor."

"Explain what? That my cousin is a mindless brute?"

Jack snickered, so she shoved an elbow into his stomach, causing his hold to loosen. "Oof. Watch it, Annie."

"Or allow them to speculate on the reasons you went to find me in Gretna Green? I will be ruined! Is that what you want, Marcus?"

"I... but... He is the one who did this! Not me!" Marcus pointed.

She had enough. Springing off Jack's lap, she marched over to the dressing screen. Hastily, she threw on a dress and tugged her hair into an unruly chignon. Shoving her feet into a pair of half-boots, she marched around the corner of the screen. "You two are to sit here and discuss this like gentlemen. If I discover that either one of you has punched the other, I am going home without you both. Work this out between yourselves. I am going downstairs."

Jack clasped her shoulder. "You will do no such thing. You are not traipsing around a coaching inn without a proper escort."

"I agree. You can wait here, we will go downstairs."

Marcus tried to block the exit until Annabelle kicked him in the shin. She yanked the handle, swinging the door wide. In the entry stood the barmaid with a bowl and towels precariously balanced on her hip. Her fist hovered in the air, still ready to knock.

"What's your name?" Annabelle half-yelled half-asked the surprised girl.

"Maddy," she replied.

Annabelle shoved the supplies into her husband's chest. "Take these. Maddy will escort me to the private dining room. I am sure Keith and his wife will be more than happy to have my company. You two no longer deserve mine."

"Oh, yes, my lady. They are most anxious to hear the whole story. I only witnessed the last part. When that big, blonde bloke punched your bonnie face."

Annabelle should not have enjoyed watching the guilt splotch her cousin's cheeks, but hearing Maddy's version of events filled her with immense joy, accentuated by the pleasure of slowly shutting the door on the two men. Mouths agape, they realized how stuck they truly were. She relished their discomfiture. She only hoped they did not murder each other while she was gone.

~

JACK JERKED ON HIS SHIRT, while Marcus poured half of the water into the bowl on the washstand. It was best to let tempers cool before talking. Jack did not know what to say to Annabelle's cousin. He was livid with the younger man's obvious high-handed nature, and for injuring his wife.

"Annabelle is mine. There is nothing short of God's own divine intervention that can change that fact." There, that made him feel infinitely better as he jammed his fist into the icy bowl. Both the law and church were on Jack's side.

Marcus balanced a bowl on his lap, sitting in the only available chair. It worked for Jack. He needed to pace or else he would treat this room like a pugilism ring.

"You are lucky the crossing from France to England was delayed a half-day. Had it not been, Annabelle would be safely tucked in my carriage and heading back home to her family where she belongs instead of with a thief who stole her in the middle of the night from her bedroom."

He shrugged. "She went willingly."

"You climbed a ladder and ran off with her. That is not the definition of willing."

Jack leaned against the wall giving his adversary a thorough examination. Viscount Oakmont was a little too perfect in his opinion, too much carefree handsomeness to lend him any serious credibility. He was shorter than Jack, fairer as well, with pale hair and startling blue eyes. Except for his nose, which was now crooked and swelling.

Marcus tried adjusting his nose but could not pop into place. Seizing the opportunity to inflict a bit more pain, Jack reached out to help. Before the man could protest, Jack popped the nose back into alignment.

"Could not resist, could you?" Marcus hissed, rubbing the bridge.

"It gives you a bit more of a rough edge."

Marcus shook his head and huffed an exasperated sigh. "Women are not attracted to a man who brawls for fun."

"Then you do not know women," Jack replied with a hearty guffaw.

Marcus scoffed. "I know women far better than you."

"Lordlings fresh from their great big adventure on the continent know nothing of real women. You might have played hide the gherkin with a prostitute, but that is not the mark of a man."

"What is the mark of a man? Whoring after widows?" That remark landed well. "How long will it take until you leave Annabelle's bed for another?"

There was more hidden within the question. A truth he did not want to name. How long would he wait until he jumped from Annabelle's bed to a lover more suited to his tastes? Titled men rarely married for love and were not loyal to wives. Yet, having a paramour would devastate Annabelle. The very thought of doing so churned angrily in his chest.

Jack's nape tingled in warning. The same battlefield alarm that kept his men alive when others perished. "What do you know of my reputation?"

"Enough," was Marcus's reply.

"Rumors are not the true mark of a man. Gossip is for women."

"I do not need rumors." Marcus did not blink.

"Then what comprises all this worldly knowledge? Why is it that you and everyone else believe I am such a reprobate? I would never harm Annabelle." Not intentionally at least. But how long could that last? He would fail her. It was inevitable.

"I know your reason for marrying Annie," Marcus said.

"So does she," Jack countered. That was not entirely true. "But it was merely the impetus for rushing the ceremony. My motivation for choosing her above all others remains my own."

"Because she is easily conned and manipulated?"

Jack's fist flexed, the desire to punch the smug bastard right in his face only increased as the younger man spoke. "You know nothing of your cousin. She may be sweet and forgiving, but she is anything but a naive simpleton. If you want one of those, try any ballroom in London."

Surprise registered on Marcus's face for an instant before it was gone in a flash. "She is mine to protect. I am not about to abandon her. She has had enough mistreatment to last a lifetime."

Jack tossed a towel across the room. It landed with a splat next to the dressing screen. "Countess Brighton was a nightmare."

"Our aunt treated her with kindness. That shows you how little you know about Annabelle."

The aunt was kind? More like desperate to be rid of her niece. "If you were worried about her well-being, she should have stayed in Hampshire. She had a season, the entire point of which was to see her wed. Which has been accomplished. Now, leave." There was no point in arguing. All Jack desired was his wife and a round two between the sheets.

"I am sending Coleman to live with you."

For the second time, he felt air leave his lungs. "I have no need of a butler. Or a footman. Or any other servant."

"He will be working for me. I will know the minute you do anything to harm Annie."

"As of now, the only man to *harm* Annabelle has been you." Jack pointed his finger at Marcus's chest.

The man blanched but continued his threat without making a comment. "My only concern is that he will dispatch you before I get the chance." Marcus set the bowl on the washstand, then retied his cravat. "Annabelle has been my responsibility. I am not relinquishing it now."

"She is my responsibility now." Jack reached for his Hessians, wanting to find Annabelle as soon as possible. He grew tired of the discussion. "I want to know one thing. How did you discover we were here?"

"Baron Crayfield," his lips curled.

Jack saw red. So much red. Blood that belonged to Annabelle's cousin. His former friend. "Did you bribe him?"

"I had Coleman pummel the man within an inch of his life. I did not ask what it took for him to spill his guts, but he did. How a wastrel like yourself managed to amass such loyalty, I will never comprehend. But understand this, I will systematically destroy everything you hold sacred if you dare harm my cousin." He shrugged into his greatcoat.

"If I see you near my wife again, you will not walk away. Do we have an understanding?" Jack wanted this man gone. Far away from his wife and the potential for the damage he could inflict. If Oakmont knew the reason why Jack married Annabelle, he had no doubt they would be dueling by night's end. "She is my wife and mine to protect."

Through clenched teeth, Oakmont spat, "Prove it."

CHAPTER TWENTY-EIGHT
A TOWNHOUSE

After the rickety ride back from Scotland, Jack was never so relieved to be home. The journey was plagued with rutted roads, torrential downpours, and the unpleasant realization that he desired his wife far more than a normal man should. He knew he had a healthy appetite, but at his rate, he was going to pull a muscle if he did not rein in his desire.

Why did he agree to a shopping trip before heading home? She should be focused on his needs, not that infernal book. She was biting the nail of her index finger. The mark of a particularly suspenseful scene when she would hold her breath, flip the page, then release the air in a puff the minute the heroine was back to safety. *How in the bloody hell could a book be so fascinating?*

"Come sit by me." Jack patted the spot next to him.

Annabelle marked the place she was reading with a ribbon, then closed the book. "You tried that maneuver five hours ago. You were left in a rather distressed state when you discovered I could not bend in the way you wanted. Then you bit poor Thomas's head off when he happened to open the door."

"He should have known to knock." Jack reached for his wife.

Annabelle swatted his hands. "He did knock! You were too *engrossed* to notice the carriage had stopped. Besides, we have no more than thirty minutes before we arrive at your home, so there is no sense in starting *that*." She circled her fingers in the air, motioning toward the tented portion of his breeches.

"I am bored." Jack pouted, stretching across the seat in front of him.

"We should converse. There is much I would like to know about you, my lord husband." Smoothing out her gown, she folded her hands in front of her. "Tell me about your childhood."

"I will if you sit on my lap." He tried grabbing her, but she squirmed away.

"You will not listen, your mind will be too preoccupied."

"One kiss."

"No."

"Two kisses."

"That is not how negotiations work!" The corners of her mouth refused to bend in a frown.

Jack counted it as a small victory.

"Come on, we have only a little while left. Good conversation makes the time go by quickly," she coaxed.

Jack's exaggerated sigh carried away his hopes of seduction as he ceded to his wife's wish. "There is not much to tell. I grew up on my father's country estate—Morefield. When he bothered to visit, which was infrequent, he found ways to make me miserable—fire my nanny, send me to boarding school, etc."

"Was there anything you enjoyed about your childhood?"

Jack flicked his gaze out the window. "I love horses. The

head groomsman taught me how to ride and how to care for them properly. I never felt as free as I did when I was riding through the woods surrounding my home. Khali, my Arabian stallion, was perhaps the most thoughtful gift my father gave me."

Annabelle reached out to take Jack's hand in hers. She curled her fingers around his in an offer of friendship. "Perhaps you will let me meet your stallion soon."

Jack used Annabelle's hand to leverage her onto his lap, settling her head under his chin. "If we get the chance. For now, you have enough to fill your schedule from arranging the household to shopping for a new wardrobe."

Her face pinched in a mulish sort of pout. Maybe these were not the desires of his wife, but did not all women dream of having their own household to manage?

The carriage rolled to a halt, drawing her attention away from whatever protest she was working on.

"It is lovely!" she exclaimed.

Jack shrugged away his concern, focusing on Annabelle's smile. "You are lovely," he said, handing her the elaborate bonnet and veil they had purchased to disguise the angry bruise.

She pinned up the side. "Surely your staff knows better than to assume you gave me this?"

He shrugged his shoulders. "They know I come home often enough sporting all manner of black and purple smudges. Allow Bertie, the coachman, to explain, I am sure the maids will love to hear about their master brawling at a coaching inn with another nob."

Annabelle chuckled. "Perhaps we can tell them a different story. Convince them it was nothing salacious."

His self-deprecating laugh filled the confined space. "My dear, you worry too much. Bertie was a bruiser himself until he decided working for a lord and chasing maids around the house was more financially prosperous. Give him a moment to tell Mrs. Cooke and all will be well."

A liveried footman held open the carriage door with his hand extended. Jack waved the servant away, opting to take Annabelle's hand. Parading his wife up the stairs to his townhome felt like the satisfying conclusion of a plan gone right.

Jack bent down, scooping Annabelle into his arms. "I believe there is a tradition where a man must carry his wife across the threshold."

"Be careful. What if the gossips catch wind of you playing the role of a besotted husband?" she warned.

The upward tilt of his lips was his answer. He shoved the door open with his foot and crossed the threshold, reluctant to set his bride down. He loved the weight of her in his arms. "The biggest danger is my housekeeper discovering me with you in my arms. She has been after me for years to settle down and bring a proper lady into the house."

"Oh dear, you poor man. What will she say when she catches sight of me?" Annabelle rested her head against his shoulder as Jack leaned to brush a kiss across her lips.

"Ahem." A throat cleared interrupting the moment Jack had imagined since stepping foot in the carriage this morning.

Seducing his wife was once more delayed, this time in the name of duty. Jack placed his bride on the floor.

"My lord, my lady, welcome home," the throaty voice greeted.

"Coleman!" Annabelle threw her arms around the butler, embracing him as if one would a friend, not a servant.

"Coleman," Jack all but snarled at the calculated gleam in the butler's muddy brown eyes. Exactly the same as a gambler who had a hand he could not lose. He could not believe the audacity of Oakmont to install a butler in another man's house.

"What are you doing here?" she asked.

"I am rather curious as well." Jack removed his gloves and handed them to a footman standing in the entrance.

Mrs. Cooke appeared, offering an explanation. "Viscount Oakmont, with the consent of your father, insisted a few of their servants come here to help our new mistress get settled." She was quick to take Annabelle's pelisse, fluttering like a mother hen over a baby chick.

It figured Jack's father was involved. Swearing to himself, Jack tried Annabelle's method of counting to calm down. He managed to get to one hundred before the twitch in his eye quickened.

"What happened to Broderick?" Jack's butler had served his family since childhood. After Jack took his own residence, the butler followed, since it was a smaller household and the servant's rheumatism bothered him.

"He has been going on for years about wanting to retire to the country. The Earl of Maitland offered him a generous severance," Mrs. Cooke said.

"No one thought to ask me, before changing my staff?" The twitch in his jaw returned, the one which never appeared until a month ago. Come to think of it, the infuriatingly persistent muscle spasm started the day of the infamous summons.

"We asked the earl, but he insisted you would not mind. After all, you promised Broderick he could retire as soon as you found a replacement." Mrs. Cooke fawned over Annabelle, paying compliment after compliment. "Besides, we want our new viscountess to feel welcomed. Your staff is quite happy with Mr. Coleman's direction."

Coleman beamed at Jack. There was no mistaking the challenge he detected.

"My lady," Mrs. Cooke said with a reverence she never offered Jack. "I am the housekeeper. Allow me to introduce the other servants."

Along the hall, Jack's staff lined up, ready to be presented to his new wife. The efficiency with which everyone moved was astonishing.

Thomas bowed regally to Annabelle, then had the audacity to wink. "My lady, as you know, I am his lordship's valet."

"I will enjoy continuing our acquaintance," she said.

"As will I."

She giggled. Great, now Annabelle flirted with his valet. Jack glared over her head, but Thomas ignored him.

"Well, I am utterly enchanted with his choice for a bride," Thomas said.

Two maids cooed while Annabelle blushed. "Oh my."

"A lovelier woman there never was."

"Thomas?" Jack growled.

"Yes, my lord?" he asked, not bothering to turn his attention away.

"Stop flirting with my wife."

Thomas flashed a wide grin and clicked his heels together. "Aye, my lord."

"That was flirting?" she asked Jack. "I have never been flirted with, I did not know."

"Nor will you. I am the only man allowed to do so." He scooted Annabelle away from his infuriating valet.

Thomas smirked. Servants should not be this irritating.

"These are Daisy and Mary Louise, they are our house-maids." Mrs. Cooke introduced the next servants.

"How do you do?" they asked in unison, dipping into perfect curtsies.

"It is nice to meet you both."

Jack stood behind Annabelle. Each person received the

same polite greeting while she repeated their names and duties. The welcoming treatment his staff gave their new mistress was a comfort. The only person who did not smile was Coleman. He continued to glare pointedly in Jack's direction.

A commotion from upstairs disturbed the last pair of footmen giving their names. An orange and white blob sailed down the stairs, launching itself against Jack. It was all he could do to hold up his arms in defense as the beast clawed and hissed. Following shortly behind was a flop-eared puppy, barking encouragement as the cat dug in further.

"Winston!" Annabelle tugged at its paws, freeing Jack's waistcoat.

As she turned to set the cat on the floor, the puppy tangled himself between her legs, causing her to lose balance. Still gripping the hissing cat to her chest, Annabelle slipped through Jack's outstretched arms, onto the marble floor. The strategic bonnet and veil slipped off her head.

Mrs. Cooke inhaled sharply. The pair of maids rushed to Annabelle's side, while a footman scooped Ginny in his arms.

Before Jack could help his bride to her feet, he was thrown against the wall. A forearm dug into his throat, choking off his air supply. Above him hovered the face of a man bent on nothing short of murder.

"Coleman," Jack choked, grappling with the butler's forearm.

"My lady!" Mrs. Cooke shrieked. "Please let us help you."

But Annabelle shoved through the crowd, coming to her husband's aid. *Just in time*. The world around him began to fade to black.

"Coleman, let go!" She yanked at the elbow crushing Jack's windpipe.

"Never," the butler roared.

"You will not harm my husband! He did not do this!" Annabelle yanked furtively at the butler's shoulder.

The pressure eased slightly, color swam before his eyes. "Oakmont," was all he could choke out before the pressure resumed.

"Marcus hit me. Not Jack. It was my fault because I stepped in between the two idiots fighting. Please, Coleman, let him go." She finally managed to dislodge the enraged man.

Jack collapsed to the floor. "Is he a butler or a trained killer?"

Annabelle was on her knees, inspecting his neck and face. "He might have spent time on a prison hulk. Before the incarceration, he worked on a merchant ship in the Bahamas."

Given his size and the menace Coleman radiated, Jack highly suspected the ship's activities might not have been entirely legal. "You and your strays. One of them will be the death of me." Pushing off from the floor, Jack took in a much-needed lungful of air. "Speaking of which, if Winston does not learn to keep his claws in, he will have to go."

Annabelle gasped. "You do not mean that! He is an innocent kitten."

Jack nearly missed the disbelief that flashed across Coleman's face. Perhaps they could agree on something. "The cat is a menace."

A footman snickered. Another one muttered his agreement. The silence of the staff was an indictment Annabelle chose to ignore.

"How could you say that!" As if on cue, Winston threaded himself around Annabelle's legs purring and rubbing his head. She cradled the cat, and it mewed plaintively.

Jack held up his scratch-covered arms. "Menace! M-E-N-A-C-E!"

Annabelle harrumphed, turning around. "Mrs. Cooke,

which way to *my* room?" The way she emphasized the word "my" let Jack know it was going to be a lonesome night.

"Apologies, my lord." Coleman extended his hand.

Jack debated for a moment before shaking it in truce. He had to respect the man's determination to protect a woman even when at odds with the lord of the house.

"Accepted." Jack tightened his grip, speaking low enough so only Coleman could hear. "However, you would do well to remember Annabelle is my wife. Under my protection."

"And you, my lord, will do well to remember I have nothing to lose should any harm befall her." With his final threat, Coleman left the entry.

Two men in the whole of existence Jack could not menace into submission, and both were connected to Annabelle. What an interesting crew she aligned with—an overprotective cousin and a pirate turned butler.

Jack stood in the tiled entry with only the puppy remaining behind. Ginny cocked her head from side to side. "It is you and me, girl." Reaching down, he picked up the pup. "I could use a drink right about now. How about you?"

It panted in response, butting her velvety head against his palm.

"Now if only all of Annabelle's rescues were like you, my little one."

That was when he felt liquid warmth spreading across his chest. The dog buried her head in the crook of his arm, whimpering.

"Ah, well despite the piddle, you are still my favorite."

Her wet tongue brushed against the back of his hand, a gesture of contrition. Jack motioned for a passing footman to bring him a new shirt and waistcoat, then carried the most agreeable member of the household into the study for a brandy.

CHAPTER TWENTY-NINE
DESIRING YOUR WIFE

J ack woke with his body thrumming with need. A need for the woman in the adjoining room. Damn inconvenient she was not lying next to him in the expansive, empty bed. Despite his raging erection, he shivered, pulling the covers to his chin, wishing she would join him.

Yanking open the bed curtains, he glared across the room at the hearth with only remnants of glowing coals. The maids did not prepare the fire. Only one solution for fighting off the chill then, the delightfully obliging creature known as *wife*.

Jack threw on his silk banyan. He forewent any other clothes, save a pair of worn woolen slippers. His insistent tumescence tented the fabric, allowing a draft to circulate around his nether region. His desperation for a cure mounted as he threw open the connecting door and was blinded by a flood of sunlight.

In defense, he threw up his arm, using the excess silk to hide the offending brightness. A gasp of surprise near the bed alerted him to the object of his quest.

"Close the curtains, Annabelle," he demanded.

"Um, my lord." The meek voice of a maid forced him to lower his arm. She stood at the head of the bed and trembled. Ah, yes. Modest maids, troublesome lot they were.

She visibly swallowed, clutching the ball of bed linens tightly against her chest. "My lord, the viscountess isn't here."

The bed, covered in feminine silks of periwinkle and ivory, was perfectly made as if his wife was merely a conjuring of his imagination. Not one item out of place. No brush with hair on the dressing table. No stray stocking. Not even a hairpin to be found.

"Where is my wife?"

"Breaking her fast, my lord. Or at least she was when I arrived an hour ago."

He rubbed his temples, the twinges of a headache pulsed. "What time is it?"

"Half past nine, my lord."

"Hast past nine?" he bellowed.

The maid flinched. "Yes, my lord."

"If you value your position, you will stop saying my lord immediately."

"Yes, my, uh. Yes."

Against his bare legs, a soft pelt brushed.

"Erp," the maid squeaked.

"Whatever is the matter?" His headache intensified. He needed relief and soon. Preferably the physical kind, but at the moment the medicinal would substitute.

"The cat, my lord."

He opened one eye; she muttered a faint apology. Interesting. His erection was less frightening than the demon seed currently winding around his leg.

"Are you scared of the cat?"

She nodded, hefting the bundle of linens higher to reveal arms covered in red welts. "'E weren't happy when I changed the sheets."

"Mangy beast." Using his foot, he lifted Winston away, but the cat sank his razor claws and single fang into Jack's bare calf. "Be gone, foul creature."

Prying the forepaws from his leg, he tried removing Winston, but their altered position only provided the harassed feline more skin to shred. The pile of bedsheets fell with a whoomph as the maid ran to his aid. Each of them took two paws, but the animal writhed and twisted, making it impossible to extract him without more punishing swipes from claws and tooth.

The door opened with a sharp intake of breath. In an instant, the chaos stilled. Winston went limp, dropping to the floor, and running through the open doorway like its tail was engulfed in flames.

The maid gathered the laundry and rushed through the door. She curtsied, before leaving with a hasty, "My lady."

Annabelle closed the door, one hand on the doorknob, a palm against the paneling to muffle the sound. Her shoulders lifted on a deep inhale, then lowered before she turned around.

Blood seeped along the scratches on his legs and hands. One trickle wound its way along his forearm, but Jack paid no attention. It was his wife who captured his thrall.

Gorgeous was not the word for her; it was not complex enough to describe the way the sunlight threaded gold in her perfectly coiffed hair. Or the slight flush of pink on her cheeks, giving her face an aura of glowing vitality.

To say Jack lost his ability to breathe would not be adequate. No, it was more akin to falling from a horse onto the unforgiving ground. The force of impact emptied his lungs of precious air, followed by a moment of panic that they would never fill again. The combination of abject fear and relief the second he inhaled, filling his nostrils with the smell of lavender and spring rain. Annabelle.

"I wanted you," he confessed, as she crossed to her dressing table to retrieve a jar of a white, sticky substance.

She dabbed her finger into goo, slathering a thin layer across the deepest cut. He did not pull back from the sting, allowing her gentle ministrations with a quiet study of his wife.

"Funny, that is not what it appeared when I walked in."

"What did you suppose happened?" he asked.

She picked up his other hand. There she covered more scratches with the stinging ooze. "You seduced a maid in my bedroom." Her wrist flicked to his banyan, where it now gapped across his middle, his erection freed and proud.

"I woke in this state expecting my wife to still be abed, but instead, found a trembling maid and an ill-tempered beast. Winston is a menace. He needs to go, or we will no longer have a staff."

She huffed, dropping his arm to slap more salve on his leg, far less gently than before. "He is *not* leaving. No creature belongs outside, a victim to the cruelties of the elements." She slammed the lid back on the jar, marching back to her dressing table before she turned on her heels, shaking a finger in his direction. "We are a package deal. You knew as much before you broke into my room, hauling me off in the middle of the night."

Jack held up his hands in surrender. "The consequences are on your head. If no maid or manservant will grace our hallowed halls, you will be left to scrub the floors." The image of his wife on her knees, her rounded buttocks bouncing as she vigorously scrubbed was nearly his undoing.

She pushed past him, but his arm snagged her waist,

drawing her against his turgid length. He nuzzled the crook of her neck.

"I missed you in my bed." He nibbled her earlobe, growling in satisfaction when she responded in kind.

The myriad of pins prevented his hands from sinking into the luxurious lengths of her hair, and the lack of time, before his lust destroyed the last vestiges of restraint, prevented him from undoing the intricate coils. Another time, then.

Instead, his hands wrenched her delicate fichu, then tore her dress in two.

"This gown was brand-new!" She slapped his hands, pulling the bodice together, but finding the dress beyond repair.

"I will buy you dozens more. Now come here." He yanked the fabric free from her body, then spun her around to untie the stays keeping her breasts bound against her chest. "You wear far too many clothes. From now on, you dress only in lacy negligees. Your wifely duties demand ease of access."

She wriggled free and crossed her arms. The action unwittingly lifted her glorious mounds, her rosy nipples straining against the thin lawn of her chemise. He licked his lips. She followed the direction of his gaze.

Lowering her arms on a gasp, she drew the fabric over her head before he had the chance to shred yet another garment.

Jack took in every available surface. The bed—too far. The window seat—she is not daring enough, not with the curtains drawn and the sky clear. The floor—soon, very soon. The image of her bent over was still fresh in his mind. Hefting her in his arms, he set Annabelle on the polished cherry wood dressing table. The mirror offered an exquisite view of her shapely back and the cleft of her rounded derriere. Already primed; however, seduction belonged to Annabelle. She deserved an equal portion of gratification, if not the lion's share.

Jack's mouth descended, her lips parted in invitation as his tongue mingled with her own. Her taste—sweetened by honey scones. Her arms rested on the breadth of his shoulders, while fingers tangled in his hair, playfully yanking on the strands to guide his head to the ideal angle. Ever the obedient lover, he followed her gentle instruction, waiting to reverse their roles. Waiting to become a teacher.

Her body was his playground, open and poised for his exploration. His hands lifted her breasts, tweaking the twin buds and eliciting a mewl of delight deep within her throat. Her eagerness, responding to every caress with equal vigor, inflamed his desire, fueled his need to settle himself firmly between her fleshy, glorious thighs.

He positioned her heels on the dressing table top, leaving the moist, hot flesh of her center exposed. How he wanted. How he needed to taste the sweet nectar on his tongue. To bring her to completion, writhing with every inch of her exposed.

He kneeled before her, taking his steely member in his hand and stroking, while two fingers parted her rosy flesh, exposing the liquid heat. His tongue swiped once, causing her swan-like neck to fall back on a moan. She tightened her fist in his hair, drawing him to the spot of her need, but he resisted, eliciting a delightful groan of frustration.

"Tell me what you need. Tell me how much you want me to lick your cunny."

The words stumbled over her tongue. A portion of innocence and naivety, he wished she would never lose. Followed by raw desire.

"Taste me with your tongue," she whispered.

He answered by doing exactly that, pushing her knees to the side, thrusting his tongue forward to sample her moist center. He laved and suckled, while she whimpered and thrashed, biting her fist to keep from crying out. But he craved her sounds, wanting to hear her moans of ecstasy fill his halls. For the people on the street to know the mistress of his home was satisfied. She was his and his alone.

His finger slid inside her tightening channel while his teeth nipped the pearl. In response, her fingers scored his back, her whimpers switching to groans, her hips thrusting forward, bringing her closer to his mouth.

So fixated on her pleasure, Jack forgot the persistent throbbing in his loins demanding immediate gratification. He relished Annabelle's response to every swipe and suckle. Driving her desire higher and higher, like a stallion galloping on open fields. She rode his mouth, his fingers.

How he needed, wanted, craved. He needed her body tightly cinched around his own. He wanted his name ripped from her throat in a cry of exaltation. He craved her flavor, her body, her soul. It was all or nothing, nothing or everything. She was his need. It was never like this, never such ferocity. Never so primal. So exquisite. So raw.

She erupted like a volcano, spewing her molten liquid over his tongue in climax. He drank her elixir. Before she reached completion, he rose to his feet, slamming fully inside. She grasped his firm ass with her nails, driving herself against him in a hurried pounding, keeping her orgasm flowing.

Her tight sheath drew him further, propelled his lust to impossible depths. His spine tingled. The hair on his neck rose. Alerting him to his impending climax. As much as he wanted this sensation for eternity, he could not stop. Would not stop if the king himself marched into the room, demanding an audience. Not fire. Not flood. Not a cannon blast would cease the erratic pounding of his flesh into his wife's.

She tightened her hold, sinking her teeth and nails deep into the layers of his skin. He welcomed the pain, grounding him in the moment. In the fucking of his wife. He shifted slightly, finding the spot deep inside of her. The one created by her maker.

Explosions within her, around him. His eardrums from her scream—his name. His seed broke through the dam of restraint, flooding her womb. His heart. Completion! But his thrusting did not cease, instead only slowing as she collapsed in a resplendent, boneless pose against the mirror of her dressing table. He still did not cease his thrusts as intruding thoughts niggled his mind, poking holes at preconceptions he held sacred.

He was not ready to recognize these feelings, to give them a voice. He abruptly withdrew, using her fichu to wipe away the evidence of their lovemaking, tossing it carelessly to the side.

"You have no regard for my clothing." She chided while placing a string of delicate kisses across his chest.

Every instinct coiled tightly inside, demanding he flee from such unrestrained affection. He stepped back. She stumbled forward, regaining her footing after his arms rose up to stop her momentum.

Her brow furrowed. A tiny, disgruntled syllable escaped. The look of confusion mixed with betrayal forced the wall around his soul a little higher. He could not let her in, there was nothing for her to find.

"Clothing is clothing. I told you before, whatever you want, I will provide. Now, I must break my fast. Ring for a maid to put you to rights. Your wifely duties are done for this morning. I should be 'round again tonight." He pinched her bottom, leaving before her mouth closed, forming the vitriol he deserved.

He left his banyan behind. He left his logic. His indifference. His armor the minute he crossed the threshold, closing the adjoining door as a slipper clattered against the wood. What the hell was this feeling, roiling around like a sickness in his belly? Rotten eels? Bad humors? Maybe he needed a leech.

"What did you do?" Thomas asked, holding out a dressing gown.

"Not now," Jack pushed past his valet, entering the bathing room. There he sat, tearing at his hair.

His heart raced. His sternum ached. Air failed to properly fill his lungs. His cock demanded his wife, still erect and throbbing. His mind railed, demanding he leave and never return.

His heart, oh, the terrible organ, it wept. It wept like the little boy he once was, when his mother lay in the wooden box, refusing to wake up and hug him. It ached like the lonely child hiding in a closet, while his tormentors taunted him on the other side.

Jack poured water into a bowl, splashing his face and cleaning the evidence of his wife from his body. Her liquid. Her scent. The memory of her flesh.

Marching into his room, he grabbed clothing from his wardrobe, ignoring the man glowering in the corner.

"I have your clothing here, my lord."

"Leave me, Thomas."

"I will not have you traipsing about like a vagrant."

Jack pulled back his fist, wanting to punch his way through his confounding emotions. Thomas threw a pair of buckskin breeches, which Jack caught, yanking them on while arguing with his valet.

"Your job is not to command me."

Thomas gathered the implements, unaffected by Jack's temper. "Sit in the damn chair, Linscott."

Jack grumbled, but obeyed, praying compliance would hurry his meddling valet along. Thomas wrapped Jack's face in warmed towels as he stropped the razor. The sound of the blade sliding across the leather stoked his ire. "Hurry it up."

"Places to be?" Jack gestured crudely in response. "Tell me, Linscott. Did my lady catch you dallying the help?"

Jack swung wide, hitting only the air.

"Ah, so it was the lovely Lady Linscott's slipper I heard. Thank goodness, else Coleman bid me to use the blade across your throat."

"I am rather surprised he is not here holding it against my jugular." Jack gripped the handles of the chair, ready to spring.

"Might have locked him in the larder until I got more information."

"So, I still have your loyalty?"

Thomas unwrapped his master's face, lathering it with sandalwood-scented soap. "I might owe you for shooting that crazed Frenchman as I carried you on a stretcher."

"Bastard bayoneted me. Thought I had done him in before you tried carrying me off in the heat of battle."

"What kind of batman leaves his officer to die?" Thomas asked as the blade glinted in the morning light.

Neither had spoken of the Belgium incident in years, opting for silent acknowledgment of the debt they owed each other. A life for a life.

The razor slid over soap-covered whiskers, soothing his anger. "What is this?" Jack asked with a thump to his chest.

Thomas lifted his gaze to meet Jack's in the mirror. "I take it you are asking about," he pointed to his chest, "this infernal organ. The one which only started functioning about a week ago?"

"A fortnight."

His valet lifted his brow. "You do have it bad."

"I do not understand these thoughts."

"Do not fight it, Linscott. You married well above yourself. It is only natural to fall so spectacularly."

"It is only sex." Even Jack did not agree with the words falling from his mouth.

"Keep telling yourself that."

Jack closed his eyes, refusing to listen anymore. After the remarkably efficient shave, he allowed Thomas to nitpick his clothing and tie a sensible knot in his cravat.

At last, he located his much-underutilized study, where he threw himself into a chair.

Coffee service came and went. Mr. Parker dropped a stack of correspondence on the blotter, mentioned a fact or two that left no impression on Jack's brain, then left him alone to sweat and stew. He raked his hands through his hair. His elbows rested on the table when the epiphany struck full force.

It was lust, pure and simple. Unbridled lust after years of searching for a partner who equaled his enthusiasm and enjoyment of the act. The others before Annabelle were bedsport, but she took the experience to the next level. The hollow feeling accompanying the so-called epiphany, he did not dare speculate on the source. Sex with his wife was enjoyable. Nothing more. Nothing less.

A faint hint of lavender wafted through the air. He sniffed his clothing, terrified he still reeked of his wife, but it was in the air. Floating around him. It stirred his loins, craving her again. Aghast, he pushed away from his desk. Perhaps a hard ride through Hyde Park would properly chase away the thoughts.

The knocker at the front door wrested Jack's ruminations away from his wife. He peered through a crack to discern the identity of the visitor. Coleman walked regally to Annabelle's parlor to inquire if they were home. It was not their usual day for calls. Best let Annabelle handle it.

A ride it was. Fetch Thomas for a quick change, then be on his way. Thunder clapped. What happened to the cloudless sky? So much for distractions, he returned to the study, cursing his terrible luck. Better avoid The Obsidian Club for a few days lest he lose more than his pride.

CHAPTER THIRTY
TROUBLE FOR FRANCINE

Annabelle dressed for the second time, cursing her husband. She knew nothing about men. One minute he desired her, the next he fled!

She wanted to forever erase the memory of their love-making on her dressing table. What possessed her to act like an absolute wanton? Biting and scratching like an animal. Of course, Jack had fled. He must be mortified to have a cat and a wife who acted the same.

The scrawny tom uncurled, elongating in a pleasurable stretch before demanding pets with a bump against her hand.

"This is all your fault."

Winston mewed, flicking its crooked tail, unbothered by her accusation.

Gathering the ruined fichu and dress, she rolled them into a ball, handing them to Daisy with instructions to throw them into the rag bin. What a waste of a finely designed gown, the first in an age to fit her properly.

Dresses aside, her confounding husband returned to the forefront of her thoughts. She stood on a footbridge of crumbling stone and uncertainty. He vacillated between passionate and distant so quickly, she could not understand what she did wrong.

It was too much like her mother. A twisting, churning whirlwind of emotions that laid waste to those unfortunate enough to be caught in her path. Annabelle could not live like that again. The perpetual creeping around on tiptoes while she waited for the next devastating insult to be hurled. Her father never stood up to her mother, and once she had died, her memory haunted their home.

Doubt crept in the corners, maybe it was not Annabelle Jack truly desired. Her mother had resented her father. Even though he was a viscount's son, he did not have the clout of the firstborn. So, she threw herself into the arms of any available man, and several not so available ones.

Jack claimed to be searching for her, but if that were true, why did he not leave the minute he discovered she was elsewhere? Why were Mary Louise and Jack standing so close, the evidence of his true desire jutting away from his body?

Oh, naive, trusting fool. The reason Jack married her was simple, she was the only one who would not say no, regardless that he had to whisk her away to Scotland.

A thick tear trickled down her face. *What had crying ever done for you before?* Perhaps Mrs. Cooke could let the maid go, with proper references. After all, it was not the girl's fault that Jack's mind tended toward one thought and one thought only. Yes, Annabelle would speak with Mrs. Cooke immediately. The girl would be gone on the morrow. No more temptations for her lord husband. With a handkerchief, she scrubbed her cheeks dry.

No, best not to let the girl go, references or not. If her husband strayed, the onus belonged entirely to him. She would not plead for him to stop. Mope around the house and be an unwanted discard. No, this was her home. This was her life. Not her father's.

She clapped her hands against her mauve skirts, knocking out the wrinkles before examining her reflection in the standing mirror. The dressing table was off-limits now. Using a powder puff, she dusted a fine layer of the scented extravagance across her cheeks before heading downstairs. As mistress of her home, she had duties to oversee.

On the way to her personal parlor, she passed the closed door of her husband's study. Should she knock? Cook wanted to bake salmon, but he had mentioned a craving for haddock. Hesitation strengthened her indecision. Perhaps it was best to allow the cook to decide, she knew Jack's tastes far better than Annabelle ever would.

Though the curtains were open, her parlor mimicked twilight. The barest of sunlight filtered through a thick layer of clouds, which had rolled in between early morning and the interlude with her husband. The darkened puffs were swollen, threatening to drench all who ventured out of doors. So much for a pleasant stroll through the park to clear her mind.

She picked up her sewing basket and selected a cushion cover for Aunt Silvia. The embroidery was a peacock and peahen, their heads nestled together in a gesture of undying love. At her heart, Aunt Silvia remained a romantic through more marriages than any one woman should have. Assuming Lord Stalworth ever came up to scratch, marriage number five waited on the horizon.

Coleman cleared his throat. "Miss MacKinnon inquired if you might be home to visitors."

Annabelle had to fight the urge to rush past Coleman and hug Francine, instead, she schooled her features and nodded. "Please have Mrs. Potter prepare a tray with refreshments."

"As you wish, my lady." With a deferential bow, Coleman left the parlor.

Francine swept into the room, a swirl of emerald skirts and cascading copper curls. She embraced Annabelle and sobbed against her shoulder. "I am ruined!"

What was a friend supposed to say to such a declaration?

Coleman stood at the door, a slight hitch to his eyebrow betrayed his thoughts. "Perhaps, I should close the door."

"I am afraid you must fill in the details, as I have been out of town." She did not want to state the obvious, they were hiding out after their hasty marriage lest people begin to ask questions.

The two plopped onto a floral settee in the center of the room that faced the bay window and the storm brewing outside. Francine gulped air and dotted the tender skin beneath her eyes with a tartan handkerchief.

Through hiccups, Francine began her watery explanation. "It was terrible. It happened at the Granworthy musicale. I had an encounter with Gladys Fitzherbert. And it was so blasted hot... er, sorry, hot, I needed a moment of solitude."

"Gladys has a way of bringing out the worst in people."

"That was not the incident I was talking about." Francine had wound the handkerchief into a tight ball.

The tea tray arrived, forcing a brief pause in the conversation while a footman arranged the offerings. Annabelle piled a plate with biscuits for each of them and poured the steaming beverage. At least in her own home, she had no one to question the quantity of biscuits she ate.

Francine slurped the tea before asking, "Please tell me you have something more bracing. Whisky, perhaps?"

Annabelle shook her head. The cellarette was in the library. "After you finish the story, I can have Coleman hunt some down for you."

Munching on shortbread, Francine continued. "I thought I was alone on Granworthy's terrace. The one on the side of the house, near the gardens."

Annabelle nodded, picturing the location Francine described.

"However, I was not alone." The woman paled considerably, setting her plate down, her hand pressing against her belly. "The Duke of Sambridge was there."

Annabelle's cup wobbled on the saucer, sloshing liquid onto her skirt. She dabbed it with a cloth. "Whyever was he there?"

"I am not sure, we hardly spoke. I offered to leave, but my skirt snagged on something."

Of course, it did. Annabelle long ago had lost track of the number of Francine's shoes, or ribbons, or dresses catching or tripping or ripping. A walking disaster of lanky limbs and towering height was the epitome of Francine MacKinnon.

"In my haste to leave, my dress snagged, and I slammed into the ground. Er, I would have if the duke had not been a convenient cushion. It was rather magnificent if it were not so utterly disastrous. As we lay on the flagstones, I felt air in places that should have been covered and a hand where no hand should ever be. Before I could right myself, and please believe me, Annie, I am talking seconds, we both heard a gasp. Several gasps."

Annabelle leaned back. This was a disaster with only one solution, one Francine would balk at. "Perhaps, whoever saw you could empathize. Did you explain what happened? No one would believe you two, I mean, ah…"

Francine waved a hand. "No, do not bother. I heartily agree. No one would ever believe 'Fumbling' Francine MacKinnon would be the Duke of Sambridge's lover, least of all his current paramour—the woman who found us."

Dread plopped from Annabelle's throat to her stomach to land with an unsettling sploosh. Last she knew, the devious Lady Anworth was the duke's light o' love.

"The countess?" she whispered while Francine nodded.

"It was all a blur." Her hands twisted in her skirts. "But it gets worse. Uncle Douglas called my brother, Leith, to London. Sambridge has refused to speak with my uncle. There is talk of dueling and all other manner of insanity. You know the MacKinnon temperament. Oh, please, Annie, you must help."

"But how? I cannot convince a duke to marry anyone," Annabelle protested.

"I do not want to marry him. He frightens me. Worse than Leith if you can believe it. No, I need to leave. Anywhere. I have money. Take whatever you need. Please help me." After shoving a reticule into Annabelle's hands, tears flooded Francine's brown eyes. Fat drops splashed against her bodice, staining the satin fabric.

Annabelle had seen a humiliated Francine more times than she could remember, often after an awkward spill, normally involving punch and a woman's dress, but a devastated and frightened Francine? This was entirely new and one of a million reasons why she could not refuse.

"Let me speak with Linscott."

Francine latched onto her wrist. "Not your husband. Please. He will make me return home. Wait for my brother. I cannot bear to go back."

"Trust me. I do not have anyone else who could help us. Marcus is refusing to speak with me for choosing not to abandon my husband. For his hatred of the duke alone, I am sure Linscott will agree."

Francine's grip loosened, but Annabelle was leery to leave her alone. "I have nowhere else to go."

"I promise, I will be right back."

It was a short journey to her husband's study.

Annabelle bit her lip, wondering if she should barge in or knock. Lifting her fist, she rapped twice. A commanding "Enter" followed.

Jack lifted his studious gaze from his paper and walked around his desk.

"About this morning," he began, but she interrupted.

"It is not why I came."

His shoulders slumped, was he disappointed or relieved? She did not have time to contemplate.

"Francine needs our help. She was caught in a compromising position with the Duke of Sambridge."

"Francine MacKinnon?" he asked, his hand hovering about chin height. "About this tall with flaming red hair?"

She nodded, her hands clenched together in prayer. He whistled, then shook his head. His mouth opened and closed, working through a decision until he declared his plan in his unique style.

His cheeks dimpled and he offered his suggestion with his trademark humor. "I will gladly call him out. Give me a minute to fetch my overcoat."

She wanted to kiss his cheek, so happy she was by his immediate agreement to help. "As much as we would both like you to shoot the man..."

"Bloodthirsty wife," he growled, pulling her in for a quick kiss.

"Francine has asked for our help."

"Who caught them?" He nipped at the skin below her ear.

"The Countess of Anworth."

The surety in his face cooled. He separated from their embrace and stomped to his desk. There he pulled out drawer after drawer until withdrawing a small wooden casket. "My hunting box in Scotland will do."

"Scotland! But what if her brother Leith hears? He is one of the men she is trying to escape."

"Yes." He pointed a finger at the casket, then his temple to highlight the genius of his plan. "For the moment. By now, he has hired the swiftest horse money can buy and is on his way south. Few know of Hull House. Neither Sambridge nor MacKinnon included. The estate to the North is Hawthorne Manor, which lies abandoned. We will send her with a guard dog of Coleman's choosing and a maid."

"Mary Louise," she piped in too quickly, drawing a speculative glance from her husband. Might as well solve two problems.

"I told you, the unfortunate creature was unlucky enough to be in the room where I sought my wife. Not me searching for a maid to dally. Annabelle, I lived alone with a full household staff for over a decade. Not once—"

She cut off his statement, reaching beneath the lid for the key. "I will tell Francine, then I will give you anything you could possibly want. Even your outrageous clothing demands."

He snatched the key from her grasp. "You will do no such thing. You do not owe me your body. You do not ever exchange yourself for a favor for your friend. For any reason, other than you want me. Do you understand, Annabelle? Your body is not for sale."

It was not possible to want him more than she did at this exact moment. He willingly gave his hunting box and servants to protect her friend. He demanded nothing from her, not even her body. He wanted her. Only her.

Her knees quaked from forcing them to remain planted where she stood. She nodded, unable to vocalize the words bubbling in her throat. Jack wanted her.

She threw herself in his arms, her mouth crashing against his. He lost balance, using the desk for support as she peppered kisses over every inch of his face, lingering along his plump mouth.

"Freely given?" he asked, between kisses.

"Freely."

He made a sound, halfway between a growl and groan, setting her away from him. "Later," was his dark promise. He snatched up the casket, stalking the hall to where Coleman blocked his path.

A quick exchange started between the two men at the door. First heated, then easing to reluctant respect. Coleman left his post, all but running for the servant's stairs, searching the rooms as he went. He passed Annabelle without a word, only lifting his chin in acknowledgment before brushing past.

Francine cowered in a corner. Jack approached her like she was a frightened horse. "Annabelle told me of your predicament."

She whimpered. "I am not a wanton."

He offered the key with a smile on his lips. "Never thought you were. I have a hunting box across the border in Scotland. It has room enough for you, a maid, and a footman."

"You are giving me all of this? But why?"

"You are in need." Jack shrugged a shoulder while Francine wept. "Please, I cannot abide tears."

Annabelle shoved an elbow into his side. "I trust Coleman's judgment. He will find you the most reliable of footmen and secure transportation."

"Stay as long as you need, when you are ready to return, you will be welcomed with open arms."

Francine took the key with trembling hands. "But my reputation. You cannot risk yours or Annabelle's by association. It is not fair to ask you to do so."

"You worry about yourself. My reputation will barely be

smudged. It might help my credibility with those who assume I am a heartless bastard," Jack assured.

Francine choked after his crude remark. "But Annabelle?"

"She will be fine. She is a viscountess and has my father's support. No one would dare snub the Earl of Maitland."

Francine bit her lower lip, indecision etched across her face. Coleman reappeared with an older footman—Bryant if Annabelle remembered correctly. The butler announced the carriage was ready with Mary Louise waiting inside.

Annabelle wrapped Francine in a hug, whispering in her ear. "Rest assured, this scandal will blow over. I will write to you often and work with our friends to find a way to restore both your reputation and place among the *ton*."

Francine shook her head with the casket clutched to her chest. "There are not enough words to thank you."

Jack waved his hand. "No need." He pointed to the rain sheeting down the window panes. "Best be off before the roads become impassable."

Annabelle watched as Francine climbed into the carriage, waving in the shelter of the doorway as the vehicle disappeared around the corner. Long after the carriage was gone, she stood on the stoop, worrying about her friend and the future awaiting her. Would she reclaim her reputation?

Jack placed a shawl on her shoulders, cradling her against his wide chest. "It does you no good to stand out in the rain."

"I am not in the actual rain."

"You know what I mean." He offered his elbow, which she clung to. "Let's go inside. In the library, a cozy fire is burning in the hearth. There is a scintillating novel for me to read, while you doze lazily in my arms."

"You are painting a picture of heavenly enchantment."

"Yes, I am. Especially if you absorb all the naughty tidbits within the book and promise to reenact them for me later. For experimental purposes only."

"Well, in the name of science, I suppose it would be acceptable."

He lifted her in his arms, scooping her feet out from under her, carrying her across his home. As promised, the fire roaring in the marble hearth removed all the chill from the air, while the rain pattering against the pane chased away intrusions. Married life promised many novelties: passion, companionship, and most of all, contentment.

CHAPTER THIRTY-ONE

HUSBANDS ARE FRUSTRATING

Married life challenged even the humblest of saints! Annabelle cursed her husband after she found yet another cheroot smoldering in an ashtray on top of a stack of unread correspondence. She needed a footman specifically tasked to follow Jack around the house in order to prevent the fires he was determined to start.

If he was not jumping out to snatch her for a quick interlude in a closet, he hovered around her like a general nuisance. Even the puppy had the sense to wander off and give Annabelle a moment of peace.

After Cissy departed from their weekly tea, Jack sauntered into her parlor and shoved the remaining biscuit from the tray in his mouth. The biscuit she had saved for herself. He fidgeted with the draperies. Smeared fingerprints on the freshly polished demilune table. Ran his fingers over the pianoforte. Rearranged a stack of books. Irritated the single nerve Annabelle held onto with her last vestiges of hope for a moment of quiet.

As he sprawled on the settee, he poked around her sewing

basket, leaving everything in disarray. "Did you have a nice chat?"

"We did," she answered curtly, picking up a novel from the table and hoping he would get the hint she wanted a moment alone without a husband asking a hundred inane questions or undressing her for the second time today.

Annabelle had such a lovely visit with her friend, much like days before married life. They discussed the latest Waverly novel, *The Abbot*, both agreeing that the escape from Lochleven was the most thrilling scene and then proceeded to examine a history treatise on Mary Queen of Scott, which only led to further questions about Queen Elizabeth.

Jack moved beside her, sitting more on her skirts than the free cushion. Without asking, he plucked the novel she was reading from her hands, flipping through the pages. At least he had the courtesy of marking her place. With. A. Sticky. Finger.

"What's this? A biography?"

"Yes," she bit out through clenched teeth, "and if you do not mind, I would like to get back to reading more about Queen Elizabeth."

"Do you reckon that she and Robert Dudley were lovers?"

"She was the Virgin Queen. No, I do not."

"Not even Robert Devereux?" Her huff only encouraged him. "Surely, she had an affair with Walter Raleigh. The man was an actual pirate. Women cannot resist the allure of a dangerous man."

She snatched back her book, marking the page she had finished with a ribbon. "A woman who resists the allure of men, especially piratical types, is wise. Elizabeth was exceedingly cunning. Especially how she dealt with all the over-stuffed popinjays trying to steal her power."

Jack was not deterred. Instead, he pulled her against his firm chest and nibbled her earlobe—it was normally the spot to melt Annabelle's resolve so she would willingly fall to his advances. But not today. She gripped her other arm, commanding her body to not yield. To give no quarter to this rogue.

"Behind every great woman is a man capable of seducing her. She might have been a mighty queen, but she was still a woman." His hand skimmed across her bodice, the feather-light touch eliciting wicked sensations.

"Perhaps a man fancies himself capable of seduction when, in fact, he only serves a purpose. It is well-documented that once the men did what she needed, they were no longer useful to her. She imprisoned Walter Raleigh if you recall."

"For betrayal, my sweet."

"For whispering sweet words in one ear and romancing another, my husband." Annabelle failed to notice the direction of his hands until her gown gaped at the neck.

"Jack, no."

"Yes, please. I've been so lonely without you."

"You spent the entire day with me. We've only been apart for one hour. Go to your club. Go riding in the park. But please, leave me be for one day." She snapped the last sentence, forcing Jack to sit up. The cold gray flash within his normally bright eyes unsettled her.

"As you wish, my darling wife." He stood, brushing the wrinkles from his trousers. Without another word, he spun on his heels, marching to the front door while calling out for his hat and cane. The door slammed.

Perhaps she could endure another round of lovemaking, it was not like it was an unpleasant activity. But married life was complicated. A balance between two people who normally spent their waking hours in solitude, now constantly within each other's spheres.

It was stifling. Suffocating. She simply needed to be for a

few hours. To allow peace in her new perpetually chaotic world. To do the things she enjoyed.

Though, sending her husband away did little to bring her any comfort or relaxation. So, she paced and fretted.

He did not take his greatcoat, and the weather was unseasonably cold with a chill lacing a brisk wind. The sky turned dark and ominous.

What if he returned with a cough or fever? Or the cold air caused chilblains? She ordered a fire for both his study and bedroom the minute he stepped over the threshold.

The book she read remained unopened on the settee. Her sewing basket was forgotten on the floor, as she stared out the front window to the street below.

The clouds opened up an hour later, drenching anyone unlucky enough to remain out of doors. The wind slung the drops against the glass. She read one page three times.

Still, no sign of her husband, even after the clock struck the hour to get ready for dinner. Daisy helped her dress, while Annabelle stared out the window—vowing to never again push Jack from his home because she was a tiny bit irritated.

She paced the parlor, dressed and frantic. Shortly before the gong sounded, the door flew open, slamming against the wall. Annabelle rushed to listen at the parlor door, pressing her ear against the paneling.

"My lord, a bath is ready for you upstairs," Coleman said.

"Who ordered it? My valet or my wife?"

A curious question to ask, the tone of his voice anxious to hear an answer, but Annabelle could not decide which satisfied him the most. She wished the door was cracked so she could read his expression.

"My lady did. Would you care for a brandy while you prepare for supper?"

"No, I drank too much at the club. Tell my wife I will be down shortly."

The last statement sounded much like the Jack she knew. Carefree and in good humor, until he sneezed. The sound echoed in the hallway.

"Very good and bless you, my lord."

Annabelle rested against the door, listening to the steady march of her husband's feet across the tile to the staircase. A relief that he had finally returned, but was confused by how she should act during their evening meal.

Did she ask about his afternoon?

Did she apologize for being short?

Perhaps she should send for a doctor, maybe he did catch a fever.

As the gong sounded, she walked with measured steps to the dining room—a bundle of nerves playing havoc with her stomach. She opened the doors, greeted by a brightly lit room and her husband standing at the head of the table, waiting.

CHAPTER THIRTY-TWO
A RETURN TO THE OBSIDIAN

J ack's return to Artie's gaming hell was precipitated by news of his recent nuptials. Apparently, his absconding with the relatively unknown Annabelle Greene earned a record purse for one lucky man, while the rest wagered against.

Winthorpe thwacked Jack's shoulder, offering a glass of brandy.

"I do not know whether to punch you or offer congratulations. I never thought you would take your father's threat seriously and marry anyone, let alone Miss Greene. Because of you, I am out fifty pounds."

"That's Lady Linscott." Jack gave the majordomo his losing bet to add to the ridiculous pot waiting to be claimed.

He did not want to be in a gaming hell. He wanted to remain with his wife reclining before the hearth while she spent the day reading and Ginny curled on his feet. Instead, he trudged through a biting wind to face a gaggle of lordly gentlemen with nothing on their empty minds but booze, women, and wagers.

Since late summer was almost upon them, perhaps he should adjourn to the country. Enjoy hunting again.

Winthorpe chuckled and saluted with his glass. "To your lovely bride. Cheers."

"Out of curiosity, who did win the wager?"

"There is speculation it was made in bad faith, perhaps the winner had inside knowledge." Winthorpe pointed to the open betting book, scratched in an elaborate scrawl was one name all too familiar—Lord Crayfield.

"The son of a bitch." He could not believe his friend bet against him, then again the odds were never in Jack's favor to begin with. At last check, it was ninety-nine to one odds against Jack marrying. "He placed the bet the day after the books opened. I would honestly say, he was working on his instincts. At that point, I was still pursuing any available debutante."

"Good to hear you come to my defense," Nigel said from the doorway. He offered Jack a cheroot. "A consolation prize. Thanks to you, I can now afford to pay my tailor and stay out of debtors' prison."

"How in the world did you have enough funds to place this bet? I thought the betting books of Artie's were closed to you after I bailed you out."

Nigel pulled Jack into a quieter room to a set of chairs facing a doorway. "I must confess, the earl gave me the funds. Said it would not be sporting for a father to bet against his son."

"I guess I should be grateful he did not bet I would lose."

"Surprised me too, but then again, if memory serves—you bet you would lose."

"I needed a sure thing in case my father followed through with cutting me off." How strange, Jack could not muster any anger toward Nigel, he was glad his friend profited off the marriage. In a way, they both did.

Nigel motioned towards a room across the hall, where a group played hazards, the table growing heated by the moment. "Care to join in?"

"I came to pay my bill, then I was not sure where I was heading next."

"Did Annabelle kick you out of the house already?" Nigel asked.

A waiter appeared with a whisky and a brandy. Their standard order.

"I am a bit of a nuisance." The way Nigel nodded along with the comment only fueled Jack's desire to punch a nose. Nigel always did have a punchable face. "We were enjoying the benefits of a recently married couple until she turned on me like her damn cat. One minute, we were joking about Queen Elizabeth, the next she was speaking about betrayal and all manner of sins."

Jack knew he was not being fair, as he was fairly certain he annoyed Annabelle with his rapt attention. The interlude in the closet was a clue—while he kissed her passionately, unbuttoning her gown, she asked: *must we?*

"I may have two sisters, but I claim no understanding of the fairer sex. One minute you are in their good graces, the next something gets up in their gander and you are mincemeat. Yesterday, Cissy accused me of purposely sabotaging all her friends by refusing to dance with them."

Jack groaned in his cup. "This is what I fear the most as a married man, having to tolerate hysterics."

Jack slouched in his chair, earning him a glare from an elderly lord in the corner. "The question is, when can I return home? The second Annabelle told me to leave, I obeyed, because I have been leeching on the poor woman since I married her. She does not get a second alone. Do you have any idea what it is like to have a willing woman in your home at all hours of the day?"

Longing flickered in Nigel's gaze. "No, I honestly do not."

Jack leaned in, confiding to his friend the benefits of marital life. "I probably should allow the woman a reprieve, but she is like opium to me. Her scent lingers on my clothing. The memory of her flesh burns my skin. It is a sickness."

"Linscott?" Nigel asked as if he was not entirely sure who the man was sitting before him.

Jack stared at his empty glass, the third in less than an hour. "Hmm?"

"Go home. But walk slowly through the rain, so you catch a fever, and I never have to listen to you wax poetically about your unbridled lust for your wife. It is rather appalling if you ask me."

Truth was, he needed a distraction from his wife. In a relatively short amount of time, he had become completely reliant on her for not only entertainment but companionship. A kinship with her he never before experienced with any human. Not even Nigel. How could it be?

"You know what I need?" Jack set his glass on the table. "A good bout at Gentleman Jackson's. Care to join me?"

"Not today, I am enjoying my good fortune for once. Fisticuffs are better suited when I am feeling low. Perhaps Sambridge has returned from wherever he fled after the incident at the Granworthy musicale. He is probably spoiling for a good fight."

Jack cracked his knuckles. "I hope so."

"Give my love to your wife for me," Nigel said with a wink.

"I would rather shove my fist down your throat."

"Ah, the Linscott we know has returned. Felicitations!"

Nigel saluted before joining a table for a friendly game of chance.

Unfortunately, Gentleman Jackson's did not provide Jack with the punishing exertion he craved. Sambridge was nowhere to be found, and the one lordling brave enough to enter the ring was laid out in five minutes flat.

Jack hired a hackney, finding himself at his father's mews. Using a bristle brush from the groom's tack, he decided Khali deserved his attention. The horse whinnied with excitement the moment he spotted Jack, his foreleg tapping against the stable door.

"Alas, I wish the weather was more suitable for a long ride, but I will not risk your health with slick stones under your hooves."

Khali snuffled his shoulder as if commiserating about their misfortune. The stallion's sleek black coat gleamed in the waning light, but Jack was not ready to leave the comfort of the stable.

Instead, he leaned against the stall door, conversing with a surprisingly attentive equine listener.

"The groom told me you were here, so I thought I might check on how you are faring as a married man." His father approached, holding an apple in his outstretched hand for Khali. "Jones scolds me when I sneak in a sugar cube or the like, but you would not betray your father?"

"How is the gray getting along?" Jack asked.

"We named him Sampson. He took to the name rather quickly and is bonding well with Khali. The two old men have become fast friends."

Sampson perked his head up from the stall where he munched on hay. His tufted ears flicked.

"How does Mayflower fare?"

"I am afraid she had to be destroyed." His father's face

twisted. "A shame, but it was her time. I could not watch her suffer, not with the farrier no longer being able to care for her. She was your mother's horse, did you know?"

"I remember well many rides on her back with mother holding the reins."

"I had a painting commissioned, wanting to capture her likeness. When you return to Morefield, I will show you."

The stillness of the evening was broken only by the clopping of hooves on wet cobblestones and the jingle of reins. The two men stood in silence, each lost to the world of thoughts clouding their minds.

His father spoke. "Losing Mayflower felt like losing your mother all over again."

The confession stole the air from the stable. A window into the world of his closeted father and the woman he never spoke of, save the odd toast with Jack. The words opened a gaping wound in Jack's heart. Feeling the loss of the old mare as a reminder of the grief he longed to forget.

It was a miracle Mayflower lived as long as she did. Nearly thirty-three years. Jack remembered her sleek tan coat and his mother's joy as she sat astride, galloping across fields.

"How is Annabelle?" His father changed the subject, closing any further discussion about Jack's mother. His father's Clara.

It used to anger Jack, how quickly his father directed the conversation away from his mother. Refusing to reminisce, but now—a part of him understood. Would he feel compelled to speak of Annabelle if she… He could not even finish the thought, such dread filled his stomach. Worse than the fear of battle.

"You would be happy to hear, she kicked me out for annoying her this afternoon."

"Trouble in paradise so soon?" His father chuckled, actually laughing with a smile remaining on his lined face. Sensing Jack's incredulity, he reassured his son. "Your mother used to send me on strange errands when we were newly married. Claimed I was the only one capable of negotiating with the butcher or picking the perfect seafood from the fishmonger. It was not until a year later when my steward informed me how astronomical the butcher's bill was, that I discovered the true reason she sent me from the house. I never told her I figured out her ruse, instead, I learned to read my newspaper at my club, and she was all the happier when I came home."

"We might have more in common than I believed."

"I hate to say it son, but you and I have much more in common than you could possibly believe."

Khali settled in the hay with a sigh, his head drooping.

"Even though the season is drawing to an end, I would like to host a ball for you and Annabelle. To introduce you properly to society as man and wife. Besides, it should undo much of the damage caused by a hasty wedding. We will simply paint you two as a besotted couple."

"It should not be difficult."

"I am glad to hear it." His father pulled out his pocket watch, flicking it open to study the hands. "I suspect you ought to be getting home. I had my groom ready my carriage. Give my regards to your wife."

Without allowing Jack a farewell, his father turned on his heels, whistling as he left the stables, strolling across the mews to his home, indifferent to the rain sprinkling his head.

CHAPTER THIRTY-THREE
DINNER FOR COUPLES

J ack bowed to his wife before reaching out for her hand to place an affectionate kiss across her knuckles. "I swear you grow prettier every day."

Annabelle expected recrimination, not affection. She felt off-kilter and chose to tread carefully. "I picked the gown because I knew you are fond of the color."

He plucked a lemon-yellow sleeve, then whispered his usual sensual promises. "The brightest ray in my dark world."

Shooing away the footman, Jack pulled out her seat to his right, helping her settle on the chair. Yet, she felt far from settled. Confused by the return of the man she married and not the angry one who stormed out of the house not five hours prior.

While footmen bustled around the room, pouring wine and preparing the first course, Annabelle studied her husband. His hair was still damp from a quick bath, slicked back from his imposing brow. The coldness in his eyes had disappeared, replaced by the warm glint of blue simmering below the surface. His cheek dimpled as he blew her a kiss from the head of the table.

A footman served turtle soup from a tureen, before returning to his post near the walkway through to the butler's pantry.

"You are quiet. Something still bothering you?" Jack was mindful of overly curious servants and whispered the question away from curious ears.

"I am only trying to figure you out."

"I am an easy man to read. Ask me a question and I will tell you no lies."

"Are you angry with me?"

True to his roguish enjoyment of uncomfortable silences, he sipped his soup before answering, his mouth breaking wide. "Direct as always. No, Annabelle. I am not. You had every right to be frustrated with me as I am not capable of giving you a moment of reprieve."

The rich soup glided along her tongue. "Perhaps, but I should have spoken of my desire for a moment of peace, instead of snapping at you. It was cruel of me to chase you out into the storm."

"My dear, you did no such thing. This house has sixteen rooms. I easily could have found another place to brood. Truth is, it did me good to leave you be. I saw Khali, who was a bit put out with me until I gave him a good brushing down."

The tightness in the air Annabelle had felt the moment the front door opened dissipated by incremental degrees. His naturally good humor eased her worries with relief washing over her chest. Normally, after such an encounter with her mother, she would tiptoe around the house for days, afraid the smallest sound might incite her anger.

"You did promise I could meet him." She purposefully

mixed a hint of humor into her chastisement followed by a conciliatory smile.

"All in good time."

He reached out to squeeze her hand. She stared at his fist, loving the feel of the warmth oozing around her. Searing her hand, not with displeasure, but with kindness and generosity.

He removed his hand, but the imprint remained. Surreptitiously, she laid it in her lap, covering it with the serviette to keep the memory of his touch alive for a moment longer.

"I have to admit my reluctance to introduce the two of you, as I rather suspect he will take to you, and I will cease to exist." He took a long sip of his wine, regarding her over the rim of the goblet.

"That's silly."

"Is it?" The question hung in the air, while the footmen cleared away the first course and served roasted pheasant.

"It is, there is no reason Kahli would prefer a person who knows nothing of horseflesh, let alone how to properly ride," Annabelle said.

"An easy remedy, you can use one of my father's mares. I will teach you to be the finest horsewoman alive."

"I do not need bragging rights. Only enough knowledge to keep me from falling off. I've always wanted to learn."

"I am yours to command." He changed the subject. "I forgot to mention my father is wanting to host a ball to introduce us as a married couple."

She poked at the uneaten portion of food occupying her plate. "I suppose it is the proper way of things, but I enjoyed not having to attend all the society affairs. I must confess, I am not fond of crowds."

"Neither am I. But he is correct. I want London to fall madly in love with Lady Linscott, the future Countess of Maitland."

He stole the protest from her lips. *Fall in love with her?* For a moment, she wondered about the possibility, then dismissed it outright. Men like Jack Davenport did not fall in love.

"Of course. It is kind of your father to offer. Did he send you a letter?"

"No, I saw him this afternoon."

"I did not realize."

"When I stopped by, he came out to the stables. Offered me fatherly advice I took to heart." He motioned for the next course.

"This is surprising," she said.

"It should not be. He was right, you know. I should apologize for not giving my wife a moment of peace. A family trait of Davenport men, I am afraid. We manage to find ourselves the perfect bride, and we are a bit reluctant to let her out of our sight. Lest she disappears like a sugar statue in a rainstorm."

"I am not going anywhere." Did he call her perfect? Surely, she misheard.

"Perhaps, and perhaps I can hardly believe my luck."

"I am nothing special."

Jack leaned against the back of his chair, shaking his head. "Someday I will meet the person who caused you to believe such a lie and punch him in the face as he deserves."

Annabelle blanched at the hint of violence. It was her mother's answer when she was displeased, and though his remark was centered on someone else, what would it take for Jack to turn against her? Best to be on her guard.

The rest of the meal was eaten in relative silence. On occasion he would remark upon a dish or regale her with silly tales of boyhood exploits. After a tray of cheese and fruit was cleared from the table, he reached out for her hand, drawing her into his arms. He kissed her softly, tilting her face upwards.

"Supper is over, for now, my sweet Butterfly. Perhaps we should turn in for the night."

For once, Annabelle heartily agreed.

CHAPTER THIRTY-FOUR

SHOPPING AND TEA

Life settled into a steady routine that Annabelle found pleasing enough. Afternoons for visits with friends or shopping on Bond Street, quiet evening suppers with only the two of them.

Even with the heat of the summer, Jack and Annabelle agreed with Maitland to stay in London instead of leaving for the country for the time being. They found it better to make the occasional appearance as a happily wedded couple instead of hiding in a secluded estate. Though the seclusion of a grand estate with stables full of animals to spoil sounded far more appealing than yet another visit to her modiste.

Madame Dubois's quaint shop was next to an exquisite milliner. There, she purchased a bonnet in the perfect shade of Prussian blue to match her new walking dress. She could not resist the impulse buy as she caught sight of it in the picture window. She reluctantly handed it into the care of Daisy when Coleman surprised her with news of a visitor.

"He insisted he needed to speak with you instead of waiting for calling hours tomorrow." Coleman took her spencer. "He has a tray of refreshments, but I could send in a fresh pot of tea."

"That sounds lovely," she said.

The last person she suspected to find was her cousin. Marcus wore a trail in the parlor's worsted wool rug.

He stopped his pacing as she entered. He raised his head, his hair falling in disarray across his brow. "Annabelle," he said.

"Marcus." She gripped his hands, which he brought to his mouth for a peck. "A pleasant surprise."

"Truly? After the abominable way, I've treated you?"

She smiled, sweeping his hair into place. "Despite the way you greeted my husband and your refusal of my invitations, I know you were hurting. We've been through too much, not to forgive when one makes a mistake."

"He is not good enough for you."

"Perhaps, or perhaps I am not good enough for him." She did not wish for an argument, but the look on his face was worrisome.

She tugged him to the center of the room, where a settee faced a pair of matching rose and cream armchairs. Marcus slumped, his shoulders limp as he ran a hand over his stubbled chin.

"Whatever is the matter?" Annabelle asked, not certain she wanted to learn the reason for his visit.

"I've recently arrived from Hampshire."

There was only one reason Marcus would travel to Hampshire.

"How is my father?"

The pregnant pause that followed caused an eruption of gooseflesh across her arm.

"He is angry."

Annabelle expected nothing less. It was no secret her father disapproved of her London season. The carriage accident. Her mother's death. The heap of notices and demands for repayment of vouchers. Her father grew more distrustful and resentful of others, even his own family. The sister whose husband paid off his debts. The nephew who was now head of the family. He shrouded himself in bitterness.

"It is to be expected," she said with a dismissive sweep of her hand. Now she wished she had lingered at the milliner, perhaps Marcus would not be here to remind her of things best left forgotten.

"He has spoken with a pair of solicitors. He believes he can have the marriage annulled."

Marcus sipped his beverage, his attention drifting around the room. The cousins were of a similar age with Marcus being a mere six months older than Annabelle. Ever since she was five years old, Marcus had taken the role of the elder and experienced relation to heart. Marcus and Aunt Silvia were the two constants in her life. That was, until a year ago when he aged ten years overnight and disappeared with hardly a word of goodbye. He left only a note, expressing his desire to finally have his grand tour.

Marcus's abdication of familial duty stirred twinges of resentment she tried to smother, but his presence fueled her desire to rage against him.

"You've never explained. Why did you leave?"

"Hmm?" His golden brow lifted in question. "Why did I go to Hampshire? As head of the family, I needed to inform your father of your marriage. I felt it was better to appear in person, help smooth the waters."

"And did you?" She allowed this perceived direction of her question to stand, she would clarify in a moment.

"No, I fear I made matters worse."

He stood, ready to depart, but Annabelle was not through.

Not by any stretch of the imagination. Not when she had him exactly where she wanted him. For a year, she had waited for his explanation; she was going to get it out of him, even if she had to call Coleman to hold him down.

"Naturally. I am sure you went there heated and out of sorts after your confrontation in Gretna Green, thus inflaming a man dead set against his daughter marrying." Annabelle's fist hit her palm.

"You deserved better," he said, taking a step back.

"I have a husband with potential."

He groaned. "You should have married Sambridge."

She reeled backward for a moment. "I had one offer, and I took it. You introduced Sambridge and I last summer. Remember the incident with the dog?"

A faint smile turned his mouth. "How could I forget?"

"Neither did he. No, the only serious pursuer was the man I married."

Finally, he sat back down, reaching for her hands. "He is not the man I would have picked."

"You were not here to help me."

His throat bobbed on a deep swallow. "I could not stay here another moment."

"Why, Marcus?"

Long minutes passed, the silence roaring in her ears as he chewed an answer he could not give voice to.

"It does not matter."

"But it does to me."

He remained contained, but she sensed the battle that raged within him. His internal torment that he refused to release. She stroked his hand, giving comfort to the grief he could not share.

"I am sorry." His words were a whisper carried across the table with a sigh. "I promise to try with Linscott."

Before she could offer absolution or admonishment, the door flew open and the object of their conversation strolled in, his energy thrummed with a barely veiled desire to attack, then ask questions. "What a cozy scene."

Jack picked up a biscuit, bit it, and flashed his white teeth. He glared at Annabelle's hand caressing Marcus'. Refusing to be cowed, she gave the hand clasped in hers an affectionate squeeze. Jack's jaw flinched. The biscuit crumbled in his fingers until she cooled his temper by rising to greet him with a simple brush of her lips against his cheek.

"I am happy to see you, husband."

He was not through with his display of masculine proprietorship. Turning his head, he captured her lips in a searing, possessive kiss.

"And I, you, wife." With mocking deference, he inclined his head towards her cousin on the settee. "Oakmont."

"Linscott," the other man returned. "I am afraid I must be getting home."

"Are things settled with my father?" Annabelle asked, knowing her question would pique Jack's interest.

"I let him know your marriage had my support and I would not fund any bills from solicitors your father might seek about the legality of your vows. Without additional income, he will not be able to afford any true petition against your union."

Jack reassured her with a caress of her cheek. "Maitland will ensure any legal action your father might take is buried swiftly. Fear not, sweets. We have the means to fight if necessary and with my father's support, the funds to make it end without a ripple registering among the nosiest of the beau monde."

Truly, it should bother her more, her father's refusal to accept her marriage, but she expected it. Expected he would not be satisfied with anything less than her returning home to care for him, as she had done since her mother's passing. The fact he allowed her a season and even a year at finishing school only spoke of Marcus' brilliance at negotiation. And probably, if she thought about it, an increase in his allowance accompanied any affirmations. A daughter provided comfort, but funds provided oblivion in the form of unlimited quantities of alcohol.

"But do we have the means to cover my most recent shopping excursion? I fear Madame Dubois was most persuasive."

Jack's blue-gray eyes brightened like clouds parting after a storm. "Did you buy frilly insubstantial bits of frippery to parade around in our chambers?"

Marcus cleared his throat, clearly growing uncomfortable with the direction of the conversation. Annabelle refused to give him a moment of reprieve. She wanted her cousin to know that she was happy. Contented.

Whispering seductively, or well, what she imagined seductive might sound like, "Sheer things in all your favorite colors, my lord."

"Oakmont?" Jack's grip tightened on her waist.

"Yes?" He coughed to cover his chuckle.

"Leave."

Her cousin muttered his farewells, making sure the door closed tightly behind him.

Her husband frantically ripped open enclosures while muttering words of passion and promise. Dishes clattered. Furniture scrapped across wooden floors. And there, with skirts flipped up and breeches discarded, Annabelle found oblivion in the arms of her husband.

CHAPTER THIRTY-FIVE
THE TROUBLE WITH GOWNS

The dresses Annabelle ordered from Madam Dubois arrived in pink and white striped packages that took three footmen to carry upstairs. Every surface of her room was covered in stacks upon stacks of boxes, reminiscent of a Christmas she had only dreamed of as a child.

Daisy helped her unpack the mountain of garments, oohing and aahing over every article of clothing. "Tis a good thing his lordship was not cut off. I've never seen so many fine things in all my days!" She held a plum-colored gown of watered silk and twirled in a circle. "I believe this is what you should wear tonight to the Marquess of Carlyle's supper."

"It is a little low cut for a supper." Annabelle fingered the lace-edged bodice, delighting in the elegant cut of the gown.

She protested the lower neckline when she tried it on in front of her modiste, but the woman clicked her tongue before speaking in her practiced French accent.

"Non, it is perfect. A little bit of flesh to keep your husband entranced by you and not the other mesdames. We cannot have his affection wandering so soon."

"But he will hate it."

"Oui. Nothing pushes a man closer to love than jealousy. Non? Well, trust me, I know about these things. A man must be reminded about what he has, or he grows too complacent."

Once the drawers overflowed with undergarments and the bonnets were stacked in their boxes inside the wardrobe, Daisy encouraged Annabelle to dress for the evening.

"You have to wear the plum gown, my lady. All the other dresses are wrinkled."

"Why do I have the peculiar feeling you purposefully allowed the wrinkles to stay in the dresses instead of finding something more appropriate."

Daisy shrugged her shoulders. "You will steal their hearts," the younger woman sighed.

"If my husband protests, let it be on your head," Annabelle chided without any heart, almost giddy with anticipation of Jack's reaction.

It had been far too many days since she inspired any sort of lustful craving from her husband. He visited her every night, but stolen clandestine kisses in the library or trysts behind doors while servants bustled around the house faded into distant memories. When a month ago, she bemoaned his behavior, now she missed it.

Perhaps Madame Dubois was correct. Jack had already grown complacent, and another captured the desire Jack once held for Annabelle. She shuddered, then snatched the gown from Daisy.

"You are correct. This is what I am wearing tonight. Cinch the stays a little tighter and dust an extra layer of finishing powder across my chest."

"Yes, my lady." Daisy hummed while she set Annabelle's hair, promising her mistress would stun the crowd.

An hour later, Annabelle stood before the floor-length

mirror in utter shock and with a twinge of horror. Not only would Jack hate the low neckline of her gown, but he would also never allow her to leave the house again.

"Be brave," Daisy whispered as the connecting door between the bedrooms opened, and Jack sauntered in.

"It appears I've opened a modiste shop in my home. How many items of clothing does one woman require?" He lifted a box, shaking it, before setting it back on the heap of empty ones.

The wide grin on his face disappeared once he caught sight of the front of Annabelle's gown. For a moment, she was tempted to wrap a shawl around her shoulders to hide her decolletage.

"Daisy, leave," he barked.

"Yes, my lord." Her lady's maid mouthed *Be brave* one more time, before closing the door silently.

"Do you like my new gown?" Annabelle held out her skirts, then spun around on her toes for him to admire the new creation, hoping the wide skirt hid her shaking hands from view.

He crooked his finger. "Come closer, so I can admire you."

Each step accelerated her heart. Anticipation for his touch tingled the tiny hairs on her arms. "I know the dress is a darker color than I normally wear, but it is suitable for a matron."

"Matron?" His hands caressed her bare shoulders. "I know being a matron simply means you are now a married woman, but my dear, you are anything but a dried-up old prune. The color is perfect for you."

A grim line slashed his face, before he tugged at her bodice, nearly lifting her off the floor. "What's this? Why can I practically see your nipples?"

She swatted his hands away. "You will rip the bodice."

"Gowns in brothels are less revealing," Jack growled and

pulled again on the bodice. The sound of a popping seam momentarily stopped him. "Change."

"No." She crossed her arms under her breasts and lifted them a tad higher. She did not know where she found the bravado to do so, but challenging Jack certainly had an appeal.

"Christ on a cross, Annabelle. You are practically naked. And do not do that with your arms."

"What? This?" She pushed them even higher, and then to torment the overbearing brute more, she jiggled.

Desire flashed. "Change," he growled once more, his fists flexing.

"No," she jiggled a little more. She found a bit of courage to fuel his torment. Perhaps he still desired her after all.

He surprised Annabelle when he flipped her onto her bed. He worked the hundred fabric-covered enclosures along her spine. "Change," he pleaded, a note of hysteria laced his command.

"No," she shrieked into the mattress.

His hands brushed her sensitive sides after he freed the buttons lining the back of the gown.

A rush of cool air breezed past her exposed limbs, as he flipped up the back of the skirts. Her merry protests faded into groans of pleasure.

"God, Annabelle. What you do to me! Change," he begged this time. His calloused hands smoothed over her freed skin, followed by his lips.

"Button me back up. We will be late."

"Not until you change." He nipped her ear lobe and finished loosening her stays and petticoats.

"How can I change my gown when I am now naked? You undid all my undergarments, it will take forever to put me back to rights."

"Do not argue with me. Change."

"Never."

"Dammit, woman, are you prepared for the consequences of you wearing this gown in public? I will be forced to murder the first young buck to stare at your tits as a warning to others. Please," he begged, pressing his hardened flesh against her.

His pleading words combined with his loving hands thrilled her in a way she had never known. Her exposed flesh chafed against the fabric of her gown. At once she felt naughty and excited. In one last measure of torment, she wriggled her exposed derriere against his throbbing phallus.

"I refuse. I love this gown. I am not changing."

His hands worked at the front of his trousers before his erection nudged along her slick folds, prodding. Spreading her legs he pressed forward with a moan.

"Change, or I torture you." His threats held no weight, instead a promise of tantalizing pleasure.

"You will only torture yourself."

He plunged fully inside her tight, wet sheath as her muscles clenched around him. He set a punishing series of thrusts driving them both towards climax until they exploded together.

Jack collapsed against her. "Change."

"No," she said, wriggling her bottom against him. "Anything that gets you this excited is worth wearing. I plan to punish you all night."

He pinched her bottom in response. "When I have no choice but skewer some young clod, know it is all your fault."

She issued another impossible challenge over her shoulder. "You know I will not let you undress me at the end of the night if you even contemplate violence."

"I've turned you into a monster. You used to be sweet and innocent."

"Your corrupting influence has been good for me."

He left her for a moment, collecting a dampened flannel. He cleaned her up, before tending to himself. With almost reverent motions, he redressed her, stealing more kisses along the way. "How has my corruption helped you?"

"I find myself capable of standing up for what I want."

"You should always feel free to speak your mind."

"With you, I do. Hopefully, in the future, I can do the same with others."

He chuckled, placing a chaste kiss on the bridge of her nose. "You might be the only person alive who is not afraid of me."

"Nigel is not afraid."

"My darling Annabelle. He is more terrified than the rest. He knows what I am capable of."

The words chilled her blood. All these hints of a darker side. Jack was once a capable officer, but did one ever truly walk away from the bloodshed unscathed?

"But perhaps, as much as you have changed me, maybe I've softened you?"

Sitting on the edge of the bed, he pulled her between his legs, his hand cupping her jaw. "I hope so. More than I would like to admit, I hope you change me. Make me a better person. So," he sighed heavily, "I will be good. No punching pathetic lordlings, who have misguided notions of lust directed toward my bride." He sealed his promise with a kiss.

CHAPTER THIRTY-SIX
JACK TO THE RESCUE

J ack followed his wife down the stairs, the guilt mocking him. He swore to himself after the fight last week, that he would give her the space she deserved, and what happened the minute he spied her wearing the tiniest bit of an alluring gown? He had his way with her like she was a dockyard doxie. Flipping up her skirts and fucking her.

She deserved better.

He needed to rein in his bestial side, not assault his lady wife before dinner with his father's oldest friend. His wife was a complicated minx, but she enjoyed her wifely duties. Thank God. Else, he might go mad with want.

Crying off the Marquess and Marchioness of Carlyle sounded more and more appealing. Why he agreed to the event when their official foray into society would be held in less than four weeks, he had no idea. Probably another lust-addled moment, when he was not listening to his wife, instead counting the minutes to when she stopped talking and he could begin seducing. He was a sick man.

Coleman carried a silver salver. He handed it to Annabelle. "My lady, a message arrived for you marked urgent."

Her brow crinkled. She looked at Jack as if asking him what the message might contain. He had no clue. The singular thought running rampant in his mind did not include hastily scrawled missives.

Sliding her gloved finger underneath the seal, she unfolded the paper. The tip of her finger moved rapidly over the words. She covered her face with a whispered *Oh dear*, pulled Jack into the parlor, and shut the door.

Jack always enjoyed being sequestered in rooms with his wife, but the pallor on her face ended all thoughts of bedsport. "What does it say?"

She spoke in a hushed whisper with the paper crinkling in her hand. "It is about Francine."

"What could possibly happen to Francine in the middle of rural Scotland? There is not another human within five miles of her!"

Annabelle claimed the woman was accident-prone. Apparently, it was an understatement.

"She does not say."

"She does not say?" His voice raised and she immediately shushed him. If only they were in bed, he would put her governess-like admonishment to work.

"Not in so many words. Simply, there has been an incident and a..." She mouthed the next word, "*Man* is now staying with her. Please, we need to help her."

"We need to help her? I am tied up with the first favor she asked of us."

"What of her reputation? A man staying alone with an unchaperoned young woman in your hunting box?"

He took one step back, then another. Distancing himself from the request he knew was coming. The plea he could not resist. Not from Annabelle. From Francine, let her mire in the muck of her creation, but for Annabelle... God, he would do anything. Any damn foolish quest she sent him on.

"Correct me if I am wrong. Did we not send her north to protect her reputation? How is it in danger for a second time?" He needed a drink, but there was none to be found.

"Yes, but..."

"But what? She has two older brothers, let them handle it."

She trapped him against a bookshelf. "But you know Leith's temper, and Rory is useless. It would end in disaster."

Annabelle fiddled with the top button on his waistcoat. Her proximity melted away any reluctance he might have felt.

"Your friend is already a walking disaster."

Her lovely pouty lips twisted into a pucker. "Do not dare say a disparaging word against my friend."

Extending his arms to the sides, he gestured widely in the empty air. "She is hopeless!"

Annabelle slapped her hands across his mouth. "Hush, the servants will hear you."

He had two choices: comply or refuse. Could he honestly give in so easily, especially when she used that voice? But refusing and allowing the servants to hear could be disastrous for everyone, including them. He chose a third option.

"Blech! Why in the devil did you lick my hand?"

"What else should I do when you are determined to silence me?"

"I was not silencing you, I was quieting your voice," she hissed, wiping her hand on the inside of his tailcoat.

He wrapped his arms around her to draw her nearer. Her scent flooded his nostrils, cooling his ire. The magic of lavender fields. "What will you have me do?"

"I hoped you had a brilliant idea?"

"Why am I always the one with the brilliant ideas?" he asked.

"You are rather ingenious when you set your mind to it. I thought kidnapping me turned out to be a rather splendid success."

Oh, how her praise churned feelings of joy within him, a practical storm of happiness. "Hmm, it rather was, was it not?"

"Indeed." She lifted on her tiptoes as he nibbled the pulse point of her throat.

"Tell Coleman to send our regrets to Carlyle and meet me upstairs in fifteen minutes."

"Why fifteen minutes?"

His lips lingered on hers, refusing to answer, or else he would cease the one activity he loved more than riding his horse. Even fighting young upstarts did not compare with one minute of Annabelle's sweet mouth and her tiny hums of contentment. Holding his wife and kissing her softly easily stole the number one spot in his mind for activities he never wanted to stop. Ever.

Damn it, she pulled away.

"Jack?" she asked, her eyes misted.

"If I am to head out at dawn to check on your friend, I want this night together with you. It will easily be a fortnight before I can hold you in my arms again."

She squealed with delight, clapping her hands together. "You will go to her?"

"Yes, but only if you agree to my terms."

She was out the door and up the stairs before he could call for Thomas. What an interesting specimen! Wife. Who would have thought being married could be this enjoyable?

CHAPTER THIRTY-SEVEN
RUMORS

Home remained eerily quiet after Jack's hasty departure to rescue Francine once again. Winston and Ginny claimed his spot in Annabelle's bed, but snuggles from furry friends did not compare to her husband's strong body wrapped around hers. She could not sleep. Surprised at how much she missed the sound of his snores, almost like a lullaby.

More like a foundry. A cacophony of snorts and rattling. Nevertheless, there was comfort found in his sleepy sounds. His presence. The scrape of whiskers on her neck from his night beard.

A stack of finished books cluttered the table tops of her room, as she hoped to find sleep between the covers of a novel. Instead, every few pages she glanced at the mantel clock, wishing anything could help make the hours fly by faster. If only traveling did not take days. What would it be like to live in a world where one could journey from the South of England to Scotland in less than a day?

After the first week, Annabelle found herself cursing

Francine's name. Though, only half-heartedly. The other half fretted over the condition Jack might find her in.

Alone at Jack's hunting box, there was no one there save for the caretaker and his wife. The walking catastrophe that was *Fumbling Francine* was incapable of ensuring her reputation. A man without scruples might take advantage of an easy situation. A woman, alone. With no protection.

On the eighth day, heavy rains plummeted nonstop from the thick cloud cover, drenching the earth. The cobbled streets grew slick with mud and waste mixing along the gutters. By the time Jack returned, the roadways of England would be a swamp. If he was lucky enough to even manage to locate the road through all the muck.

So, Annabelle agonized and paced the hallways. She barked orders to servants, then immediately apologized for her short temper. The entire staff gave her a wide berth, save for Coleman—who was never the least bit bothered by her curt tone, and Mrs. Cooke—who doted on her like a mother.

Waiting in the parlor, Annabelle stared out into the darkened streets at the sheet of rain sliding down the window. The door creaked open as a voice whispered her name, before a pair of slender arms wrapped around her shoulders.

"Coleman said you've been a veritable beast since your husband left. Wherever did Linscott go?" Cissy watched from the same window. Though typically the most unsympathetic of her friends, she was a welcome surprise.

Annabelle refrained from revealing the truth. "He had business to attend to on one of his estates, which he could not put off unfortunately. Had we known of this deluge, he might have been inclined to wait until the roads dried."

Cissy released her hold. "My dearest friend, this is England. Do you believe the roads would be in any state other than sludge and ruts?"

When Annabelle paled, turning back to the window, Cissy patted her back in consolation.

"Jack is no fool. A fantastic horseman. Rest assured, he would not push his mount more than necessary."

Annabelle sighed, allowing the curtain to fall across the window pane. Looping her arm through Cissy's, they took a turn about the room. "You are right, of course. I need to cease such ninny-headed worrying. It does no one any good. Let's talk about anything else."

"I must confess my astonishment. I never believed you and Linscott might be the least bit suited for one another. I thought by coming here this afternoon, I might find you relieved to be alone once again, not worrying over the welfare of the man who forced you to marry him."

"I believe forced might be a bit too strong of a word."

Cissy arched her perfectly sculpted brow. "He stole you in the middle of the night."

"Yes, but I could have struggled. I did not."

"Will you call for tea?" Cissy asked, taking a seat nearest the fireplace. She removed both of her peach-colored gloves, chafing her hands together.

"Oh, forgive me! I did not realize you were cold. I will call for it immediately." Before she managed to pull the bell, Mrs. Cooke breezed into the room with a tray ladened with tea accouterments and a tower of sweet cakes and sandwiches.

"Pardon me, my lady. But Coleman thought your guest might appreciate refreshments." The housekeeper took her time, humming quietly to herself while she created an appetizing display. "Will you require anything else?"

"No, thank you," Annabelle said.

Mrs. Cooke curtsied to Annabelle and Cissy, before exiting the room.

"Such thoughtful servants." Cissy nibbled at a chocolate biscuit while sipping her sugared tea.

"I am lucky in that regard."

With the horrendous weather pounding an angry tattoo against the window, it truly was puzzling why Cissy ventured out of doors. Annabelle chewed nervously at a sandwich, failing to notice the watercress she detested.

"How are the preparations for the Earl of Maitland's ball coming along?"

"Splendidly. Helping Maitland plan the event has been a welcomed distraction," Annabelle said.

"Not only does Jack appear happily married, but his father, a well-known recluse, is now hosting an event." Cissy's teacup clattered against the saucer as she set it on the table. "I always thought your talent for transforming the surliest of creatures only extended to the four-legged variety. I had no idea you could work such miracles among the two-legged kind. Perhaps you might be able to help me with Nigel, as I have long feared he is a helpless cause. Since he won the wager at the Obsidian Club, he is spending entirely too much money and will beggar us before Christmas."

Annabelle could not believe this news. "He wagered against Jack?"

"Interestingly enough, the earl gave him the funds to do it. Figured if Linscott managed to snag a bride, his friend should profit. Though, why did he pick your name as a potential spouse?"

"He wagered Jack would choose me?"

"He did."

Cissy smoothed the fabric of her skirt, fiddling with the satin trim, before speaking again. "There are other rumors I've been meaning to ask you about."

Annabelle sipped at her tea. "What sort of rumors?"

"Well, I am not sure if you are aware, being sequestered here in your apparent love nest, but our friend has gone missing."

Feigning shock, Annabelle covered her chest with her hand, purposefully picking a different name to throw Cissy away from possible suspicion of their involvement in the disappearance. "Vivian? Has she run off?"

"Vivian!" Cissy exclaimed, contemplating the woman before her. In a moment of quiet calculation, she uncovered the truth. "It was you!" She shook an accusatory finger in Annabelle's direction. "You are the reason Francine disappeared!"

"Shhh," Annabelle hushed her friend. "The servants might hear."

"I should have known she came here. At least she is safe."

"Sort of."

"Sort of!" The woman across from her yelled before tempering her voice as Annabelle waved her hands frantically. "What happened?"

"I am not sure exactly, it is why Jack left after we received a vague message."

Cissy huffed her exasperation. "I can only imagine what sort of ill has befallen our accident-prone friend." She set her cup on the table, before brushing an invisible crumb from her skirt. "Unfortunately, this is not the only rumor circulating."

Tiny hairs prickled along Annabelle's neck, as she sat back expecting to hear the worst. What the worst entailed, she could not exactly articulate, but the pleasantly comfortable room became positively chilled.

Cissy lowered her voice before confessing. "Nigel swore me to secrecy."

"Which naturally meant you would confide in me."

A reluctant smile tugged at Cissy's lips. "Exactly. Nigel

confessed to hearing rumors at the Obsidian Club and other events he has attended. Countess Anworth is claiming she is with child, and…" Cissy visibly swallowed. When she spoke next, her voice wobbled. "When I came here, I hoped you might be miserable. But instead, I find my friend glowing at the mere mention of her husband. You are happier than I could have imagined."

Was she happy? Annabelle had not thought about it. Instead, a contentment settled over her life, a feeling of belonging and being wanted. Before life resembled a careful walk around a cluttered room, always fearful of bumping into stray objects and the disaster that might befall her at any moment. But now? Life felt easy. Felt right. Until Cissy spoke again, then the rug slipped beneath Annabelle's feet, and she crashed against the floor.

"Perhaps, there is no need to tell me what you or Nigel heard. They are merely rumors."

Cissy studied her friend for a moment, before appearing to come to a conclusion. "Maybe. But if our roles were reversed…"

"I see."

"She claims the baby belongs to Jack with its conception occurring since your vows."

Annabelle scoffed in disbelief. "Can one know that quickly? We've only been back for a little over three months, and Jack has rarely left the house. I have not even wondered if I might be with child, even though…" She did not finish her confession, instead feeling her cheeks glow with the memories of her husband's attention. "Besides, he has not had the occasion to be in her company. He is always at the club or…"

Cissy shook her head. "You cannot know the truth for certain unless you are following him."

"I trust him."

Her dearest friend laid her palms on Annabelle's face. A

move a governess might do when she explained to a naive child what they did wrong. When did her friend grow so jaded that she could not possibly believe in Jack's innocence?

"This is Jack Davenport, we are talking about."

"Yes, and a person can change."

"Not that quickly," Cissy said, adding a little harumph at the end of her sentence.

Anger boiled in Annabelle's stomach, churning the watercress sandwiches. "They can change. I know you claim to understand Jack, but he is my husband, and I am telling you the countess is lying."

"Be a naive simpleton who believes only in the good of others, despite the overwhelming evidence to the contrary. Let it be on your shoulders."

Annabelle straightened, throwing her head back from the verbal attack. "I am far from naive. I know what people are capable of far more than you, living in your privileged world as the daughter of the aristocracy." She was pleased with her countered argument, finding a strength she did not know she possessed to volley back at her intimidating friend. "You assume I am easily cowed. I thought you knew better. Perhaps I was wrong."

"And perhaps I assumed you knew me better, a privileged world indeed." Cissy rose, throwing her serviette onto the tray and marching to the door before Annabelle could run after her. "No, do not bother. I came here to warn you, and I have. Jack is lying. It is what he does. He has made a fool of you. As my *friend*," she hissed, "I thought to protect you. Silly of me, I know."

Annabelle remained stunned in the middle of the room, feeling the slam of the door reverberating through her bones. She wanted desperately to run after her friend but knew she had to allow Cissy a moment to cool her temper. Could her friend be correct? Was Jack making a fool out of Annabelle? She dreaded the answer.

Winston appeared, snaking his way around her ankles. If only Jack were here with her, she would know. She could read his face, unable to hide behind a clever smile and a witty quip. But he was not here. Could this be why he willingly left after Annabelle's suggestion? To escape the rumors?

Sweat prickled the back of her neck. Was the countess pregnant? An absolute nightmare! When was Jack going to be home? Was he coming home?

CHAPTER THIRTY-EIGHT
MAITLAND HOUSE

Annabelle paced her appointed bedroom at Maitland House, stopping to peer through the curtains whenever she passed the large front-facing windows. For a normally cluttered street, it was shockingly devoid of any traffic. No sign of Jack. Nor a carriage. Or a steaming horse.

Glancing at the ormolu clock, she watched the hands barely tick the time. Annabelle resumed pacing until Daisy entered with a peacock blue gown draped across her arms.

"My lady, I am afraid we cannot wait any longer, or else I will not be able to finish your hair."

With a heavy sigh, Annabelle sunk into the chair in front of the dressing table. "You will have to move the clock next to me, else I will have to crane my neck to check the time."

Daisy hung the gown in the wardrobe. She fetched the timepiece and handed it over to Annabelle. "I understand, my lady, but I am afraid no matter how long you stare at it, your husband will not arrive any faster."

"His lordship should have been here yesterday."

An entire day had passed since Jack was scheduled to

return from Scotland, at least according to the plan he set before rushing north to check on Francine after receiving her message. Three weeks passed without a word and now Annabelle imagined all sorts of horrific disasters that might have befallen both her husband and friend.

He was not coming. He had abandoned her. That was the only possible explanation as to why he was over a day late. How could she possibly face a crowded ballroom and her father-in-law? A woman scorned.

"The six straight days of rain surely slowed him down. The roads will be washed away in places. Please, do not worry. He will be here before I've finished setting your hair." Daisy parted Annabelle's hair in the middle, smoothing the strands before twisting them into a chignon on the crown of her head. Using tongs, her maid created a series of curls to frame Annabelle's face.

The hairstyling lasted over an hour with barely a syllable spoken between the normally chatty pair. Annabelle could not concentrate on any subject except her wayward husband and the downpour outside. The wind shifted, the rain pelting the windowpane.

"The moment we spot his lordship, I want a bathtub ready. He will be chilled to the bone."

"Already taken care of, my lady. Thomas ordered a hip tub and pots of water to remain on the stove for his lordship's return." Daisy picked up a strand of pearls, weaving them around the intricate curls.

With the help of her maid, Annabelle shucked the ordinary day dress and stepped into the silk evening gown. Daisy fastened the enclosures and smoothed out the layer of net and ribbon. The high waist accentuated Annabelle's curves, while the modest beribboned neckline concealed all but a hint of decolletage. The sleeves were capped and made of silk with a net overlay trimmed with silk waves and gauzy bows.

Daisy cooed. "Utterly splendid, my lady."

Annabelle twirled, the first smile of the day widening across her face. "I feel like a fairy in a dream."

"Yes, my lovely wife. You do." Jack's baritone voice rumbled around the room, accentuated by the roll of thunder rattling the windows.

Layers of mud caked his trousers. Cravat askew. Hair matted from the rain. Never had he been more attractive. Annabelle ran towards him before Daisy snagged her arm.

"No, my lady! You cannot. Think of your gown."

"I promise you a proper welcome when I am dry." A puddle gathered beneath Jack. "For now, the vision of you in all your splendor is enough to fill my weary bones with joy."

Annabelle approached, careful of the growing puddle. "Francine? How is she?"

"Well, my Butterfly. There is much to tell you, best for tomorrow when we are lying together in bed."

"Jack!" Annabelle's hands flew to her face. She wanted to chastise him for his overly flirtatious suggestion in front of the servants, but secretly his words thrilled her.

He blew her a kiss before he disappeared through their adjoining door. His sopping clothes splattered against the floor. After a short pause, she heard his elongated groan, followed by the splash of water against the tile bath floor. Male voices mixed as valet and master discussed clothing options.

He did not leave her! Oh, what frightful conjuring of an overactive mind. She chided herself but inwardly glowed at his fortuitous return. All in one piece and happy to be with her. How wrong Cissy was, she longed to admonish her friend; instead, she focused on the joy of Jack's return.

She pasted a contented grin that itched the corners and

descended the staircase to her charming father-in-law. The Earl of Maitland exclaimed his pleasure the moment she crossed the threshold into his study.

"My dear," he greeted. He placed her hand on his elbow and led her across the room. "I have no idea how my son managed to snatch you from the hands of other eligible suitors, but I am forever grateful for his success."

A fire blazed in the hearth, removing the chill from the rainy evening. The earl motioned to the set of chairs closest to the fire, pouring drinks of sherry for them both to enjoy.

"As much as I detest hosting events, I wanted to announce to the entirety of London my approval of my son's fine choice of a bride." He tapped his glass against hers in a toast. "Cheers."

"I am grateful for such a gracious welcome, my lord."

Pursing his lips together, he clucked his disapproval. "I believe I have repeatedly bade you to call me George."

"Yes, George. I apologize."

He patted her hand with fatherly affection. "I hear my son has returned from his business up north. Care to explain his hasty departure and why he arrived looking like Pheidippides on his arrival in Athens?"

"It was a favor I asked of him. I received word from a friend who was in a spot of trouble, and he went to help her. For me, simply because I asked."

A long, silent moment passed, while George studied his daughter-in-law, his silvery eyes narrowing as he mulled over her explanation. The longer the silence dragged, the more concerned Annabelle grew. Was he disappointed in her for requesting Jack's help to rescue a friend?

"More and more surprising revelations. It does an old man's heart good to bear witness to a startling change in his only child. A strength of character I knew my son to possess, but scarcely saw evidence of. Is your friend hale?"

"Yes, she is." Annabelle kept her response short, for fear she might say the thoughts that clamored to be heard.

The object of their conversation arrived, dressed from head to toe in stark black with only a snowy white cravat to break the austerity of his dress. Magnificent—utterly composed, yet with an air of heated sensuality. He drank from Annabelle's glass, headless of any hints of impropriety in front of his father.

"Maitland," he greeted his father while he splashed chest-nut-brown liquid into a goblet. "Hopefully, tonight's soirée ends promptly. I am blast tired."

"Perhaps your jaunt north could have waited?"

"Unfortunately, it could not. Apologies, but there was little I could do. Due to the sorry conditions of the roads, I was lucky to make it back with my neck in one piece." One hand gripped the back of the chair, and the other trembled. "Horse threw a shoe an hour outside London."

Annabelle rushed to his side and tried tearing at his coat and cravat. "We will make your excuses. You need to lie down."

He straightened his clothing. "I will do nothing of the sort, especially for a couple of bruises. Nothing will prevent me from introducing my viscountess." He placed a chaste kiss on the bridge of her nose. "Let's make our entrance, shall we?"

CHAPTER THIRTY-NINE
ANOTHER BALL

Jack managed one waltz with his wife before the pain in his ribs forced him to seek refuge in a quiet corner. Thomas assured him no ribs had broken in the fall from his horse, but his side was already purple and blue. But even with the aches and pains, nothing would have prevented Jack from attending. The earl openly announcing the match declared to the entire *ton,* or at least to those that remained in town as the season drew to a close, his unwavering support and approval for the future Countess of Maitland. Jack had to be present to legitimize the marriage.

So, despite the horse with the thrown shoe, the one who went lame on the second day on his journey home, the flooded roads, the swamp of mud and goo, Jack arrived only a day and a half late. And the sight of his wife swathed in silk stole the last semblance of control he possessed. He physically ached for her.

Glancing at the watch tucked in his waistcoat pocket, he counted three more hours until they could be alone together. Three hours until he rested his head against her chest, floating off in a dreamless slumber. He wished to make love to her, even though it would be clumsy and quick. As for tonight, he did not possess the stamina for an hour-long seduction, and he nearly wept over the fact.

Annabelle was a tangible need. A week without her was a lifetime. Two weeks nigh on interminable. Though his mind conjured glorious dreams of her, helping him to fall asleep to the recreations of his brain, he remembered the weight and heat of her vividly. The scent of lavender and spring lingered in his nostrils and his brain.

Annabelle and Nigel spun around the dance floor with merry sounds bubbling around them. Jack wished for the strength to rip them apart and be the one dancing with his bride. Instead, he settled on a twinge of jealousy and reluctant appreciation for the joyful laughter ringing through the ballroom.

"I've honestly never seen her so happy." Cissy Hammond approached from the side. "I truly had no idea you would be perfect together."

"Perfect? That might be a stretch."

She was perfect, but him? Anything but. He was a greedy wretch, determined to squirrel his wife away like the miser he was.

"How long have we known each other, Jack? My entire life?"

He remembered well the curly-haired toddler with rosy cheeks and an infectious giggle. Often, he snuck into the nursery to bounce her on his knee or toss her in the air to evoke effervescent sounds. Ones so foreign in his own world. "Eons," he said.

"I remember you flirting with every woman in a skirt. Then you marched off to war, only to return more wretched than before. Furious with the world, but shrugging off the bitterness in favor of vice in every form."

"I've missed a step between where you claim I am perfect for your friend and then describe an unrepentant rogue."

"You never were a rogue, merely lost and troubled. But lately, there is a brightness in you I thought had long ago been smothered. I guess it was lurking there all along, waiting for the right person to reignite it. She brings out the best in you. And you've given her wings."

Jack could hardly believe the praise Cissy heaped on him. Where was the bitter cynic with the anger that mimicked his own? "My God. Do you actually approve?"

"Until you fuck it up, which you will."

"Language, my dear Cecilia. Such ugly words flowing from such a pretty mouth."

Her lips twisted. "They are not paying attention. They are too besotted with your wife."

He was. He could not remove his eyes from her even if the room went up in flames. A vision in blue. "Jealous, perhaps?"

"Of Annabelle? Never. A lovelier person never lived. Which is why I've come to warn you." She motioned to Jack to move further into the recesses of the alcove, away from prying ears. She lowered her voice to a little above a whisper. "Countess Anworth is spreading vicious rumors."

Jack's jaw flexed along with his fist. "About?"

She fidgeted with the spangles on the sleeve of her gown. A tell for her, as she struggled to say what she needed to, and a sharp pain stabbed his gut. "This comes directly from the countess. She is carrying and it is yours."

"Impossible."

"Truly? Because I have witnessed the way she trailed after you like a panting dog. And..."

Jack hated the way she spoke, pausing as a couple moved past them. Too close for a private conversation.

"I am not sure if you are aware," Cissy continued, once the couple exchanged pleasantries and congratulations. "This rumor is circulating swiftly. My modiste has confided in me. Whispers in the retiring room of the theater. Then there are the wagers and sniggers at the Obsidian Club. According to Nigel, the current speculation is that you would not show tonight, and you are absconding with your light o' love."

"I am here, should be proof enough it is all a load of shite."

"Perhaps, however, the countess is more determined than usual. Jack…"

The elongated pause grated on his final nerves.

"You know I have, shall we say, connections everywhere. Whether or not it is yours, she is carrying."

The floor moved beneath Jack's feet. If it were not for the quick reflexes of Graves—his father's normally phlegmatic butler, his face would have smashed against the floor.

"My lord, are you well?" the butler asked.

Annabelle rushed to his side, abandoning Nigel to the dance floor. She snapped at Cissy, stunning Jack too much to speak. "What did you say to my husband? Are you not finished spreading your damning lies?"

Cissy held up her hands in defense. "As always, I am concerned for my friends, whether they appreciate my help or not. You are the one I am protecting."

Annabelle faltered a moment, before commanding those that held Jack upright. "Graves, please help escort my husband to the library. I am afraid he might be injured far more than was initially suspected."

"Gladly, my lady. I will also locate a physician. I believe Dr. Hill is a guest of his lordship."

Despite Jack's many protests to the contrary, two footmen

escorted him to his father's library, helping him onto the orange-striped chaise lounge. Annabelle insisted on removing his cravat and coat. He remained only in his shirt sleeves and waistcoat.

"I am indecent. My father will have me bodily removed from the premises."

Annabelle rested the back of her hand across his forehead. "Your father is concerned. We both are."

"Come a little closer and give me a kiss." Much to his everlasting disappointment, she rose as the door opened for a portly man with sparse hair and spectacles perched on his beaklike nose.

"I hear you took a tumble off your horse this afternoon?" The doctor's voice grated on Jack's already thin nerves.

Annabelle excused herself, though it comforted him, knowing she hovered by the door. More than likely with her ear pressed against the paneling. At least, that was what Jack would do if their positions were reversed.

"Thrown. I do not fall off horses like a child."

The doctor ignored Jack's waspish tone. He was efficient, agreeing with Thomas's earlier assessment his ribs were merely bruised. At Jack's behest, Annabelle returned to the room to question the physician herself.

"I recommend plenty of rest and nothing strenuous over the next few days. Often, we believe ribs to be unbroken, but too much exertion after an injury, and a crack turns into a solid break."

"Thank you, Dr. Hill," she said.

"I will check on him again before I leave this evening. I must confess my reluctance to go as of yet, as it is a fine affair."

"Oh, do enjoy yourself. We are grateful for your assistance." Annabelle saw the doctor out of the library, before returning to fuss over Jack.

She was the only person he wanted to fuss over him. To find concern where there was none to be had. Fluffing pillows. Tucking blankets around him.

"Give me a kiss." He blew the air between them, but she ignored him. "I have not felt your lips on mine in far too long. A fortnight is an eternity without you. Three weeks was hell."

She leaned over, providing him with an unobstructed view down the neck of her gown to the heavenly valley between her breasts. Her lips brushed fleetingly across his before she tried to pull back. Instead, his hand stiffened on the back of her head, denying her retreat. His tongue traced the seam of her lips, while his other hand walked along her arm, nearing the bounteous mountains he craved.

"Jack." She pressed his name against his mouth.

He took advantage of the temporary parting of lips, to savor the flavor of her. With surprising force, she pushed his arms back, imprisoning him on the lounge.

"I might like being tied to a bed while you do all the work."

She blew a strand of hair from her face. "You, my exhausted husband, need rest. And since you cannot play nice, I am leaving you alone to recuperate before you break bones and do irreparable harm."

"You are being unreasonable. Let me kiss you."

She pressed harder where her hands gripped his wrists. "You are a naughty man. Listen to the doctor."

"He is an ass."

"Then listen to your wife. Rest, my husband. I will return before you have a chance to miss me."

"I miss you every second you are away from me." His confession surprised even him. Her grip loosened, so he seized the advantage by wrapping his arms around her.

"No amount of sweet niceties will get me to disobey a doctor's orders. Unhand me, you wretch." She softened the rebuff with a kiss, running her hands through his hair and cupping his face. "You are already halfway to dreamland. Please, rest and then maybe I will allow you a few tiny liberties when we are upstairs in our rooms."

"Promise? You must swear to it, or I will not obey." Even he knew there was no weight to his threat as sleep fought to claim him.

"I promise." With a tender press of her lips, she left him, dousing the candlelight as she went.

The room maintained a comforting glow from the fire burning in the hearth. Faint notes from the dances drifted through the walls, lulling Jack into a blissful surrender.

DREAMS ASSAILED HIM. Heated moments filled with lush memories of his wife. Her scent lingered on his clothing. The taste of wine and sweetness on his lips. His body craved her. Demanded release only found in the hot recesses of her body.

His mind conjured images of her bare, climbing over him with only the red glow from the firelight casting a golden gleam over her body. She peeled his clothing away and freed his overly heated body.

A wet heat scorched his lip and trailed across the pulse of his throat. "Annabelle," he groaned, waking from his slumber with the realization this was no dream. He pulled at her coiffure, threading his fingers through the length to admire it in the firelight.

But her hair was not golden honey. It was as black as raven wings. He surged to his feet, sending the succubus to tumble onto the floor in a heap of red satin.

Jack seethed, yanking at the buttons of his shirt and waistcoat. Before he could fasten the clothing, a fist knocked him to the floor while a disembodied voice screamed profanities.

"Bastard! You are with another woman on the day your marriage is announced! You could not wait one goddamn day to fuck this whore?" A punch smashed his nose, helpless to do anything but throw up his hands in pathetic defense. The man thrashed him nearly senseless, blow after blow landed against his sore ribs, his jaw.

"You are wrong!" Jack bellowed.

"It is exactly what you presume," the she-demon purred, trying to separate the two men.

"Enough!" His father's voice boomed through the room.

Two pairs of strong arms wrenched Jack to his feet, while another pair hauled his assailant across the room. From swelling lids, he recognized Annabelle's cousin—Oakmont, his newest nemesis.

"I will end you," the viscount hissed, his face unscathed.

The Countess Anworth sauntered up to Jack, her manicured nails raked over his chest, where his shirt gaped open. "Leave him to me, my lord. I will take care of him."

"You will leave." The earl's voice brokered no disagreement, firm and staid.

"This man belongs to me. He is the father of my child." Tossing her hair over her shoulder, she cupped her hand around her flat belly.

His father's shoulders rolled forward in an uncharacteristic display of age. "Graves, my son is in no condition to remain standing. Please help him to sit down, then escort this... woman off the premises via the servant staircase."

"You cannot silence me. I will tell everyone—" Valentina rose to her full height, waving an imperious finger at his father.

The surprise of all surprises, his father shouted her down. "You will say nothing. You will leave my presence, and you will abandon your pursuit of my son. You, madame, are an unmarried woman with a deceased husband." She shrunk back at his words, spitting denials. "You were never invited to this event, and I am not sure how you even came into this room. You will do what other women in your circumstances do. You will flee town with your head tucked between your knees. Threaten my son and his wife again and I will personally ensure that every door is slammed in your conniving face."

"I am the Countess of Anworth," she screamed, her face a molten red matching her gown.

"You are not welcome here!" On his father's proclamation, Graves dragged the sputtering woman from the room, her hair trailing around her shoulders.

Valentina lunged desperately to the side, snagging a handful of peacock blue skirts. "Please, do not let them do this. I am with child!"

"Jack?" The sweetest voice he knew asked. Her question broke through the din of heated voices as she twisted free from Valentina's grip. "You are hurt!" She knelt before him, dabbing a handkerchief against his face.

"It is not what it looks like." He begged her to understand. If anyone would listen, it was Annabelle. His precious rescuer of the unlovable.

"It appears that someone bashed your face in with a hammer. Who did this to you?"

Her outrage was his undoing. "I was asleep, I swear it. Please believe me." His tears splashed on her gloved hands.

"He is lying," Oakmont growled, still restrained by two of the earl's footmen.

"Elucidate for me then." She pressed the linen against Jack's cut lip to staunch the bleeding.

"Do not listen. It was not what he thought he saw. I can explain," Jack pleaded.

"Shh, let him speak." Her voice was full of reason, steady in a sea of torment.

Jack needed to hold her, wrap her in his arms, and pull her inside of him. To have her heal the wounds marring his face and soul. He opened his mouth, but she placed a trembling hand over his lips.

Oakmont yanked his arms free, pulling Annabelle away. He whispered furiously, but Jack strongly suspected his father caught every single last word by the way his jaw ticked.

"Lady Anworth was kissing your husband. He was groaning as she pawed at him." The viscount's lips curled in a sneer.

"Moaning Annabelle's name. I thought it was my wife. I was asleep. I swear it upon my life."

She stepped back. Jack rose on shaky feet, but she retreated further and further away. "I... I must go." Her knees gave out, only to fall into Cissy's arms.

Cissy took stock of the surroundings. "Jack, tell me it is not true."

"I swear it."

Cissy hesitated with her inward struggle before she helped Annabelle rise.

Oakmont shoved Jack's chest. The force sent him sprawling to the floor. "We meet tomorrow at dawn. Pistols or swords, pick your end and name your second."

"This is outrageous..."

"Name your second!" Oakmont pointed a stiff finger in his direction. "I demand satisfaction."

Annabelle fainted on a whimper while Cissy clung to her.

"Baron Crayfield is my second."

Oakmont slammed his foot on top of Jack's outstretched hand, scooped his cousin in his arms, then stormed out of the room.

"He will not demand a duel and break the man's hand. I will not have my son dishonored in my home. I will not allow it!" His father bellowed for his butler, clearing through a path of revelers that gawked at the spectacle.

Hands prodded his wounds. Staunching blood. Bandaging ribs. But internally he broke. The world he was only learning to relish disintegrated before him. He was left with nothing. Only the utter rot of his soul. Damaged beyond repair. Beyond forgiveness.

If Valentina was pregnant, the child was not of Jack's loins. The father could easily be one of ten different lovers. She was not discrete. Was not concerned with giving birth to a bastard. But he was. He used French letters, fearing disease, and always withdrew. He refused to yield his seed to a woman who owned no part of him. But not with Annabelle. No, Annabelle possessed every ounce of his humanity.

"Do not go," he whispered to the darkness overtaking him. He pleaded with the Fates to whisper the same words in her ear and hoped beyond all hope she believed him, despite the evidence to the contrary. "Do not leave me."

CHAPTER FORTY
A MEADOW

A fine mist settled over the ground shortly before dawn. Not even the wrens made a sound as Jack pushed through the copse of trees to the field where he soon would face off against Oakmont. Nothing disturbed the dew until Jack trod across the ground, leaving emerald-colored boot prints in his wake.

At the crest of the hill, he angled his head. In the distance, his father's mansion parted the fog. A lone light broke through the darkness. Did Annabelle wait for word of her husband's demise, or did she slumber like an innocent? Like the woman she was before Jack's corruption.

A million thoughts assailed his mind during the night as he stared at a blank piece of paper. A final farewell to the woman who stole his heart. But all he could manage to write was an inadequate: *I am sorry.*

Pathetic.

He rubbed the tightness in his chest. He wished he could see her. To feel her hand against his skin or the press of her lips against his. But it was better this way. To fall instead of fight.

How could he harm the family she loved dearly after he forced his way into her world?

It was better to be a victim of her cousin's bullet than risk killing Oakmont. She would never forgive Jack. He could never forgive himself.

He blew a kiss across the hill, hoping the wind carried it to lay upon his wife's cheek. One kiss before he left his mortal coil.

"You cannot go through with this." Thomas handed Jack a flask.

His hand shook as he took a long swallow, then a second, hoping to find bravery at the bottom. "Why are you here?"

"Did you expect me to abandon you when you need me the most? How many battles have we been through together?"

"I lost count." Jack offered the flask to his valet. His friend.

Thomas chugged the remains, before pulling out a second.

"You are incredibly efficient," Jack said.

Thomas chuckled, the sound mirthless in the dense fog swirling around their boots. "Why are you going through with this? I know appearances were not what they seemed."

"It is for the best, or else Annabelle will be mocked."

"How will your death save her from ridicule? You are better than this. Better than all of them."

Jack turned his back, only for Thomas to yank him around. "No, you are going to listen to me. You should be running into the arms of the woman you love, not sacrificing yourself for a misguided notion of chivalry or whatever idiotic reason has mucked up your brain."

Jack faltered, trying to regain his balance. "I am weak."

"Bullshit. You are the bravest man I know. Remember what happened after I dragged you off the battlefield?"

Jack refused to meet his former batman's gaze, uncomfortable with praise of any kind. "I did what any man would do."

"You mean shoving a junior officer out of the way of a bayonet, only to be stabbed in his stead. I found you in a pile of men, then dragged your half-delirious arse off the field. I had to hold you down while the surgeon sewed up the gaping wound in your shoulder, you slugged two orderlies before charging back to the front. There you battled like a man possessed. The only reason I joined you was because you refused to cover your back." Thomas gripped his shoulder, the one wounded at Waterloo. "Do not make me regret my decision, when I could have left you to fall in battle as a hero." His cheeks glittered suspiciously in the silver glow of the fading moonlight.

"What would you have me do? Kill her cousin?"

"Refuse to fight this duel," his valet said.

"I cannot. Thomas, I—"

"I will not leave."

Jack squeezed his valet's shoulder. "I would not have it any other way."

The neigh of horses and the jangle of reins signaled the others' arrival.

Nigel's uncharacteristically somber face wavered before him. In his hands, he clutched a walnut case, gleaming from a recent polish. He lifted the lid, revealing two Joseph Manton dueling pistols with silver filigree. Exquisite weapons.

"The last of my father's possessions that he did not manage to pawn," Nigel said as Jack selected one pistol and inspected the trigger plate. "Any chance you have changed your mind?"

Jack lifted his bloodshot eyes. "I deserve this."

Nigel inhaled sharply, trying to bite his tongue, but changed his mind. "No, I am not going to let this go. I know what you are planning. I can smell the fifth of whisky wafting from your pores. I cannot allow you to sacrifice yourself for idiotic notions of honor when we both know you did not betray Annabelle. I do not give a bloody fuck what *Lord Oakmont* believes."

"I cannot shoot her cousin." Jack acknowledged the challenger's presence, refusing to discuss the facts any further.

"Dammit, Jack. Listen to me."

"It is done, old friend."

Thomas shook his head in commiseration. "I tried to talk him out of this."

"Jack, you cannot." Nigel's shout echoed off the trees, sending roosting birds into the sky, protesting their disturbed slumber.

"Take care of Annabelle for me."

Before Nigel could utter another word, Oakmont's second approached. "Winthorpe," Nigel said by way of greeting.

Lord Winthorpe chafed his hands together, blowing on them to warm his skin against the unseasonably chilly summer morning. "Bloody awful business this. I saw Lady Anworth sneaking around, but I did not question it. I should have said something. I told Oakmont as much, tried to talk him out of this, but he will not listen."

"You know the rules, if we cannot talk them out of it, we stand by their side." Nigel handed the second pistol to Winthorpe.

The man held the weapon like it was diseased. "I do not want anyone's death on my hands."

Oakmont pushed through the group and demanded attention. "Why all the chit-chat? We have a duel to finish and a body to bury before dawn."

Jack stepped forward. "This will not solve anything and will only break Annabelle's heart. This travesty is not what she would ever want. With the consequences being the death of her husband or her cousin? Bodily injury if we are both lucky? Our fighting will kill her, and you know it."

It took his last reserve of strength to resist shoving the younger man to the ground. To not attack his adversary. When he did not so much as blink, Jack knew conversation and reason were fruitless.

Oakmont turned on his heels counting off fifteen paces.

"Shit." Winthorpe shook his head. He ran after the other man, sliding on the dew-covered ground before righting his steps.

Nigel clasped Jack's shoulder. "You were always more a brother than a friend. Do not let this be the end."

He walked to the copse of trees, out of firing range. There he stood eerily still like a soldier on watch with Thomas by his side. The wind did not even bother to stir their hair. Stoic and staid. So unlike the men, Jack knew better than himself.

"Farewell, old friends."

Oakmont counted. His smooth voice carried over the field. "One... Two..."

CHAPTER FORTY-ONE
A VOICE OF REASON

Annabelle woke with drool crusted at the corner of her mouth. The darkness outside the window faded by incremental degrees. How could she fall asleep? She leapt from the window seat with the view of the distant park.

She bade Nigel, as Jack's second, to put an end to this ridiculous duel. Then she penned two letters to her cousin, demanding he cease his foolishness. But neither of the men returned to the earl's home. No one put aside their inane amour-propre, to allow logic to prevail.

She tore open the front door, taking the steps two at a time, only to run straight into the back of Graves, bowling the poor man over. They landed in a heap at the bottom of the stairs. The butler attempted to help Annabelle to her feet, but she refused, despite the blood trickling down her forehead.

"I am sorry, I must stop them."

"But, my lady," he protested, trying to grab her arm.

"There is no time!"

A voice carried from the curbstone. "He means to wait for me. Hop in, my dear." The earl pushed open a carriage door.

"My apologies," she said over her shoulder, jumping into the vehicle. The coachman snapped the reins, and they were off before she could check to make sure the man on the pavement was still in one piece. For a moment she felt guilty, but it was assuaged as she contemplated much more pressing matters.

"I hoped you would remain sleeping, but I guess you have as much right to stop this madness as I do." The earl's leg bounced up and down. His stacked hands rested on the rounded handle of his cane.

"I assumed we would have heard that the duel was called off." It terrified Annabelle that the two most important men in her life were so diametrically opposed to one another. If they truly cared for her, they should want what was best for Annabelle. It felt too much like her parents and their selfish desires, headless of the consequences of their decisions.

She chewed on her fingernail, before realizing with a twinge of mortification that she left the house without her gloves. Her hair lay unbound around her shoulders. Nor did she wear a coat to conceal her nightdress.

Maitland was in less of a disheveled state, having never changed out of the clothes he wore to the ball.

The coachman navigated the streets with adept skill, arriving in a matter of minutes at the dueling site. Before the carriage came to a complete halt, Annabelle threw open the door and cried out for them to stop. By the time her foot landed on the dewy ground, she realized how tardy they were. The two men faced each other, but her husband's gun pointed too low. He was sacrificing himself.

"Stop!" she cried, giving all she possessed to that single exclamation. The syllable sliced through the air with more efficiency than a bullet. Oakmont's gun tipped down. It fired into the grass, while Jack dropped his and ran to Annabelle—her name echoed in her ears as the world around her went dark.

DREAMS WERE A FUNNY PHENOMENON. They played havoc with a person's sense of reality. Annabelle swore she was outside in a damp field, wearing no coat or gloves and trying to stop the duel. But daylight greeted her. Or rather, the muted gray of a cloudy day seeped in through the curtains. Curtains she recognized as her own. Home.

Her head ached terribly. The nauseating pain swirled in her stomach when she pushed herself upright. She buried her head in her hands and groaned. Which of her dreams were real or nightmares?

A cup pressed against her hand. "Drink this, you will feel better," a gruff voice commanded.

She peeked through her fingers and poked the cup skeptically. "Perhaps, or perhaps it is laced with laudanum."

The mattress depressed next to her with a familiar weight.

"Is that a problem?" the voice asked.

"When I was younger, I had a terrible reaction. My mother never forgave the nanny who administered the dose, as I was dreadfully ill the entire night. Mother fired the poor woman the next day, even though it was the nanny who stayed up the entire night giving me comfort." She inhaled deeply. Her nostrils filled with hints of cedar, tobacco, and whisky. It could only be one man, her heart raced as she glanced upward. The light cast his face in shadow, but she knew the shape anywhere.

"Good thing this is merely willow bark tea." His mouth parted, his face dimpled, but no joy could be found in his smile.

She swallowed deeply. His movements were stiff as he gathered a quilt and picked up a book off the floor.

"Are you my new lady's maid?" she asked, hoping to inject a bit of humor into the weighted air around her.

He smirked, motioning to her clothing. "Do you want me to be?"

"Hm, perhaps not. I like you better as my husband." She patted the bed next to her. "Now sit with me and help me to make sense of the whirlwind in my head."

"I would rather not."

"Why not?"

She did not want to give voice to the thoughts in her head. Since Cissy had planted little seeds of doubt that were now an overgrown forest, crowding out any ray of hope this marriage might be more than an illusion. She should have known she was merely a means to an end, but how she wanted to believe she might be more.

"Do you remember anything?" He sat gingerly on the edge of the bed, carefully putting weight on only one side of his body.

"Did you reinjure your ribs?" She threw off the coverlet, but his arm snagged her waist, pulling her back onto the bed.

"It is not my ribs. Please, lie back down. The doctor had to put stitches in your head." He stroked her cheek. His thumb caressed her forehead, a delicate brush of butterfly wings, yet stoking pangs of fire along her spine. "You frightened me."

"I frightened you?"

"Yes, even your cousin lost his desire to murder me when you collapsed, your face smeared with blood."

"Was I not with your father? I cannot make heads or tails of the events."

"He was, but he barely noticed you were bleeding."

"You terrified him with your idiotic duel." The need to scold was overwhelming, but she bit it back.

"He was terrified because I was shot. He ran past his daughter-in-law, who lay prostrate on the ground. Punched your cousin in the face for getting in his way. Hit Winthorpe in the shin with his cane and nearly tagged Nigel, who leapt out of reach before the cane could connect. All because your cousin's bullet ricocheted off the ground and skimmed my leg."

She reached for him, but Jack scooped her into his arms.

"You were shot!"

"Grazed. Nothing more than a tear in my skin. Trust me, your cat has done worse. Thomas was there to bandage it, no harm done."

He rubbed his chin over her head, squeezing her tightly. She wanted to melt into his arms, but there was a tension in the way he held her. Despite his affection, something was amiss.

"I have to know what you plan on doing now that another is to bear your child." She spoke against the pulse at the base of his throat.

He stilled his movements. His Adam's apple bobbed. "What bearing does a bastard child have on our relationship?"

She broke away from his hold. "A child needs a loving home and parents to raise him. Do you not care what becomes of your own flesh? Left in the hands of that woman, your child is destined for a life filled with agony and neglect."

"My child? There is nothing that proves this child is mine. It probably belongs to Sambridge or a footman or the fishmonger for all I know. I am not claiming a whore's child." This was the caged version of her husband. A wolf snarling at his captors as he tried to break free.

She held the key to soothe the beast, but she could not do it. "How could you abandon a helpless being?"

"It is not my child. How many times do I have to say it? I should not have to defend myself in my own home!" Heedless of his injury, he stomped across the room to the connecting door. "I will not have you dragging in more mouths to feed, because you feel sorry for the state of their birth. We are already a laughing stock with your menagerie of strays, I will not be mocked any further. Besides, it is probably the goddam antichrist!"

"How dare you say such horrible things!"

"You are a bloody fool, Annabelle. And I was a bigger one for marrying you!" he bellowed.

She recoiled, shielding her face and awaiting a blow to punctuate his anger. When nothing came, she blinked open her eyes. Steam pulsed from his ruddy face.

"Say something," he commanded.

Ginny whimpered and scratched at the door.

She lowered her hand. "Are you going to strike me?"

He took a step towards her. "I would never."

"Yet, you throw your vitriol as if you were punching in a pugilism ring. I will not spar with my husband. I will not stay in a home where I am belittled."

One breath stilled the rage she felt brewing inside. Two tampered down the need to fling hateful words in his direction. But that was her mother. She would never sink so low, no matter what he said or did. Instead, she would do the one thing her father was never able to do. She would leave.

"Annabelle, I am sorry. This whole situation has me saying things I do not mean."

"I find that people tend to say exactly what they intend during the heat of a moment. It is only later, they apologize. When the regrets are too loud to ignore." She stood, her legs wobbly, but she would never allow him to see. She could do this, draw strength from the animals she had rescued, and no longer be a victim to a bully in her home.

Grabbing a shawl draped across a chair, she ran for the door. She felt him hot on her heels, but Winston had proved invaluable. Snaking between Jack's ankles, he lost his footing, crashing into a walnut table. The calamity sent a porcelain figurine of a woman holding her cat tumbling towards the ground. Desperately, he tried to catch the sentimental objet d'art but fumbled as it smashed to smithereens, slicing through his hands as he hit the floor.

Annabelle's feet moved toward him on their own accord before she commanded herself to stand still. She called for help, and a footman arrived with suspicious alacrity.

"Goodbye, Jack," she said. It was all she could manage, shoving past the row of footmen and maids toward the front door.

CHAPTER FORTY-TWO
LOSS

J ack did not know when the summer sky had turned from azure to dingy yellow, but the color encapsulated his desolate mood. He was frozen in mute horror as any hope for his marriage faded into bleakness.

Coleman surprised him, mainly because Jack was still alive, but the butler also cared for his wounds. When the bleeding had not stopped, he left to retrieve Dr. Hill. Coleman was probably right, Jack needed stitches. However, exsanguination sounded like a better way to go than dying of a broken heart.

When did Jack become maudlin? Ah, yes, the minute his wife said, "Goodbye, Jack," then fled like he was diseased.

Mrs. Cooke brought him a tray with roast beef and vegetables. Winston was the only one remotely interested in the fare. He stared at the mangy orange and white cat as it licked and nibbled the roast.

"She left her damn cat!" Part of him wanted to run after the carriage and throw the feline misanthrope inside, but the other part held onto hope. "If she left Winston behind, she plans on returning."

There it was a tiny glimmer of possibility that this too could be mended. But what did Annabelle want him to do?

There were ways to silence Anworth, but he did not believe for a moment she was pregnant. She tried that same tactic before when her husband was alive. She attempted to convince Jack they should run away together. He did not fall for it then. He would not fall for it now. Yet, what did any of that matter when Annabelle was hurting?

Besides boyhood spats, he could not remember a single time he fought emotionally. His father stated conditions, and Jack was meant to obey or be punished. They did not argue. What made him say such hurtful words to Annabelle? He regretted the hastiness of their marriage. Had it not been for his father's demand to wed, he would not have. That was true.

Dr. Hill arrived an hour later to find Jack on the floor rubbing Winston's ears. Blood had trailed along his exposed forearm to pool on his breeches in a rust-colored stain. With the help of two footmen, the doctor half-carried and half-drug Jack to his bedroom.

Working quickly, Dr. Hill vigorously scrubbed Jack's arm, then removed the bits of porcelain. By the end of the doctor's medical rigmarole, Jack's once fine hand was a gruesome patchwork of skin sewn together—jagged remnants much like the pieces of his once beating heart.

Thomas offered laudanum to ease Jack's discomfort, but he declined. He deserved to feel every ounce of pain for the suffering he caused. He refused it all. The glass of brandy, cheroot, even blancmange.

Eventually, he succumbed to a restless sleep. During the long, dark hours of the night he reached out for Annabelle, but her side of the bed remained ice cold. As he pulled back his hand, a fuzzy head bumped against his palm. "It is you and me now, Winston." The cat curled into a ball and purred. The vibrations soothed the torment that raged in his mind until Jack again drifted into an uneasy slumber.

CHAPTER FORTY-THREE
REFUGE

Annabelle was unsure where she should go. Hampshire to her father was the last place she wanted to run to. What did he understand about relationships, other than to hide away? Marcus and her aunt were not a great alternative, considering her cousin tried to shoot a bullet through Jack's head only this morning. She chanced a new ally, one she felt a brief kinship with and knew was a gentleman. It was to George Davenport, the Earl of Maitland, she fled.

The hackney she managed to flag down outside Jack's townhouse arrived shortly in Mayfair. Not until she stepped away from the carriage did she even realize the dread she felt when riding had vanished.

Maitland's butler smiled when he opened the door. "My lady, it is good to see you." He took her shawl and said nothing about the way she was dressed.

"I apologize for my behavior this morning."

He waved away her concern. "Think nothing of it. No harm done. I was in the way. Please follow me, and I will tell Lord Maitland that he has a visitor."

Graves escorted her up the stairs to the family sitting room. There she waited. Her nerves fired as she contemplated her father-in-law's reaction to her presence here. She focused on the decor, letting her mind wander away to find her center. To hold back the tears filling her eyes.

The stately splendor of the room soothed her frazzled nerves with its papered buttery-yellow walls accented with a hand-painted motif of songbirds perched on leafy branches. A thick multi-colored Wilton carpeting covered most of the parquet flooring, inviting her to kick off her slippers and bury her toes into its soft depths. She needed a similar room in her home. One that felt calm and offered an open invitation to peace.

A table with blue and green inlay tiles stood under the window with a card tower balanced on top. Annabelle reached for the top card on the stack. The ace of hearts. Figured it had to be hearts, even the cards mocked her. Carefully, so as not to disturb the delicate balance, she placed it at an angle to create another room for the card house.

"You have a talent for building." George Davenport's voice boomed as he walked to her side to add another card to the castle.

"My mother tried to teach me all sorts of games, but I was never any good. Much to her chagrin, I was far more interested in building castles out of the decks."

A faint memory of standing like this with her father, while he praised the little card house came flooding back. Followed by her mother storming into the room.

"These are not toys," her mother said, smacking Annabelle's hands away.

"She was just playing," her father pleaded, then slunk away *from the fury in her gaze.*

Annabelle shivered, stepping away from the table.

"Perhaps, this is a more useful skill. At least, not one that would find you light in the pockets after an evening of entertainment." He took Annabelle's arm in his and escorted her to the matching blue and yellow brocade chairs.

Annabelle smoothed out her skirts and sat with perfect posture. Doubt crept into her mind. She was utterly lost.

"My butler said you arrived without my son or a maid. Did he chase you away already?" He crossed his long legs in front of him.

Much in the way he reclined, reminded Annabelle of Jack. Far too much like Jack.

"No, not exactly. Rather, I felt the need to be away for a while." Annabelle plucked at a loose thread on her dress.

George Davenport rested his chin on his hand. "Many marriages of the *ton* are conducted as nearly separate lives. Some couples choose to reside in entirely different households."

"I could not live like that. I cannot imagine being bound to someone for life and yet living as if the other half of you was so unimportant they chose a second home."

"I will admit, I was not an active father in Jack's life. After Clara died, I did not know what to do with the boy, so I left him in the care of his nannies." Lines etched the earl's face. "But it is the way of our class."

"If children are the ultimate reason people wed, should they not be the solitary focus of the family." At least then, they would feel wanted instead of a nuisance.

"Perhaps they should be. Clara stayed behind when I went to London for the season. We both believed the country air was better for a young boy. For four years we all were exceedingly happy. Until Clara and then Charlie..." He stared out the window for a long time, not finishing his thought.

Annabelle wished Jack could see his father right now. She

could only imagine such a discussion had never passed between the two men during their entire lives.

"Marriage is difficult, my dear. It takes more work than it is probably worth most days, but then again, when you have true love, I feel its value far exceeds that of any wealth a man possesses." A sparkle of blue swirled in the gray depths of his eyes.

"Love is not a factor in our marriage."

He shook his head. "Hmm, do we both recall this morning's events correctly? Perhaps I am old and sentimental, but my son appeared to be sacrificing himself for the woman he loves."

Annabelle blinked at her father-in-law. She refused to believe what he said because it was for his honor Jack dueled. Not love. It was too soon in their marriage to even contemplate the emotion.

"Why did you want Jack to marry?"

"Ah, that is the real question, is it not? I always felt marriage would save Jack. For much of his life, he wandered from place to place, indulging in all matters of sin and debauchery. I hoped a proper wife might bring out the man I knew my son could be. Then he met you."

For a moment, Annabelle feared his recriminations. She braced herself for what came next.

"He has changed, Annabelle. In the incredibly short time he has known you, I have caught glimpses of the boy I once knew. Joy radiates from him whenever you are near. I can only imagine he brings out the best in you as well."

"He does," she said with a watery smile. "When we met, I never imagined I would ever feel this, but I do."

"Why are you here, my dear?" He leaned forward, clasping her hands. "Does it have something to do with that terrible creature, Lady Anworth?"

"Yes," she admitted.

"And who do you believe? Her or my son?" He tilted his head exactly like Jack. It was her breaking point.

"Him," she sobbed.

He pulled out his handkerchief and offered it to Annabelle. "I am glad. But then I have to ask again, why are you here?"

"Because he said he does not want me. That I am a nuisance. Not only does he wish to push me aside, but he will abandon this child he created. How can he not care what becomes of his progeny?"

"Do you truly believe there is a child?"

It surprised her greatly how Jack's father denied the parentage of this child. He appeared assured with very little evidence.

"Of course, why would a woman lie about such a thing?" Annabelle asked.

He removed a letter from his pocket, unfolded it, and placed it on the table before her. "In one of the letters Lord Crayfield sent in an attempt to find a solution that did not include bloodshed, he sought the truth behind the countess's claim."

She picked up the missive, the letter irresistible. Nigel's handwriting was hurried, smeared with ink in a desperate attempt to prevent bloodshed. He engaged a man named Arthur Fox to threaten the woman, all in defense of his friend.

"She admitted the child is not Jack's?"

"According to Mr. Fox, she admits an impoverished French Comte seduced her and is the father. Together, they hoped to find a gentleman with deep pockets, and she would wed carrying a cuckoo's egg."

"Sambridge!" Though Annabelle never regarded the duke as a serious suitor, they shared a kinship. He deserved a love match, not a woman after his pockets.

"Yes, Nigel suspects Sambridge was the original target, then she came to Jack."

"But who is next? She must be stopped."

He patted her hand affectionately. "Ease your mind, child. This afternoon I received word that Anworth boarded a ship bound for Canada. Her Comte abandoned her on the docks."

Relief as she never knew filled her chest. Jack was not a father. Yet, that did not solve her problem. He did not want her.

"Now you know for certain there is not a child. But a problem remains. Does it not?"

"Yes, I am not wanted." She worried her fingernail, heedless of the commonness of the gesture.

"You are wrong, my dear. I am determined to prove it, but you must trust me."

She hesitated. "I do," she assured him but felt a niggle of doubt worming its way into her mind. "How long might it take?" What she should be doing was planning where to go long term. It would not do to remain at her father-in-law's home, nor would she return to her father. Perhaps she could afford a cottage by the shore.

"My dear, I am the most impossibly stubborn man to ever exist until Jack was born," he reassured her. "He must feel the total loss of you, and only then, will he be willing to change. Rest assured, he will come around, but you must be patient."

"I will try." She doubted this scheme. Even if he claimed to want her, she could not believe him. Not after their fight.

"You must for this to work. No matter the rumors you hear, you must trust me on this." He patted her hand as he escorted her down the hall.

How she wanted to believe the man. Hoped she might find a livable solution. There was joy to be found together if only

Jack could trust her. She had hope in the beginning and now it felt like it disintegrated before her. Love was a beautiful, but unattainable dream.

CHAPTER FORTY-FOUR
CONFRONTATIONS

A month passed and there was still no word from Annabelle. Silence as Jack waited for a sign. A whiff that she wanted him back. Yet, there was nothing.

"Why did you not leave with her?" Jack railed against Coleman one cool morning.

The butler set a tray with toast and coddled eggs on the side table. He removed an empty bottle of whisky and a goblet. Pushing open the curtains, the room flooded with bright sunlight.

Jack hissed and covered his face with his hands. "I want it dark. You will answer my questions, old man. I am the one who pays your salary!"

Coleman took his time. He straightened piles of soiled clothing and scraps. "I have ordered the footman to draw you a bath. Then your valet will help you dress. Eat something, else there will be nothing left but a pickled liver."

Jack leapt to his feet and stumbled as he righted his stance. Clawing at Coleman's lapels, he drew the butler against him.

Half spitting, half yelling, Jack repeated his question, "Where is she?"

The butler recoiled from the putrid breath wafting across his face and pried open Jack's fist. With a smooth sweep over his coat, he spoke in a surprisingly cultured voice for an ex-con. "She bade me not to tell you. Not until you have come to your senses."

"Why are you not with her? I thought you were another one of her little rescue pets, or did she abandon you as well? The heartless bitch." Jack collapsed into the chair, too unsteady to stand.

Coleman's face twisted. Though he spoke softly, Jack felt each word like a blow. "You call her that word again and there will be nothing to stop me from putting you down like a rabid beast." He shoved the plate of toast into Jack's hands. "Eat."

Jack wondered if the man might put him out of his misery. "Try it." He taunted because he wanted the pain. Wanted Coleman to beat him senseless. Then maybe the ache in his chest might make sense.

"Soak up the alcohol, you bloody fool. I am here to make sure you do not drown yourself in liquor. Her Ladyship will not return. Not if I have a say because you do not deserve her."

Jack menaced, but Coleman did not flinch. "Bring her back, now."

"My lord, I suggest a bath and basic hygiene. Then perhaps you might consider a visit to your club and spare us the pleasure of your company." Coleman did not wait to be dismissed. He marched out of the room and left Jack to simmer in his anger.

However, Jack did not go upstairs. He hastily combed a hand through his hair. Threw on a coat he found in the pile of clothes Coleman had collected and sloppily retied his cravat.

He startled a footman and frightened a housemaid as he

stormed out of the house. Through a remarkable feat of balance, he hailed a passing hackney and tumbled inside. The cab wobbled along uneven cobbled roads. His head swam, while his stomach protested the lack of food. He was grateful for the open window as he leaned out and cast up his accounts all over the slick lacquer of the vehicle.

Annabelle was close, he could feel it in his marrow. There were only a few places suitable for an unescorted woman to reside. He began with the lion's den. He hoped the meddlesome cousin was absent, so he could appeal to the more reasonable Aunt Silvia. Unfortunately, the newly hired butler would not allow Jack across the threshold.

As he turned to leave, Oakmont jogged up the steps, home after a pre-dawn ride through Hyde Park.

"Lost her already?" he asked as his riding crop beat a disjointed tattoo on his thigh.

"I know you are hiding her, where is she?"

Oakmont's judgmental gaze raked over Jack's disheveled appearance. He held up his manicured hand to pick at a nail. "I wish she had come to me. Then I would have sent her somewhere you could never find her."

"Annabelle is my wife! Right now, she could be with child. You would steal her away from me, her husband?"

"Yes," Oakmont barked. "Because you have been an absolute fool. How could you betray Annabelle with the contemptuous Lady Anworth?"

Jack's knees wobbled as he leaned against the stone entryway. Perhaps he should have eaten the toast. Come to think of it, when did he last eat? "You believe the rumors? Lady Anworth broke off our arrangement the minute my father cut me off. It was not until I married Annabelle and found a sliver of happiness that bitch tried to slither back into my life. Why does no one believe me?"

Oakmont pursed his lips and stared at Jack. "Lady Anworth approached me about a year ago."

"Does not surprise me. Even though I was her protector for three years, she was always on the prowl for the next bed. And you are exactly her type—young, virile... rich." A wall appeared just in time to catch him as he fell forward. Now if only he could stay in this exact spot until he sobered.

"Anworth left."

Jack blinked and tried to focus on Oakmont's blurred face, but there were two faces. Not one. "To where?"

"My sources said she boarded a ship with her French lover. They are heading to the continent."

Jack chuckled, surprised even more when Oakmont shared in his humor. "How unpatriotic of her."

"When did you last eat?"

"Cannot remember exactly. My meals have mostly been liquid." Shrugging his shoulders knocked Jack further off balance.

Oakmont caught his elbow before Jack tumbled on his ass.

"You need to eat. Then you need to get your house in order." Oakmont motioned to a footman, who helped support Jack's other side. Together, they maneuvered the inebriated man into the dining room and onto a chair.

Under Oakmont's direction, the footman loaded a plate with boiled bacon, coddled eggs, and toast. Setting down the hearty feast, the footman poured a cup of strong coffee. Jack forced down a piece of dry toast.

"There is someone you need to talk to." Oakmont vanished, leaving Jack to shovel food into his mouth.

He returned as the footman cleared away Jack's second plate. Where the food went, he could not say. His body simply took over the task, while his mind went comfortably numb.

"Viscount Linscott, I think it is time I introduced you to Mr. Seamus Greene, my uncle."

Jack was not entirely sure what he expected Annabelle's father to look like. Probably pot-bellied and reeking of stale ale. Instead, a bookish man with a pair of spectacles perched on his nose and several inches shorter than Oakmont cleared his throat.

"My lord," he said, "I think it would suit us both to have a conversation." He turned away from the room, heading down the hall.

"Follow me, Linscott. The library is this way." Oakmont followed his shuffling uncle through a set of double doors.

The library was a spacious room with walnut shelves filled with books. It smelled of leather and the lingering scent of firewood. Stained glass windows filtered the sunlight, casting geometric shapes across the parquet floor. At another time, he might admire the room. As it was, he wanted to be home, waiting. In case she changed her mind. In case she came back to him.

He did not wait for an invitation. He sat, wishing he had a drink to still the throb in his skull.

Mr. Greene spoke to his nephew, then took the seat across from him. He was a fussy man, and Jack took an immediate dislike to him.

He pushed his glasses up his nose. "Oakmont has informed me that my daughter is no longer residing under your roof."

"I have no idea where you heard such a rumor. She is visiting relatives." Jack cracked his knuckles, wishing the popping sound accompanied the liquid warmth of a bloodied nose.

"We know she is with your father. We have already called on her, but she was not available." Greene had a nervous habit of fidgeting with his glasses whenever he mentioned his daughter. Then he would clear his throat. "I want to know why she is there and not with her husband."

"All due respect, this is none of your concern." Jack tightened his fists on the arms of his chair. The wood protested his grip with a groan.

Oakmont pounded his fist on his knee. "You swore to protect her. Now she cannot abide residing in your home. You are a drunkard and a womanizer."

Greene's hand shot up. "Enough. We have been through this," he said to his nephew. Then turning to Jack, he leaned back, pushed up his glasses, and cleared his throat. "My daughter surprises me." Long moments passed without further elaboration.

Jack wanted to speak, but a tightness in the air stilled his lips. So he waited.

"I am not sure how much you know about her mother and about her death," he said. He did not wait for Jack to answer, choosing to continue the story at his own pace. "When we were married, I believed she was happy with our union. We were blessed shortly after with Annabelle. A clever and sweet child, she brightened my world. Her mother..." His sigh filled the room.

Oakmont tilted his head towards Jack in question. Neither interrupted Greene. This moment was important, and Jack was determined to absorb all the insight in the hopes of discovering a way to bring his wife home. He knew an apology was not enough. Not after the hateful words he spewed.

"Her mother was cruel. Mostly it was directed at me, which I accepted as I felt it was deserved. I could not give her the life she desired. As Annabelle grew, she received the same treatment and by then I was too pathetic to stop it. I am not telling you this to gain sympathy but rather, so you understand. When Annabelle was twelve, she went with her mother to

London. On the way home, there was a terrible storm. The roads were washed out. Our groom pleaded with Marilyn to spend the night in a coaching inn, but she refused. She had planned that night. Plans I discovered later. I will not burden you with the details." He tugged at his cravat, his glasses were left askew.

"She was planning on running away," Oakmont supplied, while Greene sputtered his protests. "My father told me the truth of the story. He wanted me to have sympathy for my uncle, needing me to understand my role in protecting the family. Ensuring that Annabelle made a solid match."

Greene hung his head. Red blotches spotted his cheeks. "She took the abuse that my wife grew tired of hurling at me. I found solace in the bottom of a bottle, while my daughter needed protection. Then you come along. You were not the man I would pick."

"Nor I." Oakmont's response carried far more weight than his uncle's.

"Yet, both of you have abandoned her, and I did not." The reason she left became clearer, but how to win her back did not. He had confirmed her fear that she was unwanted, spewing the same sort of hate. But Annabelle was everything. Jack had no idea a person could feel incomplete until she left him.

It should not be possible in such a short time to grow so dependent on one another. He was empty. He needed her. Her laughter. Sighs. Smiles. Books strewn across his house. Feminine smells sprinkled with lavender.

"What happened?" He had a feeling he knew the answer. From the way Annabelle paled in carriage rides and preferred to walk whenever possible to her nightmares whenever it rained.

"The carriage overturned. Marilyn died and Annabelle

witnessed it. The quick actions of the groom and a former sailor who happened to be in the right place at the right time, they managed to save my daughter." Greene only fumbled through his story when he mentioned Annabelle, otherwise he spoke with little emotion.

"Coleman," Marcus said, "was there that night. He has refused to leave Annabelle's side ever since."

"Until now." Why did the butler stay with Jack? Should he not be wherever Annabelle was?

"That should tell you, Linscott, all that you need to know. Coleman is a guard dog. He would not abandon his post without cause." Seamus stretched his hand towards Jack. "We have decided not to interfere unless you give us cause. This is our truce. Care for her in the way I should have. Protect her as I failed to do."

Jack shook his hand. "Then a truce it shall be."

If nothing else, he put right one of his wrongs. To make amends with Viscount Oakmont demonstrated his true remorse. To put right, all that he wronged with his arrogance. If he managed to smooth the waters with her cousin and father, perhaps she might forgive him.

CHAPTER FORTY-FIVE
FACING YOUR FATHER

In sobriety, things clarified. The revelations about Annabelle's mother dispersed the murkier bits. Yet, Jack still did not know how to gain Annabelle's trust. To let the single most important person in his life know she was wanted and needed.

How could he prove himself to her? He wished he had a solution. A grand gesture to make, but it all felt like a cheap ploy. No, this called for more than a declaration of love.

The buttery-soft leather of the wingback chair wrapped around him. He absentmindedly swirled the contents of his glass while mulling over these questions.

Jack grew tired of the confines of his townhouse and adjourned to his home away from home—The Obsidian Club.

The air stirred around Jack. He spied the intruder over the rim of his glass. Of course. It was his father. Without invitation, the man took the matching chair next to Jack's, motioning to the steward for brandy.

"Father." Jack lifted his glass in a mock salute.

"Son, glad you have climbed back out of the gin bottle and joined the rest of society."

"Whisky. You taught me long ago that gin was not an acceptable drink among the upper echelon." Truthfully, Jack stopped drinking gin when he turned twenty, after a rather unfortunate night of over-indulgence. He could not stomach the stuff now.

The Earl of Maitland warmed the snifter of brandy with the palm of his hand and studied his wayward progeny. "You miss her terribly. It is obvious by the amount of weight you have lost."

What exactly did the old man want now? "To whom are you referring?" Jack swam in his clothing. Even Thomas complained that he needed to take in all the seams to properly fit the clothes. And nagged Jack about his lack of sleep and the permanent purple smudges beneath his eyes. At least someone cared.

"Your wife, naturally. Annabelle has been worried sick over you." George Davenport extended his long legs in front of him and crossed them at the ankle.

"What do you know of Annabelle?" While his father reposed, Jack tensed with shoulders hunched, his fingers gripping his glass too tightly. He fought the urge to fling his drink in a juvenile gesture.

"She has been with me these last few weeks. Lovely girl you married, I am glad I gave you the nudge you needed."

"Why in the world did she go to you?" It was as much offensive as it was confounding that she sought solace with his father. He needed to see her, the temptation to throw himself at her feet and beg for forgiveness gnawed his mind. He could not find rest until he put this right.

"Annabelle felt I could provide answers to your questions.

She has fretted, pacing the halls, worried a terrible accident would befall you."

"Why did she not come to me?" He was a fool. A woman of Annabelle's caliber did not fall in love with the likes of him. She did not reciprocate his affection, even when he was desperately in love with her.

How could it have happened that such an unassuming woman captured his thrall, while other more worldly women bored him senseless? Love could be the only possible explanation for his current state. What other disease could afflict a man in such a manner? Sleepless. Irritated. And desperate for the merest glimpse of her honeyed hair and tender smile.

"Because I told her not to. John. You would not have changed if you did not feel the absolute devastation that only comes from true loss. I know too well what happens when those you love most slip through your fingers." George tried to conceal his emotion with a long sip of his drink. "Annabelle reminds me so much of your mother."

"You cannot possibly expect me to believe you miss my mother. You never speak of her." There was no comparison between his feelings for Annabelle and his father's reported love for Jack's mother.

"Sometimes the memories are too painful to put into words. I have not always been this way, but I found being around you and our home so full of memories, I could not bear it. I abandoned your education to a series of nannies and governesses, who were frankly incompetent, that I had no choice but to send you to Eton at the age of eleven."

The man resembled his father, but the anger and frustration in his words were nothing like the man he thought he knew. A husband. A father. A man who grieved for the loss of his beloved wife yet was thrown into the role of sole caretaker.

Jack's long-held resentment began to ease as compassion set in.

George withdrew from his coat pocket a short stack of folded pages wrapped in a faded cerulean ribbon. "I brought these old letters in case you did not believe me. The truth was, John, during all those years, I demanded daily updates from all those charged with your upbringing.

"Your mother was the one who made all the decisions. Duty forced me to stay in London, but you needed country air and wide-open spaces to romp around, not the stench of the city." From the stack, he handed Jack a letter so worn, the paper felt like fabric.

My dearest George,

I do not know how else to say it, my darling, but our little boy is an absolute genius. I know you laugh whenever I tell you, but he is brilliant. Simply brilliant! He has mastered his ABC's and only sometimes forgets g and n. We went to the pond today and caught two fish. He insisted we needed to wait and catch one for the baby, but it was beginning to storm, and it took all my energy to convince him to come inside.

As I write to you, he is sketching a picture of the fish to send to his Papa. My confinement draws to its end in a few months, and I cannot help but be curious about our next child. I hope she is a little girl we can spoil with gowns and dolls. And yet, I also pray it is a little boy. That he might admire his big brother John and love him as much as we do. I can imagine the two of them toddling around the garden as if I am gazing into the future.

We await your return.

With all my love,

Your Clara

∿

JACK TRACED over his mother's name. The letter's date... Probably, the last she ever wrote. Three days later, she went into premature labor. His father rushed home with mere minutes to say goodbye.

"That was the life I wanted. Had she lived? Had Charlie lived, I cannot help but wonder who we would have become. I tried so hard. I bought you a stallion and made sure you knew how to ride like a gentleman. I hired the best tutors money could buy. You went to the best schools, wore the best clothes, but it was not enough, was it?" The fingers his father wrapped around the glass turned white. Liquid sloshed against the sides, but not a drop spilled.

"No, it was not. I needed a father. Instead, I had strangers to comfort me through grief I did not understand." With a trembling hand, Jack refolded the letter and placed it in the stack with the others.

His mother's handwriting with playful arcs and loops. Cheerful and sweet as his memories of her remained. Even as he read, it was her voice that parted through the heavy veil of the past. It felt different. A weight shifted in his gut. The devastation he once felt did not ache quite as much.

"I cannot begin to make amends for not being the father I should have been. My single defense was I did not know how. However, your mother..." His lips quivered. He did not even bother to hide his emotions. "She was incredible. I did not know you could love like that. Our short time together was precious. I want more for you, and yet the same. Do not make the same mistakes I did, John."

Jack drummed his fingers along the arm of the chair. Was his father right? Could it be that simple? "Why do you not call me Jack like everyone else?"

George's lips curled into a smile. "Your mother named you after her father. When you were a baby, my nickname for you was Jack. She did not like it. Said Jack was a pirate's name, and her little John was going to be a true lord."

The remark burrowed beneath his skin. Jack was far more a pirate than a lordly. Not the type of man his mother hoped he would become. Was he truly a disgrace? As if reading his mind, Jack's father answered.

"She would be proud of you. Well, mostly. The delay in matrimonial interest and the lack of grandchildren would have been her daily lament. Your mother would be disappointed that you had not made amends with Annabelle, but she knew you would make the right choices in life. She loved you and would love you still."

"You are getting maudlin, old man." Jack choked on a hiccup. If he was not careful, he would turn into a watering pot by the end of the week. Lord, he needed his wife.

George clasped his son's hand, affection like Jack could never remember. "My carriage is waiting, would you like to come with me?"

He thought it over for a moment but then declined. "A grandiose gesture is necessary at this stage. A spectacle worthy of Annabelle." Too bad there was not a stage he could borrow. At this point, he would put on a full Drury Lane production to win her back. "Which room is she staying in by chance?"

George set his brandy snifter on a table and stood. "Your old room. Four windows to the right of center." He winked, then left Jack to plot.

CHAPTER FORTY-SIX
WINDOWS AND LADDERS

This time, Jack was sure to break his neck. The ladder he borrowed from his father was in terrible condition. He highly suspected the rungs would snap if he did not hurry off the contraption. The problem was the window was locked. He thought his father had read his mind. He was mistaken because this window was definitely not budging.

Exerting a little more force, Jack pushed against the frame, but it did not yield. Giving in, he knocked against the glass, calling out Annabelle's name. But she did not stir. Stepping up one more rung, Jack tried to leverage more weight against the window. This time, it was too much for the ladder. The rung snapped and he slid down, catching the sill before the ladder collapsed into the bushes below. He was left hanging, three stories high.

"My God, I am going to die out here." He watched the violets he brought float to the ground beneath him, praying that he did not soon follow.

The window slid open. Long honey-colored hair floated around the face Jack loved most in the world.

"Annabelle," he pleaded, still gripping the sill with all his strength.

"Jack!" she cried, wrapping her hands around his wrists. She tried to pull him through but did not have the strength. She called out for help. "Hold on, I hear footsteps and shouts."

The door flew open, and a pair of footmen stood in the doorway. One held a candlestick and the second brandished a fireplace poker. "My lady," the one with the candlestick shouted, "what is happening?"

"My husband is hanging on the windowsill. Do help him through."

The tools clattered to the floor as the footmen rushed to her side. With a heaving pull, they managed to drag their lord's son inside. Jack collapsed onto the floor and gasped out a thank you.

"Please ensure that my father gets a much sturdier ladder, and that we are not disturbed."

"As you wish, my lord." They bowed and left the room as quickly as they had arrived. If they were curious as to why the master's son crawled through a window and did not come through the door, they chose not to say.

"Jack, what in the world were you doing? You could have been killed?" Annabelle stood next to the bed. She still shook, the aftereffects of witnessing her husband cling to a window ledge for dear life.

"It was supposed to be a romantic gesture." He beat the dirt from his clothes. Approaching his wife, he gently unwound her arms. Taking her wrists into his hands, he inspected them for any bruising. "I even brought you flowers, but they are lying on top of the ladder as we speak."

"You have to stop breaking into my room at night."

Jack's hands snaked up to her shoulder, pulling her against him. "Probably, but I could not resist. I have grown a little desperate after a month-long separation from my better half."

"How desperate?" Hope colored her question.

"So, desperate, I climbed a ladder. One with all the rungs sawed through. Simply to throw myself at your mercy." He cupped her face in his hands. "I have been a fool, Annabelle, to wait so long to show you I can be the man you need me to be. I am not sure how to prove myself to you, other than to say: Ask me anything and I will tell no lies."

Her dainty fingers caressed his cheeks. "I will not share my husband with another woman, whether you love her or not."

"Done. You are the only woman I desire and will ever desire." The scent of lavender swirled around. It was all he could do not to collapse at her feet. How much he missed the smell, the feel, the sight of her.

"You may not understand why I care for animals like Winston, but you will treat them with the love they deserve." Her fingers tightened their hold on his lapels.

"Done. Winston is currently cuddled on your pillow, waiting for your return. We have entered into an agreement of sorts where he demands pets and attention. I capitulate and now do not suffer from any more vicious attacks. We are friends of a sort."

Annabelle pulled an orange cat hair from his shoulder. "He has been napping on your clothes."

"I cannot be held accountable for what Thomas might decide to do with the cat. My suggestion is to find him a comfortable bed forthwith."

"Never speak to me in anger as you did."

He took a deep breath, sucking in the hurt he had caused. Wanting to erase it permanently. "The damage from our fight is not something I can rid from your memories. I can only hope it fades and does not leave permanent damage behind as it did your father."

"My father. You speak as if you know him," she said.

"We met."

Annabelle's eyes flew open. "Met?"

"He was with your cousin. Through our conversation, I came to understand the damage inflicted by your mother and the shell that remained of your father. I swear, unto my dying day, to never cause you such pain again." He clasped his hands together in prayer. Not to a deity. But to the woman he cherished above all.

She inhaled, stilling a quiver in her lip. "I want to forget."

"I pray that you do."

"We have to move past that fight."

He drew a fingertip along her hairline. "Never again," he promised. "Never."

Her eyes fluttered open. Once filled with clouds of doubt, they were bright and clear. It gave him hope. She accepted his sworn declaration. Now he only had to prove his intention.

"I need you to tell me about yourself. No more secrets." Her hands slid up to the nape of his neck to play with the curls.

"It is a frightfully dull story, but I can start at the beginning. I was born on a balmy April day in 1795. I was quite the surprise, as I was a male and bore a full head of hair. Much of the next few years are a blur, I must be honest. But my exploits started when I was ten and figured out how to both frighten the cook and charm the housekeeper, thus my long career of amoral behavior began."

"You are incorrigible. You know that do you not?"

Jack hoped she witnessed this change in him. How fundamentally different he was. All because of her.

He playfully swatted her bottom. "I need you to keep me in

line. Annabelle, I do not work without you. I need you, all of you."

"Jack, the moment I realized you were hanging outside my bedroom window, I was ready to throw myself into your arms. In all honesty, when you stole me away in the middle of the night not so long ago, I realized you were the one I wanted."

His forehead touched hers as his request hovered above her lips. "Then come home to where you belong. Come home to me, my Butterfly."

CHAPTER FORTY-SEVEN
REVELATIONS

"I will come home again, as my place is beside my husband's. But I need more, Jack." Annabelle lit a taper candle. She reached for his hand, the one rubbed raw from where he gripped the windowsill.

Jack winced as she cleared away the dirt and grime with a cloth, still damp from her morning ablutions. "Tell me what you need. I have only the world to give you."

Annabelle's fingers lifted and smoothed his curls with gentle tugs. "You will never take out your frustrations on me. Or tell me you regret our marriage."

Jack rested his head against her belly, and she was grateful for his hands wrapped around her waist to hold her steady. How she missed the feel of him. The smell of his soap. The deep timbre of his voice.

"I have been utterly lost without you. The minute those horrid words slipped past my lips, I wanted to take them back." His hands smoothed over her silk robe, then worked at the knot until the fabric parted. They stole inside to hold her closer. "These past few weeks have been torture."

"Torture for you or for all the people you have bullied to tell you where I was?" She yanked his hair, so he playfully nipped her.

How she loved these moments together. How she missed the very feel of him. But she could not forgive so easily. Not until he understood the effect he had on her.

"For them, the torture was short-lived. For me, it was misery every single minute of every day. I dreamed of you, of how much I disappointed you. Then I would wake, not knowing where you were."

She would not apologize for leaving or the worry she caused. This was a harsh lesson for him, but she needed to know she was more than a simple solution to the demands of his father.

"Did you and Winston truly make friends?"

"He was the only one brave enough to comfort me. I am sure he expects you to remove me from my bed when you return."

"Never." She kissed the furrow of his brow until it eased.

Jack rose from the bed to the fireplace. "There are things I know I can never be, Annabelle, and I know it was unfair of me to take away your choice. For you to not find a man you loved to marry. But if you will find it enough for now, then maybe one day you can find it in your heart to love a man like me."

She wanted to declare her love at that moment, but the words were locked in her throat as she watched her husband stalk around the bedchamber.

He continued, not meeting her gaze, but keeping his body constantly in motion. He picked up her dusting powder, inhaled its scent, then he was across the room to stoke the fire. Around and around he paced as he told her what was on his mind and asked for forgiveness.

"I do not know when it was, probably the day I met you,

and you pleaded with the spider. I was a wanderer who needed a place to call home. With our first kiss, I felt a pull I never had felt before. A voice calling to me.

"I managed to find you in places I did not expect. On a city street. At a musicale. The park. It seemed I had only to anticipate your presence, and there you would be. It was as if the Fates were whispering, 'She is the one.' And I stupidly thought it was my father's conditions pushing me forward. Truth was, Annabelle, I could have asked other women to marry me. Others who would have gladly said yes."

"Valentina Anworth." Annabelle could not understand why her name came to mind, but it did. And it tasted bitter.

"No. I never even considered her. She was all bedsport, not a future partner." He raked his hands over his face and through his hair, leaving a few strands sticking out at awkward angles.

"What other names were there?" She did not want to know, rather she wanted to keep him talking. She missed this, missed his voice and their long conversations.

"I had a list," he said as a bashful smile worked the corners of his lips.

Ah, there were his dimples. It took all her strength not to cross the room to kiss it.

"Three-and-forty names were on it, and I do not remember a single one. The minute I found you across a ballroom, you had me hooked and I was helpless but to follow."

"So, we know why you pursued me." How she wanted to hear these revelations naked in his arms, but she did not dare mix in intimacies when he finally bared his soul.

"But there is more! You shine like the brightest star. So effulgent, the world pales in comparison."

She flinched, uncomfortable with the imagery he described. "I am hardly the goddess you paint me as."

"You are!" He was in front of her with three quick steps to

hold her face in his linen-wrapped hands. "Eyes of gold. Hair the color of honey. A body made for loving. I cannot get enough of you, Annabelle. It is a sickness. Know I have *never* felt like this before. Never felt this all-consuming need." He pulled her closer. "I cannot explain it. We merge, you and I. Annabelle, I do not care about an heir. I make love to you because to deny it would be depriving myself of air. I would die without you."

Annabelle did not know what to say about such a declaration, so much of it was the words that bumbled around her mind. Words that sounded a lot like love. His heartbeat against her chest became part of her.

"The truth is, I find myself falling in love with you. I cannot say I have stopped falling, because every day I find a reason to love you more."

Her world clicked into place like a tumbler sliding into a lock, but she could not repeat such declarations back to him. They clogged her throat as tears streamed.

His mouth fit over hers as he drank in her tears with each press of his lips. She told him with her body of her need, of her love for him. She allowed him to strip away the barriers of clothing. Together they tumbled onto the bed, the world around them all but forgotten.

"My dear Annabelle, does it hurt so much to love me?" Jack caressed her face to wipe away the wetness pooled there.

The response wobbled against her lips as she choked out her answer. "No. I-I..."

"Shh, let me love you." And with that declaration, Jack did.

He brought them together to melt into one being. Climaxing, they cried each other's names and shuddered their release. Long hours into the night, they made love until the sky faded from navy to magenta.

He lay with Annabelle in his arms to watch the sunrise above the rooftops.

"Jack?" Lips pressed against her neck to tell her he was listening. "I love you."

"I have always known. Who else but you could tolerate such an unlovable creature?"

Annabelle rolled over to face him. "You were never unlovable. You were far too easy to love. That was the problem."

He inhaled deeply. "Are you ready to come home now?"

"No." She hid her smile behind her hand.

"Why not?"

"Because I refuse to leave this bed and your arms. I would rather lie here for eternity than to be apart from you again."

Annabelle groaned as he settled his hardened length along her core and agreed to put off the return home for another few hours. Anything to keep them right where they were. Because this was love and all they ever needed.

EPILOGUE

Jack lounged in a chair with his cravat untied and his boots tossed in front of him. His wife brushed out her silky locks. Why the nightly ritual mesmerized him, he never understood, but every evening he watched the long strokes work their way through her hair until it crackled.

Perhaps because the hair brushing meant she was almost ready for bed. Then came his favorite part of the day when he untied all the ribbons of her nightrail. Like a present on Christmas morning, he tore away all the layers of fabric that covered his most prized gift. After every tantalizing inch of her was revealed, he would worship her with his mouth and hands. Definitely the highlight of any day.

A fuzzy brown shape skidded across a table. Before it made its way down the leg, Jack trapped it beneath an overturned water glass.

"Hand me a sheet of paper, if you will?" He reached his hand behind him, proud of the fact that he now managed to successfully trap sixteen spiders and hopefully then release number fifteen.

Poor black spider number three. Its successful extraction was thwarted by an overly enthusiastic Ginny. The pup had snuffled, then swallowed the arachnid.

"Do the men at Artie's know you are a rescuer of eight-legged creatures?" She caressed his back as he lifted the window sash to release his tiny charge.

"No, I do not believe they would be as impressed by my reluctance to squash such beings. They would view it as a touch unmanly."

Annabelle pursed her lips in displeasure. Jack kissed the steam right out of her, and she melted against his chest.

"Worry not, my love. I might not be able to save all of God's creatures, but for you, I will spend the rest of my life trying."

She glowed and tried to hide the smile that crept across her cheeks. He would spend a lifetime to guarantee she always remained exactly as she did in this moment. Love—an inadequate word to describe how he truly felt. Enraptured. Enthralled. Besotted. Mad as a hatter for his beautiful wife.

"Did I tell you, I received a letter from my father today?"

He unbuttoned his shirt and waistcoat. "Hmm? What did he say?"

"He is planning to visit over Christmastide."

He shrugged out of his shirt. "Is this a welcomed visit?"

Annabelle plaited her hair, the final step before she crawled into bed. She met his gaze in the mirror. "I have made peace. I think this is a new chapter for all of us. I intend on inviting Aunt Silvia and Marcus to stay with us at Morefield."

He nodded, stunned that his reaction did not include revulsion. "I think my father will be pleased to have a proper celebration for once." Jack yanked off his breeches and bounced onto the mattress.

"You are worse than a child, jumping into bed like that."

He pulled back the covers and patted her pillow. "Bedtime." He waggled his brows and motioned for her to come closer.

"Not yet. There is more."

"There is no reason you cannot tell me here. Come to bed, my little Butterfly, and tell me all your woes, only do it from my arms."

She untied the top ribbon in a row of pink bows starting at her throat. Jack's erection bobbed in approval.

"I am not going anywhere near you in that state." She pointed to where the sheet tented over his legs.

"I know, it has a mind of its own. I made a promise. Ignore it, eventually, it will subside. Now tell me, love, what else happened today?" He smoothed out her side of the bed and patted the pillow once again.

Winston, sensing it was time to retire, hopped onto the bed. The cat circled twice, then curled up onto Annabelle's pillow.

"Winston, move." Jack lifted the hissing orange and white feline. He set the cat carefully at the end, then retreated to the head of the bed. Winston flicked his tail before it curled between Jack's feet.

Annabelle capitulated. Jack blew out a candle on the night-stand before nestling her against his chest. He resisted the urge to undress her. Instead, he relished the simple joy of his wife enfolded in his embrace.

"I visited Dr. Hill this afternoon."

Jack's fingers stilled as they loosened the second ribbon. "Are you ill?"

She helped him untie the third ribbon before she answered. "I felt a little off for the past few weeks. He confirmed my suspicion."

Ah, perfect. She was finally free of the confines of her clothing. He peeled the material away and threw the nightrail onto the floor in a heap. Over her body, he drew naughty pictures with the tip of his fingers. Promises for what was to come.

Unintentionally, he bumped into Winston, who retaliated by biting and clawing Jack's foot through the coverlet. Grateful for the thick blanket between the disgruntled cat and his anatomy, he shoved the cat to the side. "So, what was your suspicion?" Undeterred, Jack maneuvered Annabelle underneath him.

"We are expecting."

Jack stilled. It should not have been a surprise. Not one night, since Annabelle returned, had they been apart. The only reprieve his wife had from his husbandly attentions was the month she spent living with the earl. But it was a surprise. A baby. Jack was going to be a father.

A father. It should be a more frightening prospect, but it was not. The corners of his mouth twisted into a smile.

Her brow puckered. "Say something."

But he did not, he was too happy to speak. Instead, he kissed her over and over again.

"Does this mean you are not upset?"

"No, Annie. I could not be happier. Let us hope it is a little girl. There is nothing worse than giving my father exactly what he wants." He traced over her slightly rounded belly and gave it a kiss. Then another. "Promise me. No more strays. We will have our hands full, especially if he is a little hellion like his father."

"But the baby will need a pet."

"We have a stallion. An ancient gelding. A dog. Winston." He nudged the cat, who hissed. "And Coleman."

"Coleman is not a stray."

Jack cleared his throat.

"Fine, he is a stray. But I am sure we will find another suitable pet. Perhaps a rabbit or a hedgehog..." Annabelle vibrated with excitement.

"No." He silenced her with a kiss.

"I took you in."

"Yes, you did. The last of your menagerie. Now, you get to be a mother, and if you are good, I will keep letting you have babies."

"Let me have babies." She punched his shoulder. "How many would you like?"

Jack cradled her in his arms. "Dozens," he whispered into her ear, "because I will never be able to stop loving you. Not until my dying day, and even beyond. I love you, Annabelle Davenport. The woman who stole my heart."

ABOUT THE AUTHOR

 Stacia Kaywood dabbles in all areas of romantic fiction from historical to paranormal. *Stealing Annabelle* is the first Regency Romance novel in the series Belles and Rogues. The series follows the former students of Mrs. Maxwell's School for the Education and Deportment of Fine Ladies. Francine MacKinnon's stories will appear in the second book titled *Forgetting Francine.*

Stacia's first novel, *Bathed in Moonlight,* is a historical romance set at the end of World War II and has the critics raving about the sweeping romance between Greta Müller and Jimmy O'Brien.

Stacia has several short stories available as part of anthologies with groups local to Kansas City. The first is "Of Dreams and Crossroads", part of the Midwest Romance Writers anthology: *A Kansas City Story, Volume Two.* A second short story, "Harvey's Girl" is set at Union Station and will be featured in an anthology titled *Heart of America: Kansas City Inspired Short Stories* from Woodneath Press.

Follow along on her author journey and new releases by joining her newsletter. A link can be found on her website https://staciakaywood.com/.

To learn more about Stacia Kaywood and discover more Next Chapter authors, visit our website at www.nextchapter.pub.

Printed in Dunstable, United Kingdom

66865471R00194